A New Day

Yesterday

A New Day Yesterday

a novel by

Peter Adum

A New Day Yesterday
ISBN: 978-1724569837

EDITORIAL CONSULTANT: ASHLEY M. GRAHAM
BACK COVER PHOTO: ROBERT NIZICH
BOOK PRODUCTION: WARD STREET PRESS
BOOK & COVER DESIGN BY VEE SAWYER

To my hometown, San Pedro, California, I can't imagine a better place to have grown up. Hell, Bukowski even moved there.

A New Day Yesterday

Friday
APRIL 13

▼

My friend, Randy Ferlinghetti, had asked me to take photographs of a little prank that he had planned for today. I borrowed a 35mm camera from my photography class and finished putting in a new roll of film just as the bell rang. I had to hurry to meet Randy at his van, so there was no time to stop at my locker. San Pedro High School had an open campus, so it was easy to leave school during lunchtime.

Our school's main building was a Streamline Moderne WPA structure, built in 1936, to replace a building that had been damaged during the 1933 Long Beach earthquake. I first learned of this earthquake in Mr. Johansson's local history class. I should have paid more attention to his lectures, but instead I often found myself daydreaming about his daughter, Carissa. She was a senior, and the most beautiful girl in our school. It was difficult focusing on history while I was lusting over his daughter. But since Mr. Johansson helped produce such a magnificent creature, I tried to pay attention to his lectures, assuming that he knew what he was talking about.

One thing we locals obviously knew was how to pronounce the name of our town: San "Peedrow," not San "Ped-row." If you pronounced it wrong, we all knew that you didn't belong here.

San Pedro stopped being an actual city back in 1909, when it was annexed by the city of Los Angeles for a place to build a harbor, now the largest man-made harbor in the world.

My dad, Nikola Petrovich Sr., was a commercial fisherman who came here from the Dalmatian coastline in Croatia, Yugoslavia in the mid 1930s. My mom, Nada Katnich Petrovich, had worked at a Terminal Island fish cannery for a while, but didn't like the work. They met on my dad's first visit back to the old country. After a brief courtship, they married, and a year later I was born.

When I was two, my mom and I boarded the Queen Mary for America. My father had already left earlier, to prepare for our arrival. My mom loves to tell the story that when I saw the Statue of Liberty in New York Harbor, I pointed and couldn't stop smiling, a happy new American.

But I was eighteen years old now, and with

the Vietnam War going on, I hadn't been smiling nearly as much. My draft card stated that I was "1-A," which meant that I'd likely be drafted. But fortunately for the class of 1973, President Richard Nixon ended the draft last month, in March. This allowed me to smile once again.

As a high school senior, I was starting to think about what I might do with my life, now that I knew that I might actually have one. Maybe I could go to college. I'd be the first in my family. Or, maybe I could just go fishing with my dad. The Alaskan salmon season would be starting soon. But all of these decisions would have to wait. It was the Friday before Easter Vacation, and I was going to have a whole week off from school. Important decisions could wait.

Randy Ferlinghetti sat anxiously in his red and white Volkswagen van. Randy was tall, with long brown hair, blue eyes, and a perpetual grin on his face.

My 1954 Chevrolet Bel Air was parked directly in front of his van. My '54 Chevy was made the year I was born. The color was a burnt orange called Pueblo Tan, with an eggshell white roof and accents. The car had more chrome on it than any two 1973 cars put together. As I approached my car, what I noticed, made me angry.

"My hubcaps," I shouted. "This is the second time."

I circled the car to see if they were all indeed gone. Randy got out of his van to see for himself.

"Relax, Niko," he said. "I'll get you some new ones."

"They aren't easy to find."

"Trust me, I know what I'm doing."

Randy slid behind the steering wheel of his van as I hopped in on the passenger side. He pushed an 8-track tape of David Bowie's *Ziggy Stardust* into the van's stereo.

"I've got a test after lunch," I told him. "So, I can't be late getting back."

"Don't worry," he said, tucking his hair behind both ears. "You've got film in that camera, right?"

"Yeah," I nodded, as the tune "Suffragette City" began to play.

"I've got twelve guys meeting us there."

"Twelve should be plenty."

Randy was a scammer, but not always a successful one. He often seemed to get caught in his own scams. I met him in a Catholic youth group when we were at Richard Henry Dana Junior High School. His oldest sister, Elaine, and his brother-in-law, Matt, a Los Angeles Police officer, were the group's counselors. They took the youth group to Disneyland once on a chartered bus. While the rest of us were having fun on the rides, Randy was busy shoplifting along Main Street. When he finally got caught, he had two lockers stuffed full of stolen loot. Needless to say, Randy's sister and brother-in-law weren't too happy with him. Here we all were having fun at the "Magic Kingdom," while Randy was robbing the place blind. That was his idea of fun.

"Now remember," said Randy, "you come in through the door on Bandini, and we'll all come in through the door on First Street."

"I'll be ready," I said, already feeling a little nervous.

"Just make sure you get some good pictures," smiled Randy, "Someday I'll want to show them to my grandchildren."

The pink brick, 1950s modern, Our Lady of the Harbor Catholic Church and Girl's High School filled an entire city block. Inside the girl's cafeteria, were about three hundred Catholic high school girls, all uniformed in gray and blue plaid skirts and white blouses. As they ate their lunches, the girls chatted with their friends. Two elderly priests hovered nearby, always mindful of excessive noise or inappropriate behavior. Clutching the camera to my chest, I tried to slip inside the cafeteria without being noticed. But several girls noticed me and smiled. Maybe I should start going to church again, some of these girls were cute.

It was still strange to not see any nuns here at Our Lady of the Harbor. Before 1970, they were all over the place, teachers, administrators, and staff. Now, because of some dispute with the archbishop, you couldn't find a single nun. They had disappeared like so much incense smoke. Even the nuns that had once taught me catechism were gone. One former nun, Miss Martin, was now my

U.S. History teacher at San Pedro High.

One stern faced priest noticed me, and it was obvious that he didn't like my looks. He signaled to the other priest, and like two navy destroyers, they both steamed down the center aisle right toward me. But before they could reach me, the First Street door flew open with a gust of wind. Randy Ferlinghetti bounded in, wearing nothing but a wide grin, white socks, and tennis shoes. For a moment he just stood there, proud as hell of his naked masculinity.

"Girls, girls!" Randy shouted. "You're in for a treat!"

There was a great rumble in the crowd. Gasps and "Oh my God!" could be heard as the crowd noticed Randy. The girls couldn't believe their good fortune. The two old priests were mortified. Randy first motioned the others, and then led his twelve nude champions on a victory sprint down the center aisle of the cafeteria. Waves of girls rose-up in applause as Randy's naked group raced past them. The two priests were spun in circles as the streakers sped by. The standing ovation was one you'd normally only see after a game winning home run at Dodger Stadium. I don't think even the ancient Greek Olympians, who also raced in the nude, ever got such an ovation.

I snapped picture after picture of the scene, forever memorializing Randy and his magnificent feat. When it was over, I slipped out almost unnoticed, feeling strangely envious that I was only an observer, and not a participant in Randy's little triumph.

At Alma Liquor on Ninth Street, a still naked Randy pulled his van to the curb.

"What are you doing?" I asked.

"I want to get some beer for tonight".

Randy hopped out of the van, walked across the sideway, and right into the store. The liquor clerk was reading the News Pilot newspaper when he saw Randy walk in. He blinked his eyes in disbelief as he watched Randy's naked ass move toward the beer fridge. Randy grabbed a six-pack of Coors cans and brought it to the counter. He slapped a five-dollar bill down next to it. The clerk didn't know what to say.

"That'll be it," said Randy.

After an awkward moment, the clerk finally spoke.

"I know this is a stupid question. But, do you have any I.D. on you?"

Randy shook his head. "No."

"Well, then I'm afraid I can't sell you any beer. I'm sorry."

"It's okay. Next time I just need to remember to bring an I.D. What was I thinking?"

Randy grabbed his five-dollar bill and exited the liquor store — the clerk still in disbelief.

Stephanie Davies' long blond hair draped my arm as I rested it on the back of her theater seat. She smelled really good tonight; it was some new shampoo or something. Even in the dark, her big green eyes shined brightly from the reflection coming from the screen.

The Strand Theater on Pacific Avenue was our neighborhood movie theater. I think it was originally called the Fox Strand, but no one could actually recall for sure. The last few years, we saw some really good movies there. Stephanie always called them "films." She was a junior, president of the drama club, and always in the school plays. Her dream was to some day move to Hollywood and become an actress. She even talked me into being in a play, which I actually had fun doing.

Together, at the Strand, we had watched: *Mean Streets*, *The Godfather*, *The French Connection*, *The Exorcist*, *MASH*, and *The Last Picture Show*, just to name a few.

Tonight's movie was a sneak preview of a film, which was opening this summer. It began with the sound of Bill Haley and the Comets, "Rock Around the Clock," and the image of Mel's

Drive-In Restaurant. It was called *American Graffiti*. We were supposed to fill out survey cards when it was over. The movie poster out front asked the question: "Where were you in '62?" The sound track was all great rock and roll oldies. I enjoyed every bit of the movie, but I was sad to read the postscripts about some of the characters at the end. The Beach Boys "All Summer Long" began to play as the house lights came up and the closing credits began to roll. We jotted down a few comments on our cards.

"I liked that," said Stephanie, grabbing her sweater.

"So did I," I said, standing up.

We moved with the crowd toward the Strand's small lobby, dropping our survey cards into a slotted box.

"It's funny," she said. "I used to listen to Wolfman Jack all the time."

"Me too," I said, "I think he's still on KRTH."

Once in the crowded lobby, we slowly moved toward the front door.

"What did you like the most?" asked Stephanie.

"The cruising," I smiled.

"I knew you'd say that."

Outside, we passed the ticket booth and stepped out onto the sidewalk. Looking out on Pacific Avenue, we were greeted by a common Friday and Saturday night sight — Pacific Avenue looked just like a scene from the movie *Ameri-*

can Graffiti. Low riders, hot cars, and classics all shared space on the busy street. A cacophony of rock tunes could be heard coming from the different vehicles. While most of the world had given up on cruising a decade earlier, we in San Pedro still practiced it faithfully. We were obviously behind the times.

I opened the door to my '54 Chevy for Stephanie, then for myself. The car still had only the bare wheels, no hubcaps. Hopefully, Randy will come through and find me a new set.

Stephanie never really liked the whole cruising thing. She liked theater and films, and she liked to read good books. To her, cruising was like an archaic fossil from an ancient era. A silly thing that kids did on the weekend to pass the time.

I turned the ignition key, slipped an 8-Track tape of Jethro Tull's *Stand Up* into the car's stereo, and looked at Stephanie.

"Well, do you want to cruise for a bit? "

"Sure. After watching *American Graffiti*, I think we have to."

The song "A New Day Yesterday" began to play on my car stereo as I pulled the '54 Chevy out into the stream of traffic and joined the parade of cars. I passed Bobby Routolo going the other way on Pacific Avenue in his mint green 1952 Chevy. We exchanged an acknowledging wave. Bobby had put a lot of money and work into getting his car to look as good as it did, and it looked cherry.

Chad Wagner's navy blue, 1966 Chevelle rumbled along side of us. Chad was an old friend from junior high, but since his family moved up to South Shores, I hardly ever saw him. South Shores was a more middle class part of town. Middle class was about the best you could do in San Pedro.

"Hey, football on Sunday!" shouted Chad.

"Yeah," I shouted back, "and you'd better be ready to lose."

Sitting beside Chad was Cheryl Patterson, who was in Stephanie's grade. I had dated Cheryl's older sister, Vickie. Cheryl was just a goofy kid then, but now she was tall, dark, and strikingly beautiful. Chad was a lucky guy.

"We'll see you on Sunday," said Chad, hitting the gas and leaving my car far behind in the dust.

"What does Cheryl see in Chad?" asked Stephanie.

"I think girls like his car."

At the hand car wash on Pacific Avenue and Fourteenth Street, Randy Ferlinghetti, his girlfriend, Melissa Kordich, and our mutual friend, Hank Pilsner stood alongside Randy's van. Melissa was pretty and a good student, but she always seemed to rebel against the rules. She had an angry Croatian father, who didn't like her dating Randy, but of course that only made her want to see him even more.

Hank Pilsner stood there munching a burger from the nearby hamburger stand. Hank was a big guy, with a big appetite for just about everything. He graduated from Pedro High last year. Growing up, he'd played all the sports, but suddenly dropped them all when he failed to make the school baseball team. He had lost out to guys whom he knew he was as good as or better. Instead of letting the rejection motivate him to try harder, he just gave up on organized sports. Hank lived up in South Shores near Chad Wagner.

Stephanie and I waited at the light to turn left into the car wash. As we waited, we noticed the large billboard above the car wash.

LAST NIGHT ON OLD BEACON STREET.
SAN PEDRO
SATURDAY, APRIL 21, 6 PM TO ???
DINING ; DANCING : ENTERTAINMENT

Beacon Street was the historical center of old San Pedro. Dating back to the 1800s, its waterfront businesses had provided everything that a bustling seaport had needed. It was the kind of place Jack London would have loved. But over the years it had become a collection of sad old buildings that housed seedy bars, cheap cafés, and flophouse hotels. San Pedro wanted to be respectable now. The community leaders wanted a new image. They were planning a celebration. One last night on old Beacon Street, then the bulldozers and wrecking balls would do their work.

"It's kind of sad," Stephanie said, "tearing down old Beacon Street."

"Why?" I asked, surprised at her concern. "It's a dump, nothing but drunks and bums."

"Maybe someday you'll understand," she said, sadly.

The light changed and I wheeled the '54 Chevy into the car wash. I parked it along side Randy's van. Randy beamed with pride.

"I got your hubcaps, man."

"That was quick," I said, getting out of the car with Stephanie.

Randy opened the side door to his van and pulled out four original 1954 Chevrolet Bel Air hubcaps. He handed them to me.

"Thanks."

The hubcaps were in pretty good shape. But then I noticed some numbers engraved onto the backs. It looked like a driver's license number.

"I took them off that beat up '54 on Centre and Thirteenth Street."

"What?" I asked, " Not the one with all the gray primer spots?

"Can you believe it? He never even bothers to take them off at night."

"Oh, wow," said Hank, almost choking on his burger. "That guy is supposed to be an ex-convict, and I heard he spent time in San Quentin."

"Big deal," said Randy. "Then you got some hubcaps from an ex-convict."

"What if he doesn't like me taking his hubcaps?"

"Look, man, I did you a favor."

"But I live three blocks from this guy."

"And I'm sure that he's seen your car, with the hubcaps that you just got stolen today. Right?"

"Yeah, so?"

"He'll see these on your car, and he'll think that they're the ones that you've always had."

"It's called hiding in plain sight," said Melissa.

"He'd never imagine you'd be stupid enough to drive around town with his hubcaps on," added Hank

"That would be pretty dumb," said Stephanie.

"Well," I said, "it all makes sense, I guess."

"Sure it does," smiled Randy, grabbing two hubcaps out of my hand. "Let's put them on."

He proceeded to pop the two hubcaps onto one side of my Chevy. I finally joined him and popped the other two on to the opposite side of the car.

Across the street, Jake Polanski downshifted the Hurst four-speed, and his 1967 Mariner Turquoise Pontiac GTO screeched to a stop on Pacific Avenue. "Smoke on the Water" by Deep Purple played on his stereo. Jake was a transplanted Polish kid from the Bronx area of New York City, who was now a senior at San Pedro High. All the girls thought Jake was good looking and charming. But he also had a large invisible chip on his shoulder. He rarely backed away from anything- a fight, a street race, or any other kind of challenge.

Jake had recently seen a racing film with Paul Newman, and decided that Newman was cool. Jake now watched all of Newman's movies, got his hair cut like Newman's, and wore a white T-shirt and jeans that resembled a photo of Newman that Jake kept on his dashboard. While some drivers kept a plastic Virgin Mary or Jesus on their dashboards, Jake kept this photo of Paul Newman there for good luck.

Jake noticed my '54 Chevy and Randy's van at the car wash, and then guided his powerful "Goat" onto the lot.

"What's up, guys?" said Jake, coming to a stop beside the other cars.

"Hi, Jake," I replied.

Jake turned off the GTO, and then climbed out.

"Lions Drag Strip, Wilmington!" shouted Randy. "Featuring Jake 'The Snake!'"

"Friday!" shouted Stephanie.

"Big Daddy Don Garlits!" I shouted.

"Shirley Cha Cha Muldowney!" shouted Melissa.

"Like hungry dogs on a piece of meat!" shouted Hank.

"Lions Drag Strip, Wilmington!" shouted Randy.

"Be there!" shouted everyone.

"Nice, guys," smiled Jake, "but I don't think Larry Huffman has anything to worry about."

"Hey, we tried," I said.

"Man, I miss Lions," said Hank.

Lion's Drag Strip had been called the greatest drag strip in the world. It had opened in 1955 because the authorities were sick of putting so many kids in jail for street racing. They figured that it was better to give them a legal and much safer place to pursue their high-speed passions. The Lion's Club agreed to be the sponsor and the legendary Mickey Thompson was the first manager. After they leased land near the harbor in Wilmington, the track became a home for all of the amateur drag racers, and for such professionals as Tom McEwen, Don Prudomme, Gary Gabelich, and Tommy Ivo.

"I was there last December when it closed," said Jake. "They expected a sellout of 10,000 people, and 20,000 showed up."

"Drive the highways, race at Lions," said Randy.

"I raced there every Wednesday night," said Jake,

Just then, we heard the enormous roar of a high performance engine. It was the baby blue 1967 Corvette of Dragan Mosich. "Bad Moon Rising" by Creedence Clearwater Revival blared over his stereo. Mosich was a couple of years older than my group, but an old friend of mine. He had a reputation for being reckless and a little crazy. We had been newspaper delivery boys together at the News Pilot. He had shown me the ropes, and we had become friends one summer.

San Pedro had some of the steepest hills in all of Southern California. But the first thing that Dragan did, when he got a new bike, was to remove his brakes. He said it made things more exciting. Mosich pulled his "Vette" to the curb by the car wash.

"What are you little boys and girls doing?" he asked. "Isn't it past your bed times?"

"Yeah," I said, "Our moms have milk and cookies waiting at home."

"Hey, Jake, are we racing tonight?"

"Why? Haven't you had enough?"

"I've put on some new headers; it's faster now."

"Well, good, I'm happy for you."

"I want another chance, Jake,"

"Be careful what you wish for."

Randy and Hank shared a laugh.

Mosich brought an empty RC Cola bottle to his face, then bit off the spout and began to chew it. He threw the rest of the bottle at our feet, where it smashed into a million pieces. He finally swallowed the glass in his mouth, and then looked over to Jake.

"You can run from me, Jake, But you can't hide. I'll be on the strip tonight, just waiting."

And with that, Mosich floored the gas, and burned rubber as he sped off.

"He's crazy," said Melissa.

"Yeah," said Hank, "he could have gotten a deposit for that bottle."

"Are you going to race him tonight?" I asked.

17

"We'll see. There are a lot of little fish out there that need catching." He brushed some dust off his metallic paint and then climbed into his GTO. It started up with a roar.

"Don't forget the football game on Sunday," said Randy,

"I'll be there."

"Where are you going?" I asked.

"I'm going fishing," he said with a smile.

As Jake's "Goat" roared onto Pacific Avenue, Randy turned and looked over to me.

"Sunday?"

"I'll be there."

We both then looked over at Hank.

"What about you?" I asked.

"Uh, I'll be there, sort of." said Hank.

"What do you mean, sort of?" asked Randy.

"Chad asked me to play on his team."

"Oh, man," said Randy.

"They're all from my neighborhood."

"You're playing for the other team," said Randy.

"Next time I'll probably be back with you guys."

"What a relief," said Randy. "We thought you were deserting us."

"In Miss Martin's class," said Melissa," I read that during the Revolutionary War, some of General Washington's troops were really British sympathizers, and they had red liners sewn into their blue coats."

"Yeah," added Stephanie, "and during the battle, they would reverse their coats to the British red, and fight against the Americans."

"They were called Turncoats," I said.

"And they were considered traitors," said Randy.

"Well, you can call me what you want, but this time I'm playing with Chad's team."

We all started moving toward our two cars.

"Hey," Hank shouted, "Which one of you is giving me a ride?"

"Get the British to give you a ride," answered Randy.

"Yeah," I said, "We're Americans here."

"Ah, come on. This is bullshit!"

We slammed our car doors at the same time, and then started our engines.

"You're right, man," said Randy. "It's absolute bullshit!"

And with that, we pulled our cars out of the car wash, leaving Hank Pilsner behind. We could still hear him cursing, as we pulled onto Pacific Avenue.

Cabrillo Beach rested at the foot of the federal breakwater that was built to create the Los Angeles Harbor. There were actually two very different beaches at Cabrillo Beach. On the inner side, behind the breakwater, the waves were small and it was a great place for little kids to go wading. On the ocean side of the breakwater, another sand beach faced south, and it was exposed to the ocean. In 1932, a Spanish style bathhouse and boathouse were built at Cabrillo Beach for use during the boating events of the 1932 Los Angeles Olympics. A parking lot sat beyond the bathhouse and boathouse. As on most Friday nights, this parking lot was filled with parked and cruising cars and the sound of rock and roll. Fires blazed in the fire pits on the beach. The fires gave off a little warmth and light.

My '54 Chevy sat parked looking out toward the beach and the fire pits. A low rider passed by, and "Samba Pa Ti" by Santana played over its stereo. I had my arms around Stephanie as we shared a lengthy kiss. The ocean breeze mixed with the smell of the wood fires. I'd dated other girls, but Stephanie was my first real girlfriend. We'd been together for about a year, and next month she was going with me to my senior prom.

As we kissed, Stephanie grabbed my hand, and carefully slid it over her clothed breast. It felt pretty damn good. It was small, but firm. It suited her, because she was petite. Suddenly, and very abruptly, Stephanie pulled away from me. She slid over to the far side of the seat against the door.

"What's wrong?" I asked, thinking maybe I'd

left my hand on her breast for too long.

"Nothing," said Stephanie.

I admit it. I didn't know a whole lot about women. But I knew that when they said "nothing," the way Stephanie just did, they usually didn't mean it.

"Was it something I did?" I asked.

"No," she replied, hesitantly. "It was something that you didn't do."

Now I was really confused. How could she be upset about something that I didn't do? Wouldn't I have needed to do something to upset her?

"Something I didn't do?" I asked.

"You know my mom loves you," she said, "and my dad too."

"Yeah?"

"My mom told me that I'd be a fool to lose you."

"Lose me?"

"She said, that you were a good guy and I could do a lot worse."

Okay, her mom and dad both liked me. What was wrong with that?

"I don't understand," I said.

Stephanie looked at me like I was the dumbest person on the face of the Earth.

"Was there something that you wanted me to do?" I asked.

"I'm not going to draw you a picture," she said, "if that's what you want."

I just sat there, looking out at the waves crashing onto the beach. Maybe I was the dumbest person on the face of the Earth.

"I think we should break up," she announced.

"Break up?" I asked, completely surprised.

"You're graduating anyway," she said. "Next, year, you'll be off somewhere, and I'll still be in high school. It would probably be better for both of us."

This was terrible. I really liked Stephanie, and we always enjoyed being together. Now, she was telling me that she didn't want to be with me anymore.

"And I don't think I should go with you to the prom," she said.

The prom was next month, and everything was paid for. I worked long hours busing tables at the Hungry Fisherman Restaurant to make enough money.

"What am I supposed to do," I asked, "go to the prom by myself?"

"No," she said. "You'll need to ask somebody else."

"Somebody else? But I want to go with you."

For a moment we both said nothing. We just watched the fire leap and dance in the nearby fire pit.

"It wouldn't be a good idea," she said. "I think that this will be the best thing for the both of us."

How could she say that this would be the best thing for both of us? This wasn't the best thing for either of us. But what could I do? Stephanie Davies didn't want me anymore. That was a fact.

All of the time we'd spent together, all of the things we'd shared.

"Okay," I said, reluctantly.

My insides were burning, and my heart felt like it was shrinking to the size of a pea. As we looked out at the waves washing up on the shore, tears began to well up in our eyes.

"Niko," she said, choking back emotions. "Would you please take me home?"

"Sure," I said, and then started the car. I could see that the 8-Track tape of Carole King's *Tapestry* jutted out from the car stereo. "So Far Away" began to play as I backed up my '54 Chevy.

After I took Stephanie home, I felt terrible, and I really needed a friend to talk to. I knew that if I cruised the circuit, I would find someone. On Twenty-Fifth Street, I saw Jake's GTO and flagged him down. I left my car parked and got into his "Goat." As we cruised, I told him what had happened with Stephanie. He thought about it for a moment before he spoke.

"What would Paul Newman do?"

"Paul Newman?" I asked, looking at his picture on the dashboard.

"Have you ever seen the movie *Hud*?

"No."

"Newman plays this guy named Hud who drives around this dusty Texas town in this great convertible Cadillac. He does whatever he wants to do. And when it comes to women — love 'em and leave 'em!"

"Yeah?"

"Great movie, although I did fall asleep half way through it. It was on *The Late Show*."

"Oh."

"Dating is like this giant used car lot. Sure, there's a lot of Detroit iron out there, but there are also plenty of gems."

Jake had some of the most shameless pick-up lines that I'd ever heard. But strangely they always seemed to work. My problem was that if I tried to use one of his pick-up lines I think I'd gag.

Just then, Gene Cage pulled alongside of us in his lime green Dodge Challenger. Gene had a freckled face, and a mop of blond hair that covered his eyes. The hair made him look like the sheep dog in those Looney Tunes cartoons. His dad had bought Gene his brand new Challenger for his eighteenth birthday.

"What does he want?" I asked.

"It looks like he wants to race," He motioned to Gene that the next light would be the spot.

"You can let me out right here, I don't really want to be in your race."

"Too late. I'll just play around with him a bit."

I checked my seatbelt, and grabbed the door handle. Jake was fearless and we'd had a few close calls in the past. At the red light, the two cars shook as they revved their engines. But just before the light turned green, a floodlight from a police car illuminated both cars from behind and its red lights flashed, signaling both of us to pull over to the curb.

"Crap!" said Jake, pulling the car to the curb.

"You haven't done anything yet. What could they possibly give you a ticket for?"

"They're the cops. They'll find things."

The police car pulled directly behind Jake and parked. Officer Matt Barbieri exited the driver's side of the patrol car, as his partner, Officer Hansen, exited the other side. Matt Barbieri was in his thirties, dark haired and clean-cut. He'd joined the Los Angeles Police department right out of the Marine Corp. Matt was married to Randy's older sister, Elaine. Officer Hansen looked like a blond haired version of Officer Barbieri. Both were old Pedro boys, who once were the street racers getting pulled over, but now they were the policemen doing the pulling over. Officer Barbieri approached Jake's window while Officer Hansen approached Gene's.

"Jake, Jake, Jake," said Officer Barbieri.

"Hello, Officer."

"You boys weren't about to race were you?"

"No sir, not us."

"Good, because I seem to remember writing you a speeding ticket just last week. Wasn't it for going 120 mph in a 35 mph zone?"

"I paid that, sir."

"Excellent, and I hope you learned a lesson."

"Yes, sir. I learned that you don't want to get caught."

"That's not exactly the lesson I had in mind."

Back in the early 1960s, Matt had a '55 Chevy that was a local legend. He used to tear up the streets. Now he was trying to keep us from doing exactly what he used to do.

"Where's my crazy brother-in-law?" he asked, looking over towards me.

"We saw Randy earlier tonight," I said, "but we haven't seen him in a while."

"You guys need to stay out of trouble, at least for this week. Next week shouldn't be so bad."

I didn't quite understand what he meant by "next week shouldn't be so bad," unless he was referring to school being back in session. I guess Easter Vacation was a busy time for the police.

"Officer," said Jake, "I promise we won't race tonight."

"Well, I guess that's the best I can expect from you, Jake."

Officer Barbieri motioned for Officer Hansen, and they both returned to their police car, turned off the floodlight and red lights, and then drove off.

We got out of the GTO and stepped over to the sidewalk where Gene Cage was already waiting. Gene's family owned a high performance garage in town. Jake always referred to Gene as a spoiled brat.

"Hey, Jake," said Gene. "I've got a little problem."

"And what problem is that?"

"It seems that my girlfriend still likes you."

This stopped Jake for a moment. "You mean, Hannah?"

"Who else?"

Hannah Burns was Jake's first girlfriend. They were together for a year. She was a Jewish girl from San Pedro, while he was a Catholic boy originally from the Bronx. She was as sweet as he was rough, as calm as he was excitable, and as middle-class as he was working class. They had been an odd couple.

"We had plans to go to the prom," said Gene, "but for some reason she still likes you."

"What do you want me to do about it?"

"I want you to race me."

"Why would I want to race you?"

"Because if you win, you take Hannah to the prom with my tickets."

"And if I lose?"

"Then maybe she'll see that you're really a loser, and finally stop caring about you."

"I don't know if girls think that way."

"I don't know either, but it's all I could come up with."

Jake thought it over for a moment. "Okay, let's race."

They agreed to race the next night on Westmont Avenue. I knew that even with all of his tough talk, Jake had never really gotten over Hannah, and that there wasn't anyone else he'd rather go to the prom with. After the two had broken up last year, Jake dated half the girls in the high school. It was like he was hoping that the sheer number of girls would somehow make him forget the one girl that he really cared about. Tomorrow night at midnight Jake would race with Hannah Burns as the prize. It sounded like something Paul Newman would do.

Saturday

It was Saturday morning, and I hadn't slept well. Talking things over with Jake hadn't helped much, and then he had his own issues with Hannah. I still couldn't believe that Stephanie and I were no longer together. It was like a bad dream. I staggered into the kitchen, where my dad was already busy.

"Coffee?" he asked.

"Yeah," I said, rubbing my eyes.

Since my dad had spent his whole life at sea, he always got up with the sun. He was getting older, but he was still tall and ruggedly handsome. Most fishermen were pretty rough characters, but my dad's demeanor was more like a professor than a typical fisherman. He loved to read, so he always had a book or two going. He especially liked books on world history.

"The same Russian winter that stopped Napoleon's armies," he would tell me, "stopped Hitler's armies. Fortunately for us, Hitler never learned the lessons of history."

Before he came to America, he worked as a merchant seaman, learning five languages during his travels. He had one sea going habit that really annoyed me. He couldn't just leave loose objects lying around in our garage. He had to pick them up and tie them securely with twine to the unfinished walls. Sometimes I'd have to untie a basketball, a baseball glove, or even my bicycle, and he knew a hundred different knots. It was as if he was preparing the garage for an ocean voyage. We had the only sea-worthy garage in the neighborhood.

"Here," he said, handing me a cup of coffee.

"Thanks," I grabbed the cup and sat down at the table. I scooped two spoonfuls of sugar and poured in some cream.

"Are you still coming with me on Wednesday?" he asked. "I already talked to the skipper."

"Yeah, I guess," I said, not very enthusiastically.

"Niko, you'll need experience if you want to go fishing in Alaska. You can't just show up in Ketchikan without any experience and expect to get a job."

"I know," I said, taking a sip of the coffee.

"We'll be looking for skipjack off Catalina Island."

My dad was doing all he could to help me. If I wanted to be a fisherman, he could help me get my foot in the door. I just didn't know what I really wanted to do with my life.

"Dad, I appreciate you asking the skipper for me, but I really don't know if I want to go to Alaska. I don't know if I want to be a fisherman."

My dad took a deep breath and then sighed. "I'm not getting any younger, son. I don't even know if I'll be going up next year."

He just looked at me, trying to find the right words to say.

"It's a hard life, and I don't know how much longer fishing will be around for you kids."

The fishing industry built this town. It was impossible for me to imagine San Pedro without fishing. It would be like New York without sky-scrapers or Hawaii without the beaches. We still had a fishing fleet, but it was nothing compared to its history. At its peak, our fishing industry had about sixteen canneries and about a thousand fishing boats. Tuna was first canned right here on Terminal Island. But that was then. Now, there are only a few canneries left, a small fleet of boats, and everything seems to be moving overseas.

"My problem is that I really don't know what I want to do," I admitted.

"You're young, you've got time."

"Yeah, I guess."

I heard my mom coming down the hall. I hoped

to be gone by now, but it was too late. My mom was bigger than life, a force of nature. You didn't want to get in her way. She was older now, but as a young woman she reminded people of the actress Ava Gardner. She entered the room like General George S. Patton reviewing the troops.

"Hmmm," grabbing my cheek. "Still too skinny. Why don't you eat something?"

"I eat all the time," I said.

"If you ate all the time, you wouldn't be so skinny," she said. "No girl is going to want a man who's skinny."

"Mom, I believe I'm of normal weight for my height."

"No," she shouted, grabbing my arm. "Look, skin and bones!"

"Mom, please."

"Oh, God," she proclaimed, looking up to the heavens. "All the food in this country, and he's starving!"

"Mom, I'm not starving."

She started toward the kitchen so that she wouldn't have to look at her emaciated son.

My dad had once told me that when he met my mom, she had been the most beautiful woman in their village, only unmarried because her fiancé had died during World War II. She had other tragedies during the war, but none that she would talk about. My dad would brag to his friends that he had to leave Southern California and Hollywood, to find a movie star in Croatia.

He adored my mom.

"Were you out last night with your little American girlfriend?" she asked.

She said American like it was a dirty word.

"Yeah, we went to the movies."

"I could show you a good Croatian girl, but no, you want an American woman."

"Stephanie and I broke up."

"Broke up?" she asked, not quite understanding.

"We're no longer together."

She looked at me for a moment, finally understanding what I was saying.

"It's because you're too skinny!"

"Okay, Mom," I said, standing up from the table.

"You're not eating breakfast?"

"I'm on a diet," I joked.

"A diet," she said, after looking up and crossing herself. "My God, a diet."

"Just kidding, mom," I said, standing up. "I'll eat at work."

"No," she said. "You're going to sit there and have breakfast."

She stood there glaring at me with her hands on her hips.

"Okay," I said, sitting back down.

"Good, at least you won't starve before lunch."

You didn't argue with my mom. She was an immovable force. As a child, some kid would boast: "My dad can beat up your dad." "Yeah," I'd

33

admit, "But your dad can't beat up my mom!' And the kid would have to admit I was right.

I finished my coffee as my mom went to work in the kitchen. I could hear her mumbling something to herself in Croatian.

The Hungry Fisherman Seafood Restaurant was housed in a two-story Stucco building at the end of the fish harbor, Berth 73. The Fisherman's Cooperative Association occupied the upstairs of the building, while the restaurant had the downstairs. It was decorated in the usual nautical theme. The food was prepared simply, but it was very good. What the fishermen caught that morning, we were serving for lunch and dinner that day. My friend Dean Nash, who was already a bus boy at the restaurant, had helped get me my job there.

Today was a Saturday, so both Dean and I were working lunch. He and I had met at school on the play that Stephanie and I had done together. He was about my height, but he was as thin as a rail. If his shoulders had been any narrower, or his collar any wider, his white shirt would have slid right off of him to the floor. Hank called him "The Geek." My mom was always nice to him, and never let him leave before she fixed him a meal.

If she thought I was starving, what did she think of him?

"I heard you and Stephanie broke up," said Dean, as he put out the place settings for today's lunch.

"How'd you hear?" I asked, putting empty water glasses on the same tables.

"She called me this morning. She said she felt bad about it."

"What else did she say?"

"Not much. What are you going to do about the prom?"

"I don't know."

"Women," said Dean, shaking his head. "You can't live with them, but by God, you can't live without them!"

"Right."

"She also told me that Hank isn't playing football for your team tomorrow."

"Yeah. He's playing for Chad's team instead."

"Well, do you need another man?"

"Sure. Who do you have in mind?"

"Me, of course."

I started to laugh, but stopped when I realized that he was serious.

"I'm sorry, Dean, but I thought you were just kidding."

"No, I'm not kidding," he said. "Pound for pound I'm just as tough as Hank."

"Yeah, it's just too bad he has so many more pounds."

35

"It's not the size of the dog in the fight, it's the size of the fight in the dog." Dean actually growled and then barked like a vicious dog.

"Okay," I said. "Be at Friendship Park tomorrow at ten o'clock, and remember, it's tackle. We play tackle football."

"Great. I'll be there."

"Niko!" yelled Tommy from the kitchen. "Get over here!"

"Sure, Tommy, right away." I set down the rest of the water glasses and hurried over to the kitchen.

Tommy Russo was the head chef and manager of the Hungry Fisherman. He was a Vietnam Vet, who had returned from the war a year ago. He'd gotten sent home with a Purple Heart because of wounds he'd received. Tommy was very intense, and reminded me of the young actor who played Michael Corleone in the movie *The Godfather*.

"Caesar is coming in today for lunch," said Tommy.

Caesar was Tommy's nickname for his younger brother, Paulie, who was the owner of the restaurant. He almost never came in, but when he did, he expected to be waited on like royalty. Paulie also reminded me one of the actors in *The Godfather* — the one who played Michael's brother, Fredo Corleone.

"Make sure he gets good service," said Tommy.

"Of course."

"Do you have a lighter?"

"No, I don't smoke."

"Here." Tommy handed me a Bic lighter, which I tested.

"My brother, Paulie, expects to be treated just like Caesar, and he loves a cigar after lunch. He expects someone to be there to light it. It makes him feel more important."

"I'll try my best."

"No, you won't try your best, you'll be there to light it, or else.

"Okay, but what happens if I'm late?"

"He'll probably have you killed." He said casually, and then watched my eyes grow big. "It's a joke, for Christ's sake. What's he going to do? He's a damn baby. He can't even wipe his ass without my help. Humor him, okay?"

"Okay," I nodded.

I know that Tommy was just joking, but mob killings did happen in San Pedro. It was no laughing matter. In fact, the brother of a mob boss was killed on my street. I couldn't imagine being killed for not lighting someone's cigar, but stranger things have happened.

I kind of felt sorry for Tommy. While he was off in Vietnam fighting for his country, his baby brother was busy growing and diversifying the family fish packing business. Now, Paulie had all the money, and Tommy, the older brother, had to work for him.

Marie Russo Donato, Tommy's older sister,

and her daughter, Diana showed up to waitress the lunch rush. Marie and Tommy were typical siblings, always arguing. Diana was very sweet, and the apple of her uncle Tommy's eye.

"Hi, Dean," said Diana, as she walked into the dining room.

That startled Dean, and he accidentally knocked over some of the water glasses, which shattered on the floor.

"Dean, what the hell are you doing?" shouted Tommy from the kitchen. "This isn't a Greek restaurant. We don't break plates, we serve fish!"

"I'm sorry," said Dean, bending to pick up the pieces.

"Niko," said Tommy. "Get the vacuum, we've got customers any minute."

"Okay," I said, going for the vacuum.

Diana joined Dean in picking up the broken pieces. Dean really liked Diana. In fact, he was a little crazy about her. At school, he would write her name all over his *Pee Chee* folder, with little hearts and arrows. It was all pretty disgusting. She went to Our Lady of the Harbor Girl's High School, so they never saw each other at school. Dean was trying to work up the courage to ask her out.

"Marie!" shouted Tommy. "Come here!"

"Don't shout at me, " said Marie to her brother. "I didn't break those glasses!"

I began to vacuum up the mess, while Dean

and Diana got back to work.

"Do me a favor, Marie, will you?' said Tommy, lowering his voice. "Keep Diana away from Dean. He's a good boy, but when Diana comes around, he starts to act like Don Knotts."

"They work together, Tommy!" she said. "What am I suppose to do?"

"Maybe," said Tommy, "he should work mostly with you on the floor, and Niko should work with her."

"Okay, boss!" said Marie, turning her back and walking away.

"What the hell is that?" shouted Tommy.

"What the hell is what?" she shouted back.

"That boss crap!"

"You're my boss, Tommy, I follow your orders."

Tommy held his hand up like he wanted to give her a slap across the face.

"I'm your brother, Marie! I'm your brother, first!"

"Okay," she said, "you're my brother! I didn't think you were my sister!"

Tommy made a fist and then bit it with his teeth. Vince Galasso, the assistant chef, came over and put his hand on Tommy's shoulder.

"Let it go, Tommy," said Vince. "Let's get ready for lunch."

"Okay, Dago," said Tommy. "I'll be okay."

Tommy always called Vince "The Dago," or just "Dago." I didn't like Vince. He always gave me a hard time for being Croatian, as if Italians were so much better. Most of the time I just ignored him, but sometimes he got on my nerves.

The lunch rush became busy, with most of the tables filling quickly. After Marie and Diana took the customers orders, Tommy and Vince prepared their meals, and then Dean and I delivered them to their tables. The plates of broiled sea bass, red snapper, halibut, and swordfish all looked delicious.

Just as the lunch rush was peaking, Paulie Russo strolled in. He reminded me more of a bad actor trying to play Caesar, than a real emperor. His lunch guest was a big, burly guy named Big Sal. I think Sal worked for Paulie at his fish packing company, but he looked like a thug right out of central casting.

Paulie gave his sister, Marie, a peck on the cheek, waved a quick acknowledgment to his brother Tommy, and then strolled to his reserved table. He handed me a bottle of wine that he'd brought for his meal. I quickly uncork it, and brought him two wine glasses.

After chatting a while with his niece, Diana, Paulie ordered the lobster for himself and Big Sal. When I went over to the kitchen, I heard Tommy talking to Vince.

"Look at him, he thinks he's an emperor. My brother, he's so full of shit."

Eventually, I brought Paulie and Big Sal their lobsters, and then tried to stay close to their table. I refilled their glasses and brought them more bread, but otherwise I tried to stay out of their way.

I checked my pocket, to make sure that I still had the Bic lighter. It was there. But what would happen to me if I'd lost it, or I wasn't there to light Paulie's cigar? Would they "rub me out," like in the movies? I started to imagine the worst. I could see Big Sal pouring cement into a large bucket that contained my feet. I imagined my parents finding me tomorrow morning wearing "cement overshoes" in L.A. Harbor, just like they found Mr. De Carlo, whose company's bread we still served at our restaurant, but he was "*morto.*" I guess his bread wasn't good enough, or maybe he forgot to use his Bic lighter.

"Hey, kid," said Big Sal. "Stop day dreaming!"

"Huh?"

Somehow time had passed, and it was obvious that Paulie and Big Sal had finished their lunches some time ago. Their dirty dishes still lay on the table.

"Paulie needs a light," said Big Sal, pointing to the cigar in Paulie's mouth.

I nervously took out the Bic lighter, and lit Paulie's cigar.

Paulie took a couple of puffs to get the cigar going.

"Good job, kid" said Big Sal.

Paulie blew two perfect smoke rings. He then tilted his head back in a self satisfied way. I quickly cleared their dirty dishes.

As Hank's green Ford Pinto descended Western Avenue to Paseo Del Mar, "Tell Me Why" from
Neil Young's *After the Gold Rush* played on his
8-Track player. A magnificent view of the Pacific
Ocean appeared out past the sea cliffs, and a faint
silhouette of Catalina Island could be seen in the
distance. I tried to talk with Hank, but he would
hardly answer me. I figured that I'd better apologize for leaving him stranded at the car wash
last night.

"Okay," I said, "I'm sorry."

"I had to walk three mile just to get home."

"You pissed us off."

"Well, you guys pissed me off. I can't wait until
tomorrow's game. It's payback time."

Hank was usually an easygoing guy, with a
ready joke or funny comment. It was unusual to
see him so angry.

"I like Neil Young," I said, "but couldn't we just
listen to something else?

"I have one other tape, but I never play it."

"How about the radio?"

"It's broken."

"Why do you only have two tapes?"

"I have lots of record albums at home, but
when I'm in my car this is what I listen to."

"Why?"

"Because I think it's the greatest rock album

ever."

"You think *After the Gold Rush* is the greatest rock album ever?"

"Yeah, the greatest."

"Better than The Beach Boy's *Pet Sounds*?"

"Better."

"Better than The Beatles' *Sgt. Peppers*?"

"Better."

"Well, that's your opinion, I guess."

"And that's all that matters in my car, isn't it?"

It was his car, but I was tired of listening to the same songs over and over.

"Could we please listen to your other tape?" I asked.

"I've already told you," he said. "I never listen to it. But you can get out and walk if you want to. I'd love to see how you like walking home."

We continued along Paseo Del Mar with Neil Young's "Tell Me Why" still playing. Tomorrow was our football game, and all I could think about was how I was going to smack Hank during the game. He's not the only one who wanted payback.

Hank parked his Pinto on the curb along the Point Fermin Park Annex. Randy's van sat parked at the curb in front of us. The song "After the Gold Rush" played on Hank's stereo. The Annex was a long strip of green lawn that stretched for blocks along the Paseo Del Mar sea cliffs. On the lawn, Randy and Melissa lay kissing on a blanket. When Randy heard Hank's music, he looked over to us in disgust.

"Man, are you still playing that tape?" shouted Randy.

"I don't need your permission," said Hank. "If you don't like it, tough."

"Sounds like Hank is still a little testy," said Melissa.

"Yeah," said Randy, "testy testicle."

We got out of the Pinto and walked over the grass to them.

"That one tape is all he'll play," I said.

"Why?" asked Melissa.

"He says it's the greatest rock album ever."

"No way," said Randy. "Everyone knows that *Led Zeppelin IV* is the greatest."

"Yeah," said Melissa, "Stairway to Heaven."

Hank and I sat down on the grass near their blanket.

"Next Saturday," said Randy, "Vic's having a party. He's calling it Vic's Big Blowout."

"A good excuse to drink beer," I said.

"Who needs an excuse?" said Hank.

Melissa reached over and touched my shoe.

"I need to talk to you," she said to me.

Randy and Hank looked over at Melissa then at me.

"I need to tell Niko something," she said to Randy.

"Well, babe," said Randy, "tell all of us."

"No," said Melissa, standing up. "It's about Stephanie. Niko can tell you later if he wants to."

Melissa motioned for me to follow her, which

I did.

"Let's go down to the lower park," she said.

We walked over to the path that led down to the lower park.

"Hey, no making out!" shouted Randy.

He looked over to Hank seated nearby. Randy got a silly look on his face.

"Have I ever told you how cute you are?" said Randy.

Hank put his hands up as a sign of surrender.

"Okay," said Hank. "But, no tongues!" He then puckered up.

We could still hear Hank and Randy's laughter as we walked down the hill.

"Have you finished your report for Mrs. Coleman's class?" Melissa asked.

"No," I admitted. "I haven't even started it yet. Mrs. Coleman is giving me another week."

"Oh," she said. "I turned mine in on Friday."

At the lower park, Melissa and I looked down on the rocky tide pools below. It was low tide, and a group of people was exploring the tide pools.

"So, what's all this about Stephanie?" I asked.

Melissa looked up the hill to make sure that we were alone.

"It's not really about Stephanie," she said.

"What?"

"I needed an excuse to talk to you."

"I don't understand."

"Promise you won't say anything to Randy."

"Melissa, Randy is one of my best friends."

"I thought I was a friend too?"

"You are, but Randy--"

"Is a guy!" she interrupted.

"Well, yeah. But--"

"That's too bad," she interrupted again. "I really don't have anyone else I can talk to."

Down on the tide pools, we watched as a young boy and a girl explored the pools together. They both carried small buckets.

"Melissa, you are my friend. You know that."

"Well, I thought I was."

"You are."

The little girl down at the tide pool had found something. She called the boy over for a look.

"Okay," I said, "What's your secret? I won't tell Randy."

"Promise?"

"Yeah, I promise."

Melissa smiled a naughty smile.

"I went out with Marisol's brother."

"Huh?"

"Pancho and I have been dating. If Marisol knew, she wouldn't be happy with me. She never wanted me to date her brother."

Marisol was Melissa's best friend, and they'd been neighbors all their lives. Pancho was about four years older than Melissa. He was a low rider, with a 1964 Chevy Impala. He was a rough-looking guy and a little scary.

"How did this happen?"

"What do you mean?"

"You told me yourself that you didn't think Pancho was very good looking, but now you're seeing him behind Randy's back?"

"I know; it's crazy."

"You need to tell Randy what you're doing, or you need to stop seeing Pancho. You need to be honest."

"Niko, I'm graduating, and Randy has one more year of school left."

"Now you sound like Stephanie."

"Pancho is older and kind of interesting. I'm not even sure that I want to stay a virgin."

"Melissa," I said, a little annoyed at her. "You're not a virgin."

"What do you mean, I'm not a virgin? Of course I am. Don't believe Randy's boasting."

"Randy hasn't said anything."

I looked down at the tide pools again. The little girl gave the boy a kiss on the lips. He wiped the kiss off with his shirtsleeve.

"Remember that time I showed up at Randy's, and his parents weren't home?"

"Yeah," she said, cautiously.

"After I knocked for a few minutes, you and Randy finally answered the door."

"So?"

"Come on, Melissa, don't bullshit me. You say we're friends, but then you give me this bullshit."

I looked right at her. Her eyes showed that she knew what I was talking about.

"When you two finally came to the door, your

47

hair was messed up and your clothes were only half on. I might be a virgin, but I'm not stupid."

I watched her face change to look of resignation.

"How come you didn't say anything?"

"I was just surprised, and since you guys didn't say anything, I figured that maybe I shouldn't either."

"Well," she sighed, "What do I say now?"

"Just say that you're going to stop seeing Pancho, and that you're going to start treating Randy with some respect. He loves you, and he'd be devastated if he ever found out."

Her eyes softened as she looked at me for a moment.

"Niko, I've said it before. You should become a priest."

"I don't even go to church anymore. And I don't want to be celibate my whole life, it's bad enough when you're eighteen. A priest is the last thing I want to be."

"I think you'd be a good one."

"I think I'd be at least as good a priest as Father Jason, what with all his drinking and womanizing. I can't believe he gets away with it."

"You'd be a lot better than Father Jason, he's a disgrace."

I turned to Melissa and adopted the seriousness of a priest.

"My child," I said, "You have sinned."

"Yes father," she said, lowering her eyes, "I

know, and often."

"You must say three Our Fathers and two Hail Mary's. Now go my child, and sin no more." I made the sign of the cross.

Melissa and I both tried to suppress a laugh, but in the end we couldn't.

Eventually, we went back up the hill to Hank and Randy. They were curious about our conversation, but they didn't push it. When Melissa and Randy left, Hank drove us over to his place. His *After the Gold Rush* tape played the whole way. I wanted to take it and toss it out the window, but Hank was already pissed off at me. I didn't want to give him any more motivation for tomorrow's football game.

Back at Hank's house, I got into in my '54 Chevy and gratefully popped in an Eric Clapton tape into my stereo. As the song "Layla" began to play, I headed over to Jake's apartment. Jake had his own apartment in the building where his grandparents lived. It was an old clapboard building and rents were cheap.

Jake's grandparents first brought him out for a visit to San Pedro when he was nine. They had rescued him from a bad situation in New York, where his mom, brothers, and sister still lived.

His father had left the family some time ago. For years, his grandparents would shuttle him back and forth between the two worlds. The Bronx had been a life of welfare and tenements, and crime and violence. His older brother was a small time crook and heroin junkie. Finally, in high school, Jake stopped going back to New York for visits and just remained in San Pedro. He loved his family, but knew that his life was better without them. San Pedro wasn't only a continent away in distance; it was a world away in its differences. If San Pedro was *American Graffiti*, New York was *Mean Streets*.

I turned into the alley behind Jake's apartment and found Jake in the old garage he had rented. The front of his GTO jutted out into the alley, the hood was up, and Jake's head was beneath it. As I parked my car, Jake came over to me, wiping his greasy hands on a rag.

"I forgot to tell you," he said. " I saw *The Sting* the other night at the Warner's."

"Was it any good?"

"Hell yes, it had Paul Newman. That other guy was okay, too."

"You mean, Robert Redford?

Jake nodded, and then took a deep breath before he spoke.

"You know, Niko, I still care about Hannah."

"I know. She was your first girlfriend."

"Yeah," he smiled, "Like my 'Goat,' or your '54. I guess we always have a soft spot for our first anything."

"Yeah, I guess so."

Jake slammed the car's hood shut. "I want to show you something. Do you want to go?"

"Sure, why not?"

Jake was driving, but I thought that the GTO could have found its own way here. We were in Wilmington on 223rd Street. It was an industrial area near the harbor. We finally stopped at Alameda, parked, and got out of the car. Behind the chain link fence was a large paved lot, like a shopping center's parking lot. Several cars, trucks, and vans sat parked. A warehouse building was off to the right. A few tractor-trailers were also spread around. In the distance stood an oil refinery and some high-voltage power lines. The sight was certainly not what I remembered. I closed my eyes and tried to imagine the smell of fuel and exhaust. I tried to hear the sound of dragster engines, and the frenetic voice of Larry Huffman, the announcer. But it didn't work. My imagination wouldn't take me back to the Lions Drag Strip that I remembered. Instead, all I saw was a quiet, almost empty lot. Jake was thinking his own thoughts as he stared out on what was once his Wednesday night playground. Saturdays were for the big bracket prize races, but Wednesdays were reserved for the locals "grudge" matches. Jake had taken on all comers and won most of those challenges. I remembered one certain Wednesday when Jake had beaten Dragan Mosich's Corvette and Gene Cage's Challenger all in the same night.

The eerie quiet was finally broken by the sound of a Harley Davidson motorcycle pulling up to the chain link fence. The rider had on a motorcycle jacket and a helmet with an ostrich plume. There was only one person audacious enough to wear an ostrich plume on this helmet. He was a local legend before he ever became world famous.

"Holy shit," said Jake. "That's Gary Gabelich."

Gary Gabelich was born in San Pedro to Croatian parents. The family later moved to Long Beach where he grew up. He started racing when he was fifteen. At nineteen, he reached a speed of 356 mph in a jet car on the Bonneville Salt Flats. In 1970, at age thirty, his rocket car, the Blue Flame, set the land speed record of 622 mph, making Gary the fastest man on earth. At Lion's, he had always been a crowd favorite.

Gary shut off his motorcycle, dropped his kickstand, and slipped off his helmet, revealing a haircut that reminded me of an early Beatle. The way he carried himself even reminded me of a rock star. He gazed out at the vast lot that had once been his stage.

"Man," said Gary. "A parking lot."

"Just like that Joni Mitchell song," said Jake.

"What?" asked Gary.

"You know, they paved paradise, and put up a parking lot."

"Oh yeah," smiled Gary. "It was a little slice of paradise anyway."

Jake and I had heard that Gary had been in an awful funny car crash just last year at Orange County International Raceway. His hand had been hurt badly, and his leg was so badly broken that he had a metal rod holding it together. He was in the hospital for months, yet his attitude now seemed surprisingly positive.

"We heard about your crash," I said.

"Yeah, I'm just now getting out. I had to see for myself what was left of the old track."

"There's nothing left," said Jake.

"Nothing except memories," said Gary.

In 1963, Gary had won the United Drag Racing Association title in his Double A fuel dragster, and in 1967, driving a Chevy funny car, he was the first person to hit 200 mph in a Chevy. He was known for not holding anything back and giving everyone a good show.

"You probably have a lot of memories," I said.

"You know," said Gary, "memories are great, but I'm about today and tomorrow. I don't look back."

"I was here on that foggy Saturday night, when you crashed," said Jake.

"Yeah," said Gary, "A thick marine layer had

come in. Nobody even knew that I had crashed at the end of the track."

"They didn't know you'd crashed?" I asked.

"No. Then they couldn't find me because my car had smashed through the Willow Street fence and I'm flipped over in a ditch."

"Then what?" I asked.

"They finally found me and asked me if I was okay. I said, the hell with that, did I win?" He flashed a wide grin, "of course I had."

Jake and I knew the story of how Gary had been chosen to drive the Blue Flame and try to break the land speed record. The car's owners had first gone to Craig Breedlove, who held the record in his car, The Spirit of America, but Breedlove wasn't interested. So they then offered it to another driver, but that driver was killed in a racing accident. Gary was the third choice, but he accepted the challenge; and the rest, as they say, is history.

"I can't wait to get back out on a track, any track."

Gary was pleased to learn that I was also a Croatian, and we discovered that our families were from the same region. Jake shared with Gary his history with Lion's Wednesday night races, and Gary told us that he'd started out the same way, driving his parents' 1957 Buick. He offered to share one more Lion's story before he had to leave.

"Glen Stokey had a crash like mine, but without the fog. His dragster went right through the

Willow Street fence, and it's lying across Willow Street, parachute and all. As Glen is climbing out, the first person there is some old guy in his Rambler. I don't think the old guy even knew there was a racetrack nearby. He comes over to Glen, looks at the dragster and the parachute, scratches his head and asks, "When did they start dropping these out of airplanes?"

We all shared a laugh.

"It's too bad Lion's had to close," I said.

"Just too many noise complaints," said Jake.

"That's not why it closed," said Gary. "That was the excuse."

"Then why did it close?" I asked.

"It was money."

"Money?" asked Jake. "But Lion's always made money."

"Yeah. But somebody found out that they could make even more money if it was something else," pointing out past the chain link fence. "Like maybe a parking lot."

We talked a while longer, then Gary said his goodbyes and got on his Harley. Growing up, Gary Gabelich had been one of our heroes, and meeting him did nothing to change that. As he rode off, we got in the "Goat" and headed back to San Pedro.

When we got back to Jake's, I left him there, got in my own car, and went over to the nearby Chevron station for some gas. Dave, the mechanic, left the service bay when he saw my car at the pumps and headed toward me. Dave was from Boston, wore his Red Sox cap with his Chevron uniform, and still had his working class Boston accent. He was a Vietnam vet, who lost a leg there. His artificial leg gave him a noticeable limp. For some reason, Dave never returned to Boston after Nam. Maybe he didn't want his friends back home to see what had happened to him.

"There's cheap Niko," said Dave. "How much gas today, a buck?"

"Dave, I'm rich today, two bucks."

"A regular J. Paul Getty."

As Dave turned on the gas pump, I heard a car pull up behind me. I could hear "Tequila Sunrise" by The Eagles playing over its stereo, and I could see Dave's face as he watched the car come to a stop. His eyes almost popped out.

"Look at that!" said Dave, staring.

I turned to see what had caught Dave's eye, and found that Carissa Johansson had pulled up in her white Volkswagen convertible. She was her usual gorgeous self.

"That's Carissa," I whispered to Dave as I gently waved to her.

"Jesus, you know her?" he asked.

"Yeah, kind of."

"I might have to change my opinion of you, Niko."

"Relax, we were in journalism together, that's it."

As Carissa stepped out of her VW, the sunlight hit her flowing blond hair and her blue eyes glistened. She looked amazing, and the truth is that she was as smart as she was beautiful. Life wasn't fair, why couldn't I ever rate a girl like Carissa Johansson?

"Hi Niko," she said as she smiled her magnificent smile.

She wore a tight burgundy top and a pair of faded jeans.

"Hi Carissa," I stammered.

She looked over my '54 Chevy as if it had some kind of disease. "You still have this funny old car," she said, shaking her head.

"Yeah, but not for long, maybe."

"Oh, really?"

I didn't really have any plans to get rid of my car. But this was Carissa Johansson. The truth was pretty boring, so I figured that I'd better make something up.

"When I go to college next year, I'll want something else." I said.

"Oh, where are you going to college?" she asked. "I might be going to Berkeley."

"Uh, I'm not sure yet." I said, "I still need to decide."

"Are you going to take journalism?"

Carissa and I had been together on the staff of the *Fore-n-Aft*, our school newspaper. She was an editor, while I wrote about sports.

"I'm not sure what I'll major in."

"I liked your articles about our school's sports history," she said. "They were very interesting."

"Your dad's influence, I guess. After his class, I now seem to look at everything from a historical perspective."

She stared at me for a moment, sizing me up.

"He'd be very happy to hear that," she smiled.

"Please tell him then, because it's true."

"I will," she said, running her fingers through her hair. "It might make him feel better, he's been out sick for a week."

"Nothing serious, I hope."

"He's a tough old guy," she said, "and he doesn't like doctors."

"Neither does my dad, and hospitals even less."

I paid Dave for my gas. Then Carissa asked him to fill-up her car as well. She then looked back over to me.

"Are you going to the prom?"

"I was, but my girlfriend, Stephanie, and I broke-up. Now, I don't know."

"Really," she said thinking for a long moment. "You know Tony, my boyfriend, he's still in a cast for his broken leg."

Tony Sorrento was San Pedro High's All Marine League tight end/defensive end. He went through the entire football season uninjured, but broke his leg one Sunday going up against my friends and me at Friendship Park. Tony had a scholarship offer from UCLA, but Hank Pilsner, was the man that day. He covered Tony when he was playing tight end, and blocked him when he was trying to rush the quarterback. Hank made him look absolutely foolish.

"Yeah, I know Tony," I said.

"Well, he told me that he wouldn't mind if I went with someone else to the prom, since he couldn't dance or anything. Maybe you and I could go together."

I looked over to Dave, and saw that his chin was almost touching his Adam's apple.

"Oh, yeah?" I asked.

"Yeah," she smiled.

I couldn't believe all this. Was I dreaming? Was Carissa Johansson really asking me to the prom? Yeah, she did have a boyfriend, and it wasn't like we were seeing each other, but this would definitely solve my problem of having to find a date.

"That might work out," I said.

"Well," she paused. "Do you want my number?"

"Sure, yes, definitely."

I reached over to Dave, who was still pumping gas, and pulled a pen and a credit card form from his shirt pocket. I then handed them to Carissa. As she used the hood of her car to write down her phone number, I noticed that Dave had a little drool actually starting down the corner of his mouth.

I pulled the shop rag out of his back pocket and dabbed at the corner of his mouth. He yanked the rag out of my hand.

My mom tore open the blue Air Mail envelope as she sat with me at the dining room table. While I finished my dinner, my dad cleared his dinner plate and moved into the kitchen to help with the dishes. I assumed that the Air Mail letter was from my mom's sister, Darinka, my spinster aunt who still lived in the family home back in Zlarin, the island village off the Dalmatian coast where we were from. Since I was only two years old when we left, I don't remember anything about Zlarin, although I've seen endless photos and postcards. It looked like a lovely and idyllic place, sunbathed and rustic. An island where no one owned a car, but everyone owned a boat. My dad had sailed those waters as a boy, and dived for coral in its bays, and my mom had swam every beach on the island. They were always telling me how wonderful the waters were, warm and crystal clear.

"I've been waiting for this." My mom gushed, looking into the envelope.

"What is it?" I asked between forkfuls of mostaccioli.

"Look!" she said, showing me a photo.

The picture was of what looked like a twelve year old girl. The photo was obviously taken somewhere in Yugoslavia.

"Well, do you think she's pretty?" she asked.

"Mom, this girl looks about twelve years old."

"So, when you're twenty-six, she'll be twenty."

"Mom, what are you up to?" I asked, somewhat suspicious.

"I was just hoping that you would say she's pretty."

"And why is it important that I say she's pretty?"

"Because, you two are engaged to be married."

"What?" I asked, almost choking on the pasta.

"I made an arrangement with my best friend. She won't let her daughter marry anyone else, but you. Don't tell me that you never plan to get married."

"I do hope to get married some day. But that day is somewhere in the future, and it's not with some girl that I've never even met."

"In a few years she'll be fifteen, maybe you'll have met her by then."

"And I'll be twenty-one. I'll still be six years older than her."

"Niko, back in Zlarin, we have a saying. Sometimes the saying is about how you go about making a good meal, and other times it's about how you go about finding a good bride."

"And what is this saying?" I asked, putting down my fork.

"If you want tender and flavorful, better a young lamb than an old goat."

I couldn't believe that I was having this conversation with my mother.

"Yeah, mom, and in this country, we have a saying too," I said. "Underage girl equals jail. It's called statutory rape."

"What is this statuary rape?" she asked. "I'm not talking about a statue."

My dad finally came out of the kitchen to put a stop to the conversation.

"Enough of this talk," he demanded. "Niko is not getting married anytime soon, right Niko?"

"Right," I answered.

"I was just trying to help," she said, sheepishly.

"Let the boy find his own bride when he's ready."

"I only want what's best for him," she said, sulking her way into the kitchen.

"She's only trying to help," said my dad, putting his hand on my shoulder.

"I know," I said. "But with a twelve year old?"

"She's certainly a young lamb," he said.

"I guess that makes me the old goat."

"So, the skipper needs to know, are you going fishing with us on Wednesday?"

I still hadn't made up my mind yet about whether I wanted to go fishing, but since my dad rescued me from mandatory jail time, how could I say no.

"Okay, sure."

"Good. I'll call the skipper right away."

It was to be a busy Saturday night. First, I was supposed to meet everyone at the car wash in the early evening. Next, Dean Nash and I were supposed to go up to Averill Park for a little underage beer drinking. And finally, I was supposed to be at Westmont around midnight for Jake's street race. It was almost sundown as I turned my '54 Chevy onto Pacific Avenue and headed toward Point Fermin Park to watch the sunset.

Jethro Tull's *Stand Up* poked out from my 8-track player, and "Jeffrey Goes to Leicester Square" began to play. I remembered the first time I heard this song. It was in Tom Helm's 1948 Chevy Fleetline, and it was the first time I'd ever gone cruising. Tom was about eighteen then, while Jake, Randy, and I were about fifteen. Tom would let us ride around with him while he cruised the circuit. This was pretty cool, since we were just little punks. There were twice the number of people cruising back then, and there were at least a dozen car clubs. Tom had been a member of the Coachman Car Club. Their claim to fame was that they actually got Mama Cass, of the Mamas and the Papas, to pose nude with "The Coachmen" written across her ample ass.

Tom's black '48 Fleetline was a beauty, and it was in perfect stock condition, except for an 8-track player that he added under the dash. Unfortunately, the player had a loose wire or something, because the sound didn't always come out of both speakers. But whenever both speakers decided to miraculously work, Tom would take out whatever tape was playing, and pop in Jethro Tull's *Stand Up*.

A year later, when I bought my '54 Chevy, I showed it to Tom. He really looked it over closely, running his hand along its curves.

"It's nice, Niko," he said. "How many miles?"

"Twenty-four thousand," I said proudly. "Not bad for a sixteen year old car."

"That's great," he smiled. "That's really low."

"The old man kept it in a garage," I boasted. "And only drove it to the market once a week."

"You know, Niko," he said. "You're the last of us. It's great that you're carrying on the tradition, but we're not long for this world."

"What do you mean?"

"We're dinosaurs, Niko, we're just about extinct, even though we don't know it yet. But I don't think the dinosaurs had any idea they'd be extinct either."

I really didn't understand Tom, because even two years later people still cruised San Pedro. In fact, I imagined that people would still be cruising San Pedro forever. I didn't really understand what Tom was saying.

At Point Fermin Park, I parked my Chevy across from Walker's Café, a 1930s era café. It was quiet now, but on Sunday afternoons, Walker's became a busy biker hangout, with Triumphs, Nortons, and Harleys all parked diagonally along its curb.

From Walkers, I strolled over to Point Fermin's white and green Victorian era lighthouse. Built in 1874, the lighthouse operated until 1941, when it became a lookout point during World War Two.

After the lighthouse, I walked over to the short wall along the sea cliff for an unobstructed view of the Pacific Ocean. The sun was just setting and it looked like it was going to be a spectacular sunset.

"Is that your '54 Chevy?" a voice called out from behind me.

I turned around to see who it was. I didn't know this guy. He looked like he was in his twenties, had short hair, and looked Mexican-American. He was dressed like a "*cholo*," a Mexican low rider.

"Did you say something?" I asked.

"Yeah," he said, "Is that your '54 Chevy over there?"

He pointed over toward Walker's and my car. There, parked near my '54 Chevy, was another '54 Chevy. This one had gray primer spots, and it was missing its hubcaps. "Oh, crap," I thought to myself.

I knew right away who this guy was, and even though it was Randy who took the hubcaps off his '54 Chevy, I was the one who had them in my possession. And since they had his driver's license number engraved on them, he could prove they were his. If I was lucky, he'd call the police, if I were unlucky, he would take the law into his own hands. I wonder what they do to you if you steal something from them in prison? I don't think I really wanted to know.

"Yeah, that's my '54 Chevy," I said, trying to remain calm.

"Nice ride," he said, without any emotion.

The guy certainly looked the part of an ex-convict. Although I had to admit, I didn't really know what an ex-convict even looked like.

"Is that your '54 Chevy over by mine?" I asked, already knowing the answer.

"Yeah," he said. "I got it after I got out."

I wonder what he'd been in prison for? It was probably for some violent crime, like assault or murder. I don't think they put you in prison for unpaid parking tickets.

"It looks like it's being worked on," I said. "But it has a lot of potential."

"I had some nice hubcaps," he sighed. "They were just like yours."

"Really?" I gulped.

He looked at me for a moment, trying to decide what to say.

"Anybody try to sell you any hubcaps lately?"

"No," I answered quickly.

"Not that you need them, yours look pretty good."

"They do," I said, "there's nothing wrong with them."

"Some bastard stole mine. And right in front of my apartment."

"I've had two sets stolen myself," I said, realizing that I probably shouldn't have said that.

"Really?"

"People want the '54 Bel Air hubcaps, they're popular."

"I know," he said, looking me over.

I realized that I probably shouldn't say anymore than I had to.

"I guess you wouldn't want to sell your hubcaps, would you?" he asked.

"Uh, no, I wouldn't."

"Before I had my Chevy," he said. "I used to see yours parked in front of your place."

"Oh, yeah?"

"Yeah. It's one of the cleanest Chevys in Pedro."

"Thanks," I said, and then tried to change the subject. "So, you live in Pedro?"

"Yeah, I graduated from Pedro High in '67. I've been away, but after I put in my time I knew that I wanted to come back home."

"Your time?"

"Yeah, it was hell. I thought I'd never get through it."

"That bad?"

"I almost got killed a few times," he said. "Of course I had to kill a few of them myself just to stay alive."

"Of course. It's probably a dangerous place."

"It can be, it can also be beautiful."

"Beautiful?" I asked, surprised at his choice of words.

"Yeah, the dry season is warm, but nice. It's the wet season that makes things miserable."

Was he in prison in Seattle? What did it matter if it was the dry season or the wet season? Didn't every prison cell look the same, just three solid walls and gray bars?

"I didn't think you guys got out much?" I said. "I know that you go outdoors for exercise, but I thought that was about it?"

He looked at me with some confusion.

"You have to go out to find the enemy," he said, mystified.

"You mean in the yard?"

"What yard? If you wanted to find Charlie, you had to go into the jungle."

"Charlie?" I asked. "The jungle?"

"I was in the 101st Airborne, Vietnam. I just got out."

His name was Danny Sanchez, and he had no idea how the rumor started about him being an ex-convict. He said he'd never spent time in prison, or even in jail. In high school, he'd been a bit of a loner, but identified with the low riders. He'd been drafted right out of San Pedro High into the army. We sat and talked in the old band shell area of the park. He had a lot of stories about Nam that he shared — the bad times, the funny times, and the scary times. He became very somber when he told me that he was at the Battle of Hamburger Hill.

"It was really just called Hill 937," he said. "The grunts gave it the name Hamburger Hill, because so many of us were turned into Hamburger."

He explained how the terrain and foliage protected the Viet Cong from U.S. air power.

"Half the time, our own Cobra helicopters fired on us. We had a lot of casualties from friendly fire."

Danny told me all this in a very matter of fact way. He didn't seem bitter about the years he'd spent in Vietnam, he was just happy to be home and in one piece. He found his '54 Chevy in a Lomita used car lot.

"I'm taking auto body classes over at Harbor Occupational Center," he said. "So I'm able to do the body work myself."

"Is that what you want to do?" I asked.

"Yeah," he said. "I'm also learning how to do custom auto painting. I want to be able to do the fancy stuff you see in the custom car magazines. I want to be the Mexican Ed "Big Daddy" Roth."

"That's great," I said.

Danny gave me his phone number. He wanted me to call him if I ever came across some cheap '54 Chevy hubcaps. I almost confessed about his hubcaps right there and then, but for some reason I didn't. I don't think I wanted Danny to know what a worthless piece of crap he'd been talking to. I was so damn lucky and I knew it. I missed going to Vietnam by one year, while so many guys had gone before me. Danny wasn't some rich white kid with a deferment. Yeah, it's so easy to be gung ho about war with a college deferment, knowing you wouldn't ever have to back up your tough talk. Danny, and Tommy Russo at the Hungry Fisherman were Vietnam vets who were willing to fight and maybe die for their country, regardless of whether their country appreciated their sacrifices or not. Boston Dave now had to wear a plastic leg just so that he could fix cars and pump gas. They were the lucky ones. The unlucky ones never made it back. They were also just guys from our neighborhoods. They were our brothers and our friends. And they had parents who would never see them again, and girlfriends who would cry when they learned what had happened. We shouldn't forget them, but we probably will, because we have short memories, and we will move on with our lives, because we can.

Even though it was early evening, cruising cars were already passing the car wash on Pacific Avenue. I wiped the last drops of water from my bumper, while Randy finished drying his van. Hank, Dean, and Melissa stood nearby, while Jake admired his now clean and shiny G.T.O. "All the Young Dudes" by Mott the Hoople played over my car's stereo. When I'd first bought my Chevy, I made sure that I washed it twice a week. Now, that was down to just once a week. Did that mean that I loved my car any less? I hated to think that it did.

I'd first told everyone about meeting Danny Sanchez, and what I had found out. And then I told them all about Carissa Johansson and the prom.

"No way!" said Randy.

"She needed a date," said Hank, munching a burrito. "Her boyfriend has a broken leg."

"Yeah," said Melissa. "You should know; you broke it."

"That's football," said Hank. "If he didn't want to get hit, he should have worn a dress."

"Carissa Johansson is not of this world," said Dean, starry eyed.

"And what world is she from?" asked Melissa, incredulously.

"I don't know," said Dean. "Maybe Mount Olympus; she's a goddess."

"Like Aphrodite?" asked Melissa, sarcastically. "The goddess of love and beauty?"

"Maybe," said Dean. "I'll bet you that she doesn't even use the bathroom."

"And what does she use?" asks Melissa, in disbelief.

"I don't know," said Dean. "I just can't imagine her sitting on the toilet."

For a moment, we all tried to imagine just that.

"She's just a girl," said Melissa.

"She's not just a girl, babe," said Randy. "She's a fox."

"A stone fox." said Hank.

"A goddess." said Dean.

"Well, whatever she is," I said. "I might be taking her to the prom."

"Let me give you some advice," said Jake, putting his hand on my shoulder. "Whatever you do, just don't be yourself."

"Thanks for the great advice," I said.

The rumble of twin exhaust pipes filled the air as Chad Wagner pulled his Chevelle into the car wash. His girlfriend Cheryl Patterson sat beside him. After I stopped seeing Cheryl's older sister, Vickie, I managed to stay friends with her family. For some reason, the girl's parents always seemed to like me more than their daughters. Cheryl's friend Monica Morgan sat in the backseat. I guess she was Hank's date.

"What's up, guys?" said Chad.

"Just washing our cars," said Randy. "That's what we little people do down here. We don't have butlers to do it."

"Yeah," said Dean. "You don't want a dirty car when you're trying to pick up chicks."

"Well Dean," said Chad, "that's an awfully good idea."

"Hi Niko," said Cheryl, smiling.

"Hi Cheryl," I replied.

Hank tossed his burrito wrapper into a nearby trashcan, and then joined Monica in the backseat of the Chevelle.

"I'm sure glad Hank is playing for us," said Chad.

"Yeah," said Randy. "You losers need all the help you can get."

"We'll find out who the losers are tomorrow," said Chad.

"Yeah," said Dean, putting on his game face. "Be there, or be square."

Chad laughed at Dean's remark, then pulled out of the car wash and joined the traffic on Pacific Avenue.

"Be there, or be square?" I asked.

Dean just smiled and shrugged his narrow shoulders.

"Good Times, Bad Times" by Led Zeppelin played over my 8-track as Dean and I headed up Thirteenth Street to Averill Park.

Randy and Melissa said they had other plans, and since Randy's parents were out of town, I figured out what those other plans might be. Also, Jake wanted to get a few warm-up races in before his big race that night. So that left Dean and me alone to start the evening.

Averill Park closed at dusk, and there were no lights. During the day, the park was pretty, with green sloping hills, lots of old trees, and a creek that ran through the center. There were several picnic areas with built in barbeques.

Dean and I parked near one of the picnic areas. He carried in some firewood, while I carried in the ice chest filled with the beer that his older brother had gotten for us earlier. Dean put some firewood in one of the barbeques and made a small fire. This gave us a little heat and light.

Diana Donato was supposed to meet us here, because Dean had finally mustered up the courage to ask her out. In fact, he was going to ask her to the prom.

"What if she says 'no?'" asked Dean.

"Don't get ahead of yourself," I said, reaching into the ice chest. "Maybe she'll say 'yes.'" I pulled out two cans of Lucky Lager and handed him one.

A lowered 1964 Chevy Impala with a custom purple paint job rumbled up to the curb behind my Chevy. "Evil Ways" by Santana played over its stereo. Inside were Pancho Rodriguez and two of his Chicano friends, Luis and Chuy. As they exited the car, they exchanged some Spanish profanity and then headed into the park. They saw our fire and headed over toward us.

"*Orale*, Niko," said Pancho, "*Que onda guey*?"

"Not much," I said. "What are you doing?"

"*Nada, vato*."

"How's your sister, Marisol?"

"She's doing okay for a *chica*," smiled Pancho.

"*Hola, amigos*!" said Dean, proudly. "I've had two years of Spanish."

"*Fabuloso*," said Pancho, "And I've had twenty-two years of *gringo*, and I still don't know *pedo*!"

"Well don't give up," said Dean. "Maybe you Mexicans are just a little slow."

"Slow?" asked Pancho, shaking his head. "What a *pendejo*!"

"I'd offer you guys some beer," I said, "but we're expecting some girls."

"That's okay," said Pancho, pulling two marijuana cigarettes from his shirt pocket. "We got *mota*!"

His two friends laughed.

"Is that really marijuana?" asked Dean, surprised.

"No, *gabacho*," said Pancho. "*Es mi mierda*."

His two friends laughed again.

"So, what's up?" I asked Pancho. "You guys didn't come here to share your weed."

"You're right, Niko. Luis here wants to buy your car." He pointed to the taller of his two friends.

"How come you never lowered it?" asked Luis. "It could be a fine *cholo*."

"I'm not a low rider, I just like classic cars."

"How much?" asked Luis.

"It's not for sale."

"I'll give you double what you paid for it."

"Really?" I asked, a little surprised.

"Yeah, really."

I'd originally paid three hundred dollars for my Chevy, and double that would be six hundred. The car only sold for about fifteen hundred brand new. Luis' price was very tempting.

"Why don't you let me think about it, I wasn't really planning to sell it just yet."

"Sure, vato," said Luis, "think all you want."

I couldn't imagine ever getting a better price for my car.

"So," said Dean to Pancho, "you're Marisol's older brother?"

"Yeah, *gabacho*, you know my little sister?"

"She's Melissa's best friend, right? I know Melissa pretty well."

"Yeah, I know Melissa pretty well too," smiled Pancho.

Luis and his other friend laughed.

"What's so funny?" asked Dean, a bit confused.

"She's his *sancha*," said Luis, laughing.

"*Sancha*?" asked Dean, trying to translate. "Hey, doesn't that mean secret girlfriend?"

"It means what it means," said Pancho.

Fortunately, instead of talking about Melissa, Pancho started to tell us all about the new hydraulics he'd just had installed on his Impala, and how he could raise and lower the car now by simply pressing a button. He also mentioned that he was looking for someone to do some custom painting on his car. I remembered Danny Sanchez, and dug out his phone number. I tore the paper in half, borrowed a pen from Luis, and wrote the phone number for Pancho.

"*Gracias*," said Pancho.

"You're welcome."

Pancho motioned to his friends that it was time to leave. But before they left, I managed to get Luis' phone number.

"Let me know about your car," said Luis, as he was leaving.

"I will," I said.

"*Hasta la vista*, amigos!" shouted Dean. "Hey, don't worry, if I can learn Spanish, you guys can certainly learn English."

"*Besa mi culo!*" shouted Pancho.

"What's that?" asked Dean.

"Kiss my ass!" shouted Pancho. "*Amigo!*"

The song "Evil Ways" began to play again as Pancho started up the Impala and pulled away from the curb. Just as they were leaving, Diana drove up with her friend Nancy McClay, who also attended Our Lady of the Harbor Girl's High School. I didn't know Nancy very well, but she looked too sexy for Catholic school. Her red hair and makeup made her look a little older. I'd been raised Catholic, but I had to admit that my exposure to Catholic schoolgirls was limited. Although I very much liked what I'd heard.

"Do you girls want a beer?" asked Dean.

They both nodded yes. Dean reached into the cooler and pulled out a couple of beers. The fire was dying down, so I put on more firewood. Dean handed each of the girls a beer.

"Are you guys working Monday?" asked Diana.

"Yeah, I'm working dinner," said Dean.

"I'm working lunch," I said.

"I'm working both," said Diana unhappily.

"You'll get a lot of tips," said Nancy.

"It's Easter Vacation, I didn't want to work that much," said Diana. "But Uncle Tommy wants to keep me busy."

"Is Tommy married?" I asked. "I was just wondering."

"No," said Diana. "While he was in Vietnam, his girlfriend married someone else. He's never really gotten over it."

"That's too bad," I said.

"Yeah," said Diana. "Her name's Karen, and they're still friends. She comes into the restaurant all the time."

I thought about Tommy as I took a sip of beer, and wondered how serious he and his girlfriend were when he went off to war.

"Do you know Jim Pallente and Howard Funcich?" asked Nancy. "We went to elementary school together."

Jim and Howard transferred over to San Pedro High this year from the boy's Catholic high school that was closing. They were only attending San Pedro High School for their senior year.

"Yeah," said Dean. "We know them."

Howard was okay, but Jim had lots of issues with the girls. He would always say inappropriate things, and even try to grope them. It was as if he didn't respect the girls as people.

"Diana," asked Dean, "could we take a little walk?"

Diana looked over to Nancy, who nodded her approval.

"Sure," said Diana.

Dean and Diana both got up and made their way to one of the park's dark walkways. Dean grabbed Diana's hand and they strolled into the darkness together. Nancy looked over at me for a long moment.

"You look familiar," she said. "Were you one of the guys who streaked our school?

"No." I said. "But I was there taking pictures, I was the only guy with his clothes on."

"That's probably why you stood out."

"Yeah, that's probably why."

"I wouldn't mind seeing your pictures some-time," she smiled.

"I'll bet you wouldn't."

"All those naked male bodies," she said, "Yum!"

I guess she wasn't interested in the photography.

"How come you didn't streak?"

I wanted to tell her that the other guys demanded that I keep my clothes on because I was so well endowed, but instead I decide to be somewhat truthful.

"Somebody had to take the pictures," I said, with a shrug.

"Would you ever want to take pictures like that of me?"

"You mean, running naked through a cafeteria?"

"No, silly," she smiled, "just naked."

Thank you Jesus, Mary, and Joseph. Maybe some of what they said about Catholic schoolgirls was true.

"My dad," she said, "has a whole collection of Playboy magazines in his closet. He doesn't know that I've looked at all of them."

I wondered if they were the same issues of the magazine that I'd seen over at Randy's house. The women in them were absolutely beautiful. Once, when we were in junior high, Randy slipped a Playboy centerfold into the school's main display case. It caused quite a stir.

"How would you get the pictures developed?"

she asked. "Would you have to take them to A-1 Photo?"

"No. I'm taking a photography class. I can use the school's photo lab whenever I want to."

"I dream about being one of those girls in the magazine."

"Yeah, I sometimes dream of them myself."

"Well, then," she smiled. "Let's take some pictures."

"Are you sure?"

"Very sure. If the pictures look good, I could send them to Playboy."

"Are you eighteen? I think all the models in Playboy have to be eighteen."

"I just turned eighteen."

This was perfect. She was eighteen, beautiful, and wanted to be a centerfold. Back in junior high, Randy had asked me over to his locker to see his Bobby Sherman pictures. Back then, the girls would take their teenage fan magazines, cut out photos of Bobby Sherman, the latest teen idol, and tape them inside their lockers. I knew Randy was joking, but followed him to his locker anyway. He opened his locker to reveal that it was wallpapered with Playboy centerfolds. Bobby Sherman never looked so good.

"When can we do this?" she asked, excitedly.

"Sometime this week would be good," I said. "I still have a camera checked out, and there's no school."

"Great. We can do it at my house, my parents are usually gone during the day."

"What do your parents do?"

"My dad is an attorney for the Catholic archdiocese, and my mom works for my uncle, the Monsignor."

"Your uncle is Monsignor McClay?"

"Yeah. Didn't you know that?"

I'll be lucky if I don't burn in hell for this. I'm going to be taking nude pictures of Monsignor McClay's niece for Playboy Magazine. If I were a devout Catholic, I'd be worried. But fortunately, I was a fallen Catholic. Nancy and I exchanged phone numbers and planned to meet later in the week at her house.

After a few minutes, Dean and Diana returned from their walk, and let us know that they would indeed be going to the prom together. They both looked very happy. I was of course happy too, but not just for them. I was going to be photographing an attractive girl with her clothes off. If I was going to be Hugh Hefner for a day, maybe I should go out and get a smoking jacket and a pipe.

Westmont Avenue was a long stretch of four-lane road on the northern end of San Pedro. Most of the land around it was undeveloped, making it a good place for Jake and Gene's race. It was almost midnight, and the full moon cast its glow down on the roadway, which by now was filled with what seemed like half the town. I was standing there with Jake, as Gene's Challenger pulled in behind the "Goat." Seated beside Gene was a somber looking Hannah Burns. They both got out, and Hannah walked directly over to Jake. I met Gene and pulled him aside to allow Jake and Hannah some privacy.

"Hi, Jake," she said, without smiling.

"Hi, Hannah," said Jake.

"Why are you two doing this?" she asked.

"Ask Gene, it was his idea."

"I'm asking you," she said.

Jake seemed to be sailing into a headwind.

"I guess we're racing to see who takes you to the prom."

"Really?" she asked, shaking her head. "Am I some kind of trophy?"

Jake searched for the right words.

"Gene says that you still like me."

"Yes," she said, hesitantly. "I still like you."

"Good, because I like you too, and I thought that maybe--"

"Jake," she interrupted. "Just because I still like you doesn't mean that I want to get back together."

"Oh," he said, sadly.

"I'm with Gene now and I'm very happy."

The wind seemed to leave Jake's sails.

"I told him all this, but he's so insecure," she said. "I guess that's just how some guys are, but, of course, not you."

"No, of course, not me."

Jake looked at Hannah for a long moment, going through a range of emotions. He just wanted to grab her, kiss her, and hold her. He wanted to fight for her, if fighting would do any good. But he knew that fighting was not the answer.

Gene and I finally walked over and joined them.

"Well, are we still going to race?" Gene asked.

Jake thought about it before he answered.

"Yeah," he said, finally. "Let's race."

As Jake and Gene positioned their cars on the starting line, everyone began to find good spots to watch the quarter-mile drag race, Jake would be in the middle lane and Gene would be in the lane by the curb. I would be the starter, and Chad Wagner and Randy Ferlingetti would be at the finish line. Somebody handed me a white t-shirt to use as the starting flag. When everything looked ready, I got between the two cars and looked toward the two drivers. I looked at Gene, and he nodded. Then I looked at Jake, and he did the same. Finally, I raised the t-shirt in the air and held it there for a moment. When I dropped my arm, the cars let out a thunderous roar and their spinning tires screeched loudly. A cloud of dust and smoke enveloped us. From the smoke, the cars leapt out, like two lions attacking the same gazelle.

Within just seconds, Chad was signaling that Gene's car was the winner of the race. "Wow." I thought to myself, it had been years since I saw Jake lose a race. After both cars had slowed down, they made u-turns and headed back to the starting line.

In the distance, I could see the red lights and hear the siren of a police car approaching quickly. Jake stopped for me to hop in, and then sped away. There was great confusion as everyone else scrambled to get out of there. After we were several blocks away, and with no sign of the police, I finally looked over to Jake.

"Too bad about the race."

"Yeah. You can't win them all," he said with a shrug.

"You must really like Hannah."

He gave me a curious look.

"What do you mean?"

"I've seen you race enough to know that you weren't pushing it. You let Gene win. Why?"

"Maybe now Gene will feel better about Hannah."

"But you don't even like Gene?"

"I just want Hannah to be happy, even if it's not with me."

Jake obviously wasn't happy, but he looked down at his picture of Paul Newman and forced

a little smile, then looked out at the open road ahead of him.

Sunday

APRIL 15

▼

It was a quiet Sunday morning. The marine layer was just starting to lift. From the hilltop observation area at Friendship Park, the city grid of San Pedro seemed to make sense. The east-west streets led from the hillsides to the harbor, while the north-south avenues ended at the sea cliffs near Point Fermin and White Point.

I don't remember how these football games first got started, but they involved most of the town's neighborhoods. There was Chad's team from the middle class South Shores area, another similar team from the hills above Western Avenue, our own working class team from Midtown, a Mexican-American team from the Barton Hill area, and an all black team from the area north of First Street. It wasn't an organized league, and there weren't any uniforms or requirements. There wasn't even a real schedule. We met weekly at school and planned games with the other teams. We all just liked to play football.

Just after World War II, San Pedro had two semi-pro football teams, the Longshoremen and the Athletic Club. The two teams were made up of the fathers of some of these kids. The players would work all week at their jobs, then play football on the weekend. These semi-pro teams were so popular, that when the Cleveland Rams move to Los Angeles in 1946, they initiated a game against a Pedro team made up from the two teams. The Longshoremen were a more blue-collar team, while The Athletic Club was more a white-collar and middle class team. But both teams put their differences aside for their game with the Rams. The Rams won of course, but the Pedro players didn't embarrass themselves and even earned the Rams respect. Respect was just about all we played for ourselves, that and bragging rights.

The park's small parking lot was starting to fill up. Several players and their girlfriends unloaded coolers and bags of food and snacks. A few girls laid down blankets and set up small lawn chairs.

Chad gathered up his players, all South Shore boys. I could see Billy Bliss, Steve Woodward, Paul Wilcox, Rick Kelly, Tim Young, and Larry Williams. There was also our old buddy, Hank Pil-

sner, and their not so secret weapon, Kerry Krauthammer. Kerry had been a punishing power
running back at the Catholic boys high school
that had just closed. We all expected him to start
at San Pedro High, but because he refused to cut
his long hair, our Neanderthal coaches refused
to allow him on the team. Instead, Kerry just sat
in the stands and watched. But he still loved to
play football, and these sandlot games were his
chance to remind everyone how good he was.

Randy gathered our team together on the
grass. Besides Randy and me, there was Manny
Ortega, Chris Camello, Neven Tomich, Bobby
Jefferson, and Jake Polanski. Jake and Bobby
Jefferson were on San Pedro High's track team
together. Bobby, who was black, called Jake
"White Lightning," and warned the black runners
on the other teams that a white boy was going
to kick their ass. Bobby was fast also, and had
pretty good hands. Jake didn't have great hands,
and had problems catching the ball, but as a running back, he was amazing. Oh, yeah. I almost
forgot, Dean "Lean and Mean" Nash. Ninety-nine
pounds of potential road kill. Dean was our only
substitute, so the rest of us needed to stay healthy.

"Tails never fails!" shouted Chad as he made
the call for the coin flip. Gene, Randy, and I stood
watching as he tossed the quarter into the air. The
coin did in fact land tails on the grass. So Chad's
team would receive the football to start the game.
Randy gathered us in a huddle before we kicked

off to the other team.

"Remember," he said, "they might be bigger and stronger than us, but we have something they don't have."

"Speed?" asked Dean.

"Yes," said Randy, "We do have speed, but we also cheat and play dirty."

"We do?" asked Dean.

"Yeah," said Randy. "So, let's go out there and cheat and play dirty, then maybe we'll have a chance to win this game."

"Thanks, Coach Rockne," I said with a smirk.

We ran out to take our places on the field for the kickoff. Neven, who was also a soccer player, kicked off for our team. With the ball in the air, I raced as fast as I could down field. But before I could get to the ball carrier, Hank stepped right in my path. I tried to stop, but only managed to slide. His feet were anchored, and it was like hitting a brick wall. I went down hard. Hank stood over me, tauntingly.

"That's just the beginning."

I got up slowly, trying to clear my head. I noticed that someone on my team had made the tackle, but I had no idea who. We were on defense now, so I managed to take my position at defensive end. When they broke the huddle, Hank lined up right across from me. We were almost nose-to-nose.

"I've been waiting for this for a long time," he sneered.

"Oh, crap," I thought to myself.

Before the ball was snapped, I came off the line swinging my forearm and connecting with Hank's head. Then Hank swung back at me with his forearm. I was knocked back about three feet. I came out swinging again, and again he knocked me back. Meanwhile, everyone was just standing there watching us. The ball hadn't even been snapped yet. Hank and I finally notice this and stopped. Everyone was smiling, except Gene who finally spoke up.

"Are you two going to fart around, or are you going to play football?"

Hank and I assured everyone that we were here to play football, so that's just what we did. No more personal vendettas.

From the sidelines, someone's portable stereo blared Jethro Tull's "Locomotive Breath," as both teams made some good plays and some bad plays. Chad fumbled the ball early, but then recovered it. Krauthammer was a beast; it took about three guys to bring him down. The first guy just barely slowed him down, the second guy slowed him down some more, and finally, the third guy would help bring him down. Krauthammer scored their only two touchdowns. There were no goal posts, so we didn't bother with extra points or field goals. For our team, Randy spread the ball around as the quarterback. He hit Bobby, for a long touchdown pass. Then Jake ran for a long touchdown himself. It was fun to watch the other team trying to catch Jake. All they managed to do was grab at the air as he went racing by. Unfortunately, he fumbled the ball once, which allowed Chad to tackle him for a safety. At half time, the score was 14 to 12, and we were behind.

As we came off the field for a short break, Cheryl Patterson, Chad's girlfriend, handed him a cold beer, and then handed me one, too.

"Thanks, Cheryl." I said, opening it and taking a thirsty gulp.

"I heard about Carissa and the prom. Is that true?"

"It might be, I need a date."

"My parents still haven't forgiven Vickie for breaking up with you."

"We were too young. Your sister is a terrific girl."

"She said you weren't so bad yourself."

I thanked Cheryl again for the beer, and then joined my teammates over on the grass. Everyone sat drinking their beers.

"Two points," said Randy, "that's nothing!"

"Yeah. That's just one more than one," said Dean.

We all looked over at him.

"Thanks, Dean," said Randy. "I think we can all do the math."

Jake had an intense look in his eyes. "I want the ball," he said. "I lost that fumble, so those two points are my fault."

"Okay," said Randy. "We'll get you the ball."

"Have Bobby back with me to catch the kick-off. Then hand me the ball and get out of my way."

We all liked the "I'm going to kick some ass" look in Jake's eyes. After the half time was over, we took the field for the kickoff.

Jake and Bobby were back to receive the ball. Gene was kicking off for their team and kicked it right to Bobby. Bobby handed the ball to Jake, and then Jake did his thing. We blocked for him, but I don't think he even needed us, because everybody on the other team looked like they were stuck in mud. It was like one of Jake's high hurdles races, nobody could catch him. I think the old Longshoreman team would have loved to have Jake when they faced the Rams.

After that, both teams stalled, nobody could put a drive together. Chad's team got their chances, and our team got its chances, but nobody could get the ball over the goal line. When the game was almost over, we were starting to think that we might win this game.

But then our chances took a hit, both liter-ally and figuratively. Krauthammer was running around his right end, when Randy was there to tackle him. Randy's tackling form was good, but Krauthammer caught him right in the head with his knee. Krauthammer had been forced out of bounds, but Randy lay unconscious on his back. We called time out and tried to revive him, but it didn't work, he was out cold.

"Grab his leg," I told Jake, as I grabbed the

other one. We dragged Randy just out of bounds and left him there.

"Dean," I shouted, "you're in!"

"You're not going to just leave Randy there?" asked Dean.

"Why not?" I said, "He'd do the same thing if it were one of us."

"Okay," said Dean, shaking his head.

Dean came out on the field and took Randy's position on defense. We knew we had to stop them from scoring, since the time was almost up for the game. But this time, Krauthammer was not to be denied. He powered past two would be tacklers, right across the goal line. The score was now 20-18 in their favor. Chad looked at his watch, then informed us that the game would end after our next possession. So, we had one last chance. But without Randy as our quarterback, we were in trouble. I would have to take his place, and I was not nearly as good a quarterback.

For the kickoff, we tried to do the same stunt with Bobby and Jake, but this time, they squib-kicked it to one of the linemen, who was quickly tackled. On first down, I tried a pass to Bobby, but it was batted away. On second down, I tried a handoff to Jake, but I fumbled the exchange, and I had to fall on the football. On third down, I tried to go back for another pass, but I got sacked for a loss. Finally, it was fourth down, and our very last chance.

Going back to the huddle, I wondered to

myself what Randy would do in this situation. Well, he would cheat, I thought. But how do I do that? That's when I came up with a plan, a trick play. We would use Jake and Bobby as decoys, and I would do a little diversion with Dean. If it worked, we would look brilliant. If it didn't, then we would look foolish and lose the game. "But, no guts no glory." Is what Randy might say, if he wasn't knocked out as cold as a frozen halibut.

At the line of scrimmage, I had Jake at left wide receiver, and Bobby at the right. I had Dean as the lone running back behind me. Before I took the snap, I turned and looked at Dean.

"Get out of here!" I yelled, motioning that he needed to get off the field toward the left side-lines. Dean hesitated and acted confused. That's when I turned again and yelled, "Go, now!" and pointed to the left sideline.

As Dean ran left, Jake turned and ran back across to the right side, pulling his defender with him. Dean stopped before he exited the field and turned toward me. I took the snap, and gently tossed the ball right to him. There wasn't a defender within twenty yards. Dean caught the ball and raced for the goal line. Chad's entire team ran in pursuit of Dean, but they never caught him and he scored the winning touchdown. Making the final score: 24-20 in our favor.

Randy had managed to come to just as the game ended. He was still very groggy as he staggered out onto the field.

"We won!" I shouted to him.

"Won what?" he asked, trying to clear his head.

We offered to take Randy to a doctor, but he didn't want to go. He wanted to stay and share this victory with his team. When we told him that Dean had scored the winning touchdown, he almost passed out again.

I admitted to Hank that he had gotten the better of me physically, but the final score was my victory, no matter how beat up I was. Everyone on Chad's team got over the loss quickly. We all shook hands, grabbed beers, and sat tired on the grass. We either boasted or made excuses about the game. The beer flowed, and food was passed around generously. Maybe this was how the Longshoremen and the Athletic Club felt after their game with the Rams? They were proud that they competed, regardless of whether they won or lost.

Even during a long hot bath, the muscle in my body still ached. But as I sat there soaking, I thought about this morning's football game and how we'd won. I smiled and my aches and pains didn't seem quite so bad. As I towel dried my wet hair, I remembered one thing that was still hanging over my damp head.

I had a term paper that was due last Friday, which I hadn't even started yet. The assignment was to write a short biography about any non-fiction author. Fortunately, Mrs. Coleman, my English teacher, had extended my deadline until after vacation. Today, I should probably start doing my research. But unfortunately, I also had to work dinner at the Hungry Fisherman.

Over lunch, I mentioned my writing assignment to my dad. He suggested that I might want to talk to Cousin Vlatko. My Cousin Vlatko was an interesting guy and he was very well read. He could talk books and authors with anyone. It was difficult for me to believe some of his real life adventures, but my parents swore that they were all true. They said that back in the old days, Vlatko had socialized with some Hollywood types at the Los Angeles Yacht Club, where he was a member, and even romanced a Hollywood starlet or two. Visiting Cousin Vlatko would be a lot more interesting than just doing my research at the local library.

I got into my '54 Chevy and headed south on Grand Avenue toward Twenty-Second Street and the outer harbor. At Fourteenth Street, I noticed a woman standing on the southwest corner. I quickly realized that it was Miss Martin, my U.S. History teacher. As I approached the intersection, Miss Martin also recognized me and hurried out into the crosswalk, blocking my path. I had to quickly slam on my brakes to avoid hitting her.

"Niko," she said. "You're such a dear for stopping. I need a ride."

Everyone knew that Miss Martin didn't drive, and she got around San Pedro either by walking, taking the bus, or by flagging down anyone who could give her a ride. She wasn't shy about it. I reached over and unlocked my passenger side door and Miss Martin got in.

"Where are you headed?" she asked.

"Twenty-Second Street Landing."

"Perfect, you can drop me off at the Pacific Central Market. They have the best fruit and vegetables in town."

Miss Martin had hazel eyes, and wore her sandy colored hair in a pageboy cut like one of those silent-movie stars. Her clothing also suggested the 1920s, except for the peace symbol button that she wore, which made her seem like a 1960s radical. Since I was always annoying her with my attempts at humor, giving her a ride was the least that I could do.

"How is your vacation?" she asked.

"Good."

I told her about how our team had just beaten the South Shores boys in football, and she told me that she'd just returned from Mass. That reminded me of a question that I'd always wanted to ask her.

"Why aren't the nuns still over at Our Lady of the Harbor?"

"It's a long story," she sighed.

"Well, give me the 'Cliff's Notes' version. That's my speed anyway."

She thought about her answer for a moment before she finally spoke.

"Do you remember Vatican II?"

"Yeah, sort of. It got rid of the Latin Mass, right?"

"Among other things. They were reforms that the Catholic Church passed in order to bring the church into the twentieth century. It allowed nuns to modernize their dress and play a larger role in the church."

"That's good, right?"

"Yes. But Cardinal McIntyre of the Los Angeles Archdiocese refused to accept the changes and dug in his heels against them. "

"Why?"

"Who knows? In the past, our order had always been autonomous, we hadn't answered to the Cardinal. But now he claimed authority, and ordered us to go back to the practices of the past, or else."

"What did you do?"

"After tasting the sweetness of the future, we couldn't return to the bitter taste of the past."

She started to choke-up but caught herself.

"The Sisters of the Immaculate Heart of Mary Order was started by a nun during the time of the California Gold Rush. We had always tended to the poorest and sickest, ran a college and high school, and we staffed hospitals and schools.

There were some 500 sisters. The artist Sister Corita Kent was one of us."

Miss Martin's classroom at San Pedro High was covered with silkscreened posters by Sister Corita Kent, who was now a famous artist, with some people comparing her to Andy Warhol. One poster read: "Stop the Bombing" in letters that seemed to cascade down like the very bombs they wanted stopped. Another held a quote from Camus: "I should like to be able to love my country and still love justice." And another written over the drawing of a sunflower read: "War is not healthy for children and other living things."

"So what did the Cardinal do?" I asked.

"He had The Immaculate Heart of Mary Order dissolved. An order that had stood for over 100 years now simply ceased to exist."

"How sad."

"Yes. It was, because we all still loved the church and we didn't want to leave."

This was very confusing for me. Why would Cardinal McIntyre sacrifice 500 of the most devoted women in the Catholic Church? It wasn't like they weren't doing their jobs. They just weren't doing their jobs his way.

"How are you doing in your classes, Niko?" she asked, changing the subject. "You have so much potential, but you have to stop messing around."

"I'm suppose to write a biography this week for Mrs. Coleman's class; it's overdue."

"What type of biography?"

"A biography on any non-fiction author."

"Really?" she said, as she thought a moment. "You should write about Louis Adamic."

"Who?"

"Louis Adamic. He was a famous writer back in the 1930s and 40s. He's pretty much forgotten now, but he lived right here in San Pedro."

"San Pedro?" I asked. "I've never even heard of him."

"Well, maybe it's time you did."

I dropped Miss Martin off at the Pacific Central Market.

"Thank you, Niko," she said, opening the car door.

"Miss Martin, I'm sorry for always being the class clown," I said, contritely. "I'll try to do better."

"Good," she said, smiling as she got out of the car. "I'll expect more from you now. And don't forget, Louis Adamic."

She closed the car door.

Cousin Vlatko cut a dashing figure. He was tall, with slicked back black hair and a pencil-thin mustache. Although he was my first cousin, he was closer to my dad's age. Vlatko reminded me of a movie swashbuckler, like Douglas Fairbanks, or Errol Flynn, whom he swore he knew. In another time, he probably would have been a pirate. To tell you the truth, I really didn't know what he did for a living. He was always sailing his boat, the *Illyrian Queen*, or preparing it for another adventure. His boat was a beauty, a 45-foot wooden hulled schooner, built over at the Wilmington Boat Works in the 1930s. Although a member of the Los Angeles Yacht Club on Terminal Island, Cousin Vlatko liked to keep his boat here at the 22nd Street Landing.

As I walked down the ramp to the narrow dock, I marveled at the beauty and variety of the boats tied in their slips. Each boat was more beautiful and sleek than the previous one. When I reached the Illyrian Queen, I found Vlatko on the deck, gathering up a loose line. He wore a skipper's cap, and had a cigarette between his teeth.

"Hi, Vlatko."

He looked up and smiled when he saw me.

"Niko, my favorite cousin."

"I think I'm your only cousin."

"And that's what makes you my favorite." he said, tying the line he had gathered. "You're just in time, I'm taking her out. You want to come along?"

"I'd love to, but I have to be at work soon."

"Work," he frowned. "What a vile word. The worst four-letter word there is."

"Yeah, but I need the money."

"I know, there is no shame in honest work,"

he said, stroking his mustache. "It's just that so much work these days is not so honest."

It's funny to hear Vlatko talk about honest work, because his father had been a rum runner back during prohibition, and that Vlatko had often helped him with his boat. Back then, large cargo ships would come down from Vancouver, Canada loaded with liquor. They would anchor just outside the legal waters, where a fleet of powerboats would greet them, and then transfer the cargo to trucks waiting on the shore. Vlatko's father's powerboat was called the Quicksilver, and they were never caught, although the Coast Guard had fired on them more than once.

I told Vlatko about the writing assignment that I was supposed to do, and then I mentioned the writer, Louis Adamic, that Miss Martin had mentioned earlier.

"An interesting choice," he said. "When I was a kid, I met Louis Adamic, he used to work at the Port Pilot's Office just down the road."

"Really?"

"He knew this town and its people. He was here in the 1920s for the IWW strike. He wrote about it."

"What's the IWW?"

"Don't they teach you kids anything at school anymore?"

"Evidently not."

"The International Workers of the World. They had this crazy idea that if all of the workers were joined together in one giant union, they would have some clout with the bosses. A lot of people thought they were Communists. They took anybody, they didn't care about their color or their nationality."

"Huh."

"Louis Adamic wrote about the worker's struggles. He tried not to take sides, but how could you not?"

From down the wharf, I could hear some talking and laughter. I saw two pretty girls making their way toward us. They both carried towels and beach bags, and they both looked to be about college age.

"Ah, my dates," said Vlatko, smiling.

"Those girls are your dates?"

"My friend, Errol Flynn, used to always say, 'I like my whiskey old, and my women young.'" He stroked his mustache. "I told him, Errol, you could at least wait until they finished teething." He let out a big laugh. "Are you sure you don't want to skip work?"

"I wish I could, but my boss wouldn't like it."

"Bosses never like it."

Cousin Vlatko was right; work was a four-letter word.

Cousin Vlatko had set sail with his two cute girl friends, leaving me all alone at the dock. Maybe that was going to be my life story, watching pretty girls sailing off into the horizon. I knew I needed to change that story line. Hopefully, Carissa Johansson or maybe even Nancy McClay could help me change it.

Since it was still too early to go to work, I decided to drive over to Berth 68, and look at the Port Pilot's Office, where the writer Louis Adamic had once worked. Oil tanker facilities and warehouses lined the wharf road that led to the water's edge. Once there, I noticed the pilot's boat tied nearby. The office's many windows gave it the look of an airport's control tower. But unlike an air traffic controller, who merely relays instructions for landing, the port pilot actually boards the large ships and safely guides them to their dock. Without an experienced port pilot, these ships could easily run aground. As I stood out at the point, I could see the main channel of the harbor on my left and the outer harbor to my right. It was a perfect spot to monitor all the port's comings and goings. Louis Adamic certainly had an excellent view of things.

When I arrived at the Hungry Fisherman, I was still almost a half hour early. I thought maybe I'd be able to grab some dinner and talk with Tommy, but instead, Vince Galasso was the only one in the kitchen.

"You're early," he said. "Can't you dumb Slavs

tell time?"

"It was foggy, my sundial wasn't working too well."

"Oh, now you're a comedian." He said, stirring some clam chowder on the stove. "Does this look like the Tonight Show?"

I looked over to the dining room, and saw Tommy sitting and talking with a woman. She was pretty, about his age, with medium length brown hair. They were the only two in the room.

"Who's that with Tommy?" I asked.

"First you're Jerry Lewis, now you're Joe Friday," he said, putting some dirty pots and pans into the sink. "Her name's Karen, she's an old friend of Tommy's."

Tommy and Karen really seemed to be enjoying each other's company. I'd never seen Tommy so relaxed and happy. He was usually very surly.

"They make a nice couple," I said.

"They were a nice couple," said Vince, sliding a tray of foil-wrapped potatoes into the oven. "Now she's married to someone else."

"Did that happen while he was in Nam?"

"Yeah, he told her not to wait for him, so she didn't. I think she's the only woman he ever loved."

The way Tommy looked at Karen, I could tell that he still loved her. Poor Tommy, because of Vietnam, he got a Purple Heart instead of a wife. It didn't seem like a fair trade.

The phone on the wall rang and Vince

answered it.

"Who? Oh, you mean the dumb Slav." He handed me the phone.

"Thanks," I said, grabbing the phone. It was Randy on the other end.

"Man, I need your help."

"I'm working dinner, I just got here."

"Okay, tonight then. My van got impounded yesterday. Pick me up at home."

"Okay. I'll be there after work."

Vince gave me a dirty look as I hung up the phone.

"We're not an answering service for your stupid Slav friends."

"He's not a Slav, he's a dumb dago, like you."

"Oh, then he's okay," smiled Vince. "Tell him to call anytime."

"What do you have against Croatians, anyway?"

"Croatians are just crazy," he said, pulling loaves of sourdough bread from a box. "You seem too normal to be a Slav. You must be part something else."

"I'm 100% Croatian."

"Then I feel sorry for you."

Vince was definitely getting on my nerves. Of all the Italians I knew, he was the worst.

After work, I picked Randy up at his home. It was starting to get dark. "Stairway to Heaven" by Led Zeppelin played on my stereo.

"Why would they impound your car for no reason?

"I have a few unpaid parking tickets," he said, pulling his long hair behind his ears.

"Oh."

"But this isn't the Soviet Union, man! They just can't take your things!"

"Did you call your brother-in-law?"

"Yeah, he just laughed at me."

"Cops have a strange sense of humor."

"He also said something about things changing after this weekend. I had no idea what he was talking about."

"He said something like that the other night."

"Hey, what's going on with Melissa?"

"What do you mean?"

"She's been ignoring me, making excuses why she can't see me, she's like a different person."

I wanted to tell Randy about Melissa and Pancho, but I promised her I wouldn't. Poor Randy looked confused and a little hurt. Obviously Melissa hadn't told him anything.

A ten-foot high chain link fence surrounded the Seventh Street Garage's police holding lot on Centre Street. Inside the fence were the impounded vehicles. We could see that Randy's van hadn't been blocked in yet by other cars. I parked my Chevy and we walked over to the padlocked gate.

A sign on the fence read:

"Pay inside to release your vehicle from impound."

"Stay here," said Randy, as he began climbing the fence.

"What are you doing?"

"Just keep an eye out for cops."

"You need to go in and pay the fine."

"I'm not paying jack!" he said, dropping to the ground on the other side.

Randy walked over to the van and got in. He started it up and drove to the locked gate. He then got out and opened the rear hatch. From under a blanket, he pulled out a large pair of bolt cutters. Randy took the cutters and snapped the lock, which fell to the ground.

"Don't just stand there," he said. "Open the gate."

As I opened the gate, he got back into the van.

"You'd better get out of here. The cops won't like it when they see that I took my van back. They might take it personally."

"I know I would."

I hurried back to my car as he drove off. Randy and I both attended Sunday school as kids, but we obviously hadn't learned the same lessons. The nun who taught my class would have frowned at the idea of stealing back your car from a police impound lot, but maybe Randy's nun had been a little more open-minded.

I don't know if it was holy retribution, but I hadn't even driven one block up Seventh Street, when a Ford sedan blew through a stop sign and slammed right into my car. I was stunned, but I thought that I was physically okay. I could see that the Ford was full of people. I stumbled out of my car to survey the damage, and found that my right rear quarter panel had been smashed in. The Ford's right headlight was shattered and the right side of its front bumper was pushed in.

From the driver's seat, a redheaded woman wearing an evening dress staggered out. She was barefooted, and she smelled of liquor.

"Oh, I'm so sorry," she said, slurring her words. "I was being distracted."

"You'd better put your shoes on," I told her. "There's a lot of glass."

As she went back to get her shoes, the man in the front passenger seat got out. I recognized him immediately. It was Father Jason from Our Lady of the Harbor. He was wearing his collar, and he was obviously drunk.

"You look like you're okay," he said, walking toward me. "I'm very glad."

In the backseat of the Ford, I could see that two other women were also dressed up for the evening. They didn't seem anymore sober than Father Jason and the driver.

"Maybe we should call the police," I said.

"No, no, no," he answered, digging in to his coat pocket. "It will be fine." He handed me his business card. "Just take your car to a body shop, we'll pay for it."

When he said, "We'll pay for it," I didn't know if he meant he and the women, or he and the church. But it didn't matter, because someone was going to pay to fix up my damaged car. The red-headed woman returned with her driver's license and insurance papers. I handed her mine, and we both wrote down the information.

"No need to involve the insurance companies," said Father Jason. "We know it was our fault."

"Okay," I said. "I guess if you're going to pay for everything."

"It will all be taken care of," he grinned. "Is your car drivable?"

I looked at the rear wheel to see if it was rubbing against the fender, it wasn't.

"Yeah," I said. "I think it is."

"Good. Let me know how much it will cost and we'll get you a check." He staggered back to the Ford, then stopped and looked at me before getting in. "Bless you, my son."

I didn't think they should drive, but what was I going to do. Father Jason already asked me not to call the police. I just headed home, my car looking like hell.

Monday

▼

In the morning, I took my car over to Pacific Body Shop, which was right across Pacific Avenue from our car wash. After they gave me an estimate for the repairs, I called Father Jason's office and told him what the cost of the car repairs would be. The price didn't faze him at all, and he told me that the body shop would get a check later that day.

The body shop told me that it would take a few days to get my car fixed, so during that time I would have to get around on foot. I walked the few blocks back home. Once home, I grabbed my notebook, and headed to the public library to find out what I could on writer Louis Adamic. I was a little resentful that I had to do this during my vacation, but I also realized that I only had myself to blame.

I hadn't even walked two blocks, when the aroma of baked goods coming from Pilato's Bakery seduced me inside. Mr. Pilato, a short, bald, Italian man, smiled when I entered his business. On the walls were photographs of beautiful multi-layered wedding cakes, and the display cases were filled with an amazing variety of Italian pastries, cakes, and cookies. Past the freezer of Italian ice, and the display case of various biscotti, my eyes focused on the cannoli, cream horns, and Napoleons. I licked my lips and chose a cannoli. After Mr. Pilato took my money, he placed the cannoli on a sheet of waxed paper and handed it to me. I took a large bite. "Momma Mia!" I thought to myself. Mr. Pilato smiled at my obvious satisfaction. I then poked my head into the kitchen. Nunzio the baker was busily decorating a wedding cake.

"Hi, Nunzio."

"Oh, Niko," he replied, "hello."

I'd known Nunzio since I was a little kid, when my parents would send me to pick up a pizza we'd ordered. While waiting for the pizza to bake, we would often talk. But Nunzio rarely said much, and he rarely smiled. He never seemed happy, like he'd led a difficult or sad life. But his baked goods were a work of art. My father said that Nunzio was an artist, and artists could be temperamental.

"How's you momma and poppa?" he asked.

"They're good, Nunzio, very good."

I finished the cannoli, said goodbye to Nunzio and Mr. Pilato and headed toward the library.

Our local branch of the Los Angeles Public Library was in a nondescript stucco building, built to replace a red brick structure that had preceded it. Both of these libraries had replaced our lovely 1905 Carnegie Library, which once stood on the park that overlooked the harbor. It had fine Roman columns, a granite exterior, and an impressive dome. When the Carnegie finally stopped functioning as a library, it served as offices for the Chamber of Commerce, until it was finally torn down in 1966. As a kid, I watched some of the demolition.

Inside the current library, I found the card catalogue and began to look up Louis Adamic. I thumbed through the "A" section, but with no luck, then I went to the librarian and finally asked her for help.

"How do you spell that name?" she asked.

"A-D-A-M-I-C," I replied.

She pulled out a bound catalogue from behind the counter. There she found a long list of books by Louis Adamic. Unfortunately, they were all at the central library in downtown Los Angeles. She could have most of them transferred to the San Pedro branch, but it would take a few days. I handed her my library card and asked her to please have them sent.

"Hi, Niko," said a female voice directly behind me.

It was Stephanie Davies, my ex-girlfriend. She held a handful of books, and tried to produce a smile.

"How are you?" she asked.

"I'm okay. How are you?"

"Okay, I guess."

After the librarian returned my library card, Stephanie asked me if we could talk for a minute. We found an empty table with two chairs and sat down. She laid the books, *An Unfinished Woman*, and *Pentimento*, on the table before her. I noticed that Lillian Hellman had written both of them, and remembered that Stephanie had always liked her stage plays.

"I didn't expect to run into you here," she said.

"I have that biography to write for Mrs. Coleman's class."

"Wasn't that due last week?"

"She gave me this week to finish it."

"How's it coming?"

"I haven't started, and they don't have any of the books I need. They're being sent from the central library."

"Have you tried Seaside Books?"

"No, but that's a good idea."

Stephanie looked at me for a long moment.

"I miss you," she finally said.

"I miss you too."

"I'm sorry if I messed up your prom plans."

"It's okay. I might have found someone to go with."

"Yeah, I heard," she frowned. "Carissa Johansson."

"She has a boyfriend, it would just be a prom date."

Her eyes looked sad. "I hope you're not angry with me."

"How could I be angry with you? You were my girlfriend, I never wanted to breakup with you."

"That's what I mean, I thought you might blame me for everything."

I don't know why, but I felt that she wanted me to somehow absolve her of any guilt. "Stephanie, you obviously weren't happy. It takes two people to make it work."

She looked at me with sadness.

I didn't blame her, and I wanted her to know it. "You're an amazing girl," I said. "And I don't know if I'll ever meet anyone like you again."

Stephanie's green eyes softened and she looked so beautiful.

I pointed at her two books. "Someday, you're going to be performing in one of Lillian Hellman plays on a stage, and I'll be sitting in the audience, just thinking of what a wonderful actress you are. And I'll be so proud of you, and I'll feel so lucky to have just known you."

Her eyes filled with tears. "Oh, Niko."

"Maybe this breakup is just what we need, or maybe it's the worst thing we could do. I don't really know. But we're just kids, and we both

117

need to do some growing up."

She managed to force a smile. "Something tells me that you're already starting to do that."

"Maybe I am, maybe we both are."

It was painful to see Stephanie again, because I still liked her. We could have easily gotten back together, but what would that have fixed? Like she said, I'll be graduating, and she'll still be there. We just needed to get on with our lives. We shared a long hug and finally said goodbye.

The Seaside Bookstore had been located at the same location for almost a hundred years, but recently they had to move into another building two blocks away. Their old building was to be demolished as a part of the Beacon Street Redevelopment. Mabel, the old woman who owned the bookstore, had to be at least a hundred years old herself, or maybe she just looked that way. Her thick horned-rim glasses couldn't conceal the cataracts that had formed on both her eyes, and her wrinkled up face looked like a relief map of a rugged coastline.

The bookstore occupied the entire first floor of its new building, while cheap apartments filled the top two floors. Her grown son, Henry, and their black cat, Steinbeck, also helped out. Stein-

beck loved to lie on the front counter, daring anyone to disturb him.

When I asked Henry for help finding books by
Louis Adamic, Mabel heard the name and seemed
to come to life.

"Christ, Louis Adamic," she said. "I haven't
heard that name in years."

"You've heard of him?" I asked.

"Hell yes, I used to know him."

"You knew Louis Adamic?"

"I got to know Louis in the 1920s, while he still
lived in Los Angeles. He came down to San Pedro
to cover the IWW strike as a reporter."

"Yeah, I heard about that."

"Then he moved here himself. He would come
into the old bookstore often." She smiled. "I was
a pretty young dame back then, helping out my
father."

"Oh, yeah?"

"My father ordered books for him. We probably have some of his books in the used section.
He's been out of print for years. Henry can show
you where they are."

"Thanks," I said, following Henry past the
new book section, to the used books in the back.
There in the non-fiction area was a shelf full of
books by Louis Adamic. I looked over the titles:
The Native's Return, *My Native Land*, *A Nation
of Nations*, *What's Your Name?*, *Two-Way Passage*, *My America*, *From Many Lands*, *Laughing
in the Jungle*, and *Dynamite*.

"Wow," I thought. He wrote a lot of books, and these might not even be all of them.

Nearby, a man wearing a suit was looking through the books in the section labeled "Business." He glanced over at me and seemed to scowl. He then picked a book from the business shelf and began to look it over.

I picked up *A Nation of Nations* and turned it over. There on the dust jacket was Adamic's photo. He had a serious, but kind face, with a receding hairline and dark eyes. The information on the jacket stated that he had come from Yugoslavia in 1913 at the age of fourteen. He spent time in the American army during World War I, and published his first book, *Dynamite*, in 1931.

"Why are you reading that crap?" asked the man in the suit, referring to the book in my hands.

"Excuse, me?" I asked, confused.

"That bastard was a communist. And he sympathized with those IWW crooks. He's the last person you should be reading."

"I'm just trying to learn something about him for school." I said.

"You won't learn anything from his books. You should be reading books like these." He showed me the books *How to Win Friends and Influence People* by Dale Carnegie and *Capitalism and Freedom* by Milton Friedman.

"I'll keep that in mind," I said.

"You young people have your priorities all messed up. This is the free enterprise system.

Back in my day we didn't put up with commies. Hopefully you'll learn something before you're too old." He sneered, then took his books and walked up toward the front of the store.

Well, he certainly doesn't know how to win friends, I thought. It's a good thing he's reading that book. It might help him.

I gathered a copy of each Adamic title from the shelf and then carried the stack out to the front. The man in the suit was still paying for his books at the counter. He turned and looked at me as he was leaving.

"Come and see me at the Chamber of Commerce," he said. " I'll give you a real education." He then took his books and walked out the door.

I looked over to Mabel and Henry. "What's his problem?"

"He doesn't have any problems," said Henry. "He's the richest man on the peninsula."

"Really?" I asked. "Who is he?"

"J. P. Watterson Jr.," said Mabel, "Watterson Construction Company."

"And he's buying used books?"

"He's a cheap son of a bitch," said Mabel. "How do you think he stays so damn rich?"

"His father, J.P. Watterson Sr. partnered with Frank A. Vanderlip back in the 1920s," said Henry.

I'd learned about Frank A. Vanderlip in Mr. Johansson's class. He and a group of wealthy associates had financed the development of the Palos Verdes Peninsula. Before that, he had been assistant secretary of the U.S. Treasury under President McKinley.

"Watterson Construction is part of the Beacon Street Redevelopment Project," said Mabel. "He's also president of San Pedro's Chamber of Commerce."

"Huh," I said, dropping the stack of Adamic's books on the counter. Steinbeck hissed at me for disturbing his slumber. "I'm writing a biography on Adamic for school. I need these books, but I don't have a lot of money."

"I'll give them to you for fifty cents a piece," said Mabel.

"Okay," I said, still hurting from even that reduced price.

On the wall behind the counter, was an old, framed photograph of a tussled haired seaman wearing a pea coat and standing on a waterfront dock.

"Who's that?" I asked. "I've never seen that picture before."

They both turned to see what I was referring to.

"That's Jack London," answered Henry. "We found that picture when we were moving."

"My father got that photo when London came to San Pedro in 1913," said Mabel. Supposedly he even bought a book in our store.

"He came here?"

"Hollywood was filming *The Sea Wolf* on the waterfront," added Mabel. "London played a seaman in the movie."

So, Jack London actually spent time on Beacon Street. I thought that was great. Seeing London's picture made me think of my friend Ronnie Zankich, who worked nearby at the City Fish Market. Jack London was Ronnie's favorite writer, and he had written his biography on Jack London for Mrs. Coleman's class. It couldn't have been too difficult for him, since he'd already read most of London's books. But here I was, carrying a bag full of books that I haven't read yet, written by an author whom I knew nothing about. I had a lot of work to do.

The City Fish Market was a large open room with bare concrete floors and faded and chipped paint on its walls. There was one display case, but most of the fish were kept on ice in large wooden crates, that rested on pallets. Local housewives poked around, looking for the freshest fish to buy. Ronnie Zankich, who wore an oilskin apron and rubber boots, was happy to see me. He and I had grown up on the same block, playing all of the different sports together. His father, whom I never saw without a cigar in his mouth, was a machinist over at Todd Shipyard and a shop steward for the union. Besides Todd, there were several other shipyards nearby, including Bethlehem Steel and the Long Beach Navel Shipyard. These shipyards provided the area with many well paying union jobs. Ronnie's dad had been saving money for years to send him to UCLA. He wanted him to someday become a labor attorney and practice here in town. I told Ronnie about the Jack London photo, and he said he wanted to see it. Then I told him about meeting J. P. Watterson.

"He's president of the Chamber of Commerce," said Ronnie. "And owns a big construction company."

"Yeah, I heard."

"His father was very anti-union and would finance strikebreakers whenever there was a strike. At least, that's what my dad told me."

"Really?"

"I think he had some connection to the local Ku Klux Klan."

"What?" I asked, in disbelief. "The KKK in San Pedro?"

"Yeah, my dad said that he watched them march."

I couldn't believe what Ronnie was telling me. I thought that the KKK was something you would see in the Deep South, not in Southern California. Of course things were different back then. And it's not like all of the racial issues have been solved by the civil rights movement, but hopefully things were improving. Recently, Bobby Jefferson's dad won a lawsuit against the ILWU, the longshoreman's union; finally opening up regular, full-time longshoremen jobs to minorities. I couldn't imagine that Ronnie was right about the KKK. Maybe Bobby's dad, Solomon Jefferson, would know for sure.

Solomon Jefferson's shoeshine stand sat in a parking lot just behind Pacific Avenue. It was really nothing more than a small shed with two chairs. But it was a meeting place of sorts for many of the old time fishermen and longshoremen. They would come to get a shine, but then they would stay to share stories and laugh. Besides English, Mr. Jefferson, a black man, spoke a fair amount of Serbo-Croatian and even some Italian. He'd learned the languages while growing up in the town, and by working for years on the docks with the Slavs and Italians.

During World War II, when most of the white longshoremen were serving in the military, minorities had no difficulty working full time on the docks. But after the war, when the white stevedores returned, the minorities were released. They had always been excluded from regular union membership because of the nepotism requirements, which had been a long time longshoremen tradition.

Mr. Jefferson tried for years to join the ILWU as a regular longshoreman, but was only able to work as a "casual," a temporary worker.

The shoeshine stand was only for when there was no work as a casual, and casuals only worked after all the regular longshoremen jobs were taken. Mr. Jefferson and a few others filed a federal lawsuit claiming discrimination. The lawsuit went on for years, but was now settled. Finally, blacks, Mexican-Americans, and other minorities were able to become regular full time longshoremen. A "For Sale" sign hung on the wall of his shoeshine stand.

"*Dobar dan, mladi,*" he said, wishing me a good day in Croatian.

"*Dobar dan, Gospodin* Jefferson," I replied, wishing him the same.

Mr. Jefferson had been my first Little League coach, with his son Bobby and Ronnie Zankich also on that team. We almost didn't get a chance to play that season, because no one else had signed up to coach us. But when he heard that we wouldn't be able to play, Solomon Jefferson signed up as our coach, and even acted as our sponsor. I was surprised to see that his shoe rack was almost empty of shoes. He wore a stained work apron, and was just finishing shining a pair of black wingtips.

"Things are pretty bare," I said, looking at the empty shelves.

"Everyone knows I'm closing up," he said,

setting the wingtips on a shelf. "They've already brought in their shoes for one last shine."

"Congratulations on your lawsuit."

"Thanks, Niko," he said, with a sigh. " It's been a long time coming."

His son, Bobby, had told me how a lot of white longshoremen had actually supported his dad's lawsuit, because they knew that it was the fair thing to do. While others, liking the way things were, never came aboard. Some were still bitter that the federal government was telling them what to do. As if discriminating against others was somehow their birthright.

"I just heard something from Ronnie Zankich that I find hard to believe."

"What's that?"

"He said that as a kid his dad saw the KKK march in San Pedro."

"Yeah, what about it?"

"Is it true?

"Hell yes, it's true," he said. "They burned a damn cross on our front lawn."

"Just because you were black?"

"That, and because my dad had become a Wobbly. He was black and a Wobbly, can you imagine that?" he said with a small laugh.

"What's a Wobbly?"

"A member of the IWW, the International Workers of the World."

"Why were they so hated?"

"Some of them were communists, some of them

were radicals, and some of them were agitators. But the main reason why the IWW was hated was because they were effective, and they had a dream, and it's damn hard to kill a dream."

"I heard that they held a strike at the harbor."

"Yeah, it started in May of 1923," he informed me. "According to my dad, they bottled up the whole harbor. Nothing got loaded or unloaded. Their demands were for basic things — a little more money, a little better working conditions."

"Did they win their strike?"

"No," he said, sadly. "I told you that it was hard to kill a dream, but unfortunately it's not impossible. Especially if you have all of the money, the police force, and vigilantes like the KKK all working together against you."

"It doesn't sound like a fair fight."

"No, it wasn't."

We talked for a while about how he believed that some of the IWW spirit still lived in today's ILWU. After all, they long ago borrowed the IWW slogan: "An injury to one is an injury to all."

"My union brothers are now doing the right thing and becoming inclusive. They're finally getting back to the way the IWW was fifty years ago."

"That's good, right?"

"Hell yes! That's damn good."

We talked for a while about how he didn't expect anyone to buy his shoeshine stand, but he didn't care. It had been something he had to do to make a living, because everything else was denied him. It wasn't something he ever wanted to do, or something he ever wanted his son Bobby to do. He was now going to be a full time longshoreman. That's all he ever wanted, just that opportunity for a good job.

"You know, Niko, if the KKK came back today, and wanted to set my shoeshine stand on fire," he said, with a smile. "I'd probably hand them a match."

I believed him, because he was done.

With the Adamic books still under my arm, I headed toward the Beacon Street area, passing many businesses that were now boarded up and just waiting for next week's demolition. Signs for Watterson Construction and Demolition were everywhere Amazingly; some businesses were still open and operating. Among them were a few bars and a pool hall.

The Beacon Street Redevelopment office sat just south of the area to be torn down. On their large window, was displayed an artists rendering of what the Beacon Street area would look like after the redevelopment. The new Beacon Street looked bright and beautiful, with lovely people strolling and window shopping. The proposed future sure looked appealing. Inside I saw a pretty blonde woman seated at a desk. She looked over at me and smiled.

A block over from the redevelopment area was the Chamber of Commerce office. On its window, was a sign reminding everyone of the "Last Night on Old Beacon Street Celebration," which was this Saturday night. Several shiny new Cadillacs were parked in front. Through the large window, I saw J.P. Watterson standing and talking to a group of businessmen. They all seemed to be listening intently to what he had to say.

At the nearby A-1 Imports Italian Market, the owner was out front polishing his new Buick. He made sure everyone noticed his fine purchase. Inside the market, I bought a foot-long Italian torpedo sandwich and a Coke, and carried the food over to the Plaza Park, which overlooked the main channel of the harbor. I stopped at the spot where the old Carnegie Library once stood. In the vacated spot, the city had built a covered sitting area that clung down along the hillside. It was an excellent place to sit, read, and look out at the ships. A Catalina seaplane was just gaining speed, then finally taking off toward the south. As a kid, my dad would walk me down here from the little house we rented on Twelfth and Centre. He would identify the flags of all the nation's ships that passed through the main channel. I was amazed that he knew so much.

Sitting inside the ghost of the old Carnegie Library, I removed the books from their bag. Then, I unwrapped my Italian sandwich and ate as I looked through the books, my notebook open and nearby.

Thinking maybe that I should start at the beginning, I picked up Adamic's first book, *Dynamite*, which was subtitled, *The Story of Class Violence in America*. I read the introduction; then thumbed through the book, glancing at each chapter's heading. Chapter 16 was titled "The Wobblies." I read it, hoping that it might mention San Pedro and the 1923 longshoremen's strike, but unfortunately it didn't.

Then I picked up *Laughing in the Jungle*, which was subtitled: *The Autobiography of an Immigrant in America*; it was his second book. I started at the beginning, figuring that his book might give me the material I needed.

First, the book told of Adamic's youth back in Slovenia, which was a part of Yugoslavia. It reminded me of my dad's life, and his decision to come here. Then, the book told of Adamic's trip to Ellis Island and America. Of course that reminded me of New York Harbor, and our seeing the Statue of Liberty. Finally, the book told of Adamic's wide-eyed observations of his new country, which both fascinated and confused him. He equated his new land to a "jungle," borrowing the term from author Upton Sinclair, whose book he admired. Adamic felt that the only sane response to his new land's strangeness and contradictions was to laugh at it, as if he were watching a three-ringed circus. At times *Laughing in the Jungle* was a story of his life, but at other times it was a social commentary. He wanted to be an impartial observer, but his sympathies seemed to be with working folks. He wrote:

"Of late I find it hard to laugh at things and conditions in the jungle, although I know it is essentially ridiculous, for instance, for shoe workers to walk ill-shod, for woolen-textile workers to have no warm clothes in the winter, for coal miners to shiver in cold shacks." Obviously some things were no laughing matter.

During World War I, Adamic spent time as soldier in the U.S. Army, eventually becoming a U.S. citizen. To get to Southern California, he signed up as a mess-boy on an oil tanker headed for San Pedro. After arriving here, he made his way to Los Angeles. On his first day in L. A., he was mugged and lost what little money he had. Sitting on a park bench in the rain, he started to laugh:

"This is funny," I said to myself, half hysterical. "It's all a joke."

He called Los Angeles "The Enormous Village," and was amused by the con men, religious phonies, and civic boosters that all seemed to populate the place and he was fascinated with the city's many contradictions.

After working as a laborer and other jobs, he

became a reporter for a small L. A. Newspaper. In May of 1923, he was sent to San Pedro to cover the IWW dockworkers strike. He wrote:

"I came to San Pedro on the day that Upton Sinclair was arrested and jailed there for attempting to read the Constitution of the United States on a privately owned piece of property. 'None of that Constitution stuff here,' was the edict of the chief of police."

It seems that Sinclair was there to speak in support of the IWW strikers, but he was never given the chance. Adamic continued:

"When the strike was about two weeks old, and threatening to go on for another two weeks or longer, the police began to round up the Wobblies, herding them into P. E. trains like so many cattle, and shipping them to various jails in Los Angeles. To belong to the IWW was a crime in violation of the so-called Anti-Criminal Syndicalism law."

Why would the U. S. Government make it illegal for people to join the IWW? I didn't understand that. Adamic went on:

"When the strike was thus being broken, the Wobblies — rough, strong men; native-born and foreigners — sang their songs. They sang in the prison stockade in San Pedro, on the way to the trains, and finally in jails. 'God!' another young newspaperman remarked to me. One feels like singing with them. They got guts!"

They were singing as they were being hauled

off to jail. I thought that was amazing, and I wondered what songs they sang? Then I suddenly remembered something from the *Dynamite* book. I opened it to the Wobblies chapter, and there it was:

"In 1914 there was the Joe Hill case in Utah... The IWW songwriter, Joe Hill... was arrested in Salt Lake City for the murder of a local grocer, of whom, no doubt, Joe had never heard of before. He was tried and convicted... On November 17, 1915, Joe Hill faced a firing squad... His body was sent to Chicago for burial."

This Joe Hill might have written some of the songs that the Wobblies sang? I went back to reading *Laughing in the Jungle*. Adamic continued:

"The two weeks in San Pedro, when I covered the Wobbly strike, were the only agreeable part of my journalist career in Los Angeles... So one day late in June 1923, I quit the job and, with fifteen dollars in my pocket, moved to San Pedro. I had no definite idea what I would do there. During the strike I had taken a liking to the town. It was so unlike Los Angeles or Hollywood. It looked sane."

He wrote more:

"Coming from Los Angeles, with its phony beauty, I thought San Pedro was a clean place. I liked the mingling smells of crude oil, fresh lumber, oranges, lemons, spices, coffee, fish, and other cargos, which were handled over the wharves."

Adamic found a small bungalow on the edge of the bluff that overlooked the outer harbor.

"By and by I got work on the docks and made a living at it for nearly six months. One week I was unloading lumber; the next, as likely as not, trucking coffee or canned goods, or carrying bunches of green bananas off some boat just arrived from Guatemala. It was hard work, sometimes, from seven in the morning till past midnight, or until the particular cargo was loaded or unloaded so that the ship could sail. The wages were nothing to brag about, often I was in physical danger, and there were annoyances and indignities which every sensitive laborer must endure; but even though it was better than being a reporter."

It doesn't sound like he liked being a reporter. He continued:

"Every once and a white I worked for a few days in some gang which was half white and half black. The Negro stevedores were a great lot. They talked incessantly, kidding one another, the while pushing their trucks. And they sang and laughed. Their laughter was marvelous."

One of those black stevedores could have been Solomon Jefferson's father, I thought. After all, he was a longshoreman then.

Working on the docks wasn't always steady, and it gave him a chance to rest and relax a bit. Adamic continued:

"I had time to read. There was a decent, if

small public library in town and after a while I became acquainted with the local bookseller, who within a few days, was able to procure for me whatever book I desired."

A strange chill went through me and I shuddered. Adamic was describing the very Carnegie Library where I was sitting, and probably Mabel's father and the old Seaside Books. I felt like an archaeologist, having just opened up a long sealed tomb. I started to tear up, but fought back the tears. Here was this old book, by a writer who nobody even reads anymore. Why was it making me so emotional? I dried my damp eyes and continued reading. He went on about his four years as a port pilot clerk:

"The pilot station was a small building on the edge of the outer harbor, near the entrance to the main channel, with a full view of the Bay of San Pedro, and the powerful telescope which we had in the office was capable, on clear days, of stretching one's vision to the horizon. My work hours were from eight to five, with Saturday a half-day and Sundays and holidays off. My duties were simple, my salary good, and I was practically my own boss... There was about a half-hour of clerical work, which I did first thing in the morning; then I answered an occasional phone call from some ship's agent, telling me the time of her arrival or departure, so that we could have a pilot available for her. The pilots were elderly ex-sea-captains. They were seldom at the station, and I got along with all of them. When their services were needed, I summoned them by phone. Alone in the office I read and wrote most of the day."

Adamic started to get articles published. He often wrote about the people he met in San Pedro and Los Angeles. His clerk job gave him this opportunity. It was late afternoon when I finished the book.

On my way home, Louis Adamic's books weighed heavily in my arms, but his words also weighed heavily in my thoughts. His writing on San Pedro had hit a nerve. Here was someone writing about my town in a way that I could relate to. I thought I could write a decent biography using what I already knew.

As I once again passed the Chamber of Commerce office, I noticed that most of the Cadillacs had gone, leaving just one parked in front, a red one. After I'd passed the storefront, the door opened and J.P. Watterson stepped out onto the sidewalk.

"You there," he called out. "Stop."

"Are you talking to me?" I asked, turning around.

"Of course." He held the door open and

motioned me inside. "Come in. You may bring your subversive literature with you."

I suddenly felt like I was being called into the principal's office.

"My mom's expecting me for dinner," I said, all the while knowing that I actually had plenty of time.

"This won't take long," He stood there holding the door.

"Okay," I said, hesitantly, and then went inside.

The Chamber of Commerce's outer office had a woman and two men busily working behind their desks. On the walls, were paintings of some of the town's landmarks; the Fish Harbor, Angel's Gate Lighthouse, and the Vincent Thomas Bridge were among some of the paintings.

Watterson led me into his private office.

"Have a seat," he suggested, while he took a seat behind a large desk. I sat down at one of the two chairs in front of the desk and set my Adamic books on the other.

The room was covered with photographs of sailboats and sailing yachts. Watterson was pictured on what must have been his own yacht, and I could see the boat's name: "Carpé Diem," which I knew meant, "seize the day." A few impressive trophies sat on a shelf. Nearby, there was a large black and white photo portrait of J.P. Watterson Sr. on the wall. I could see that he had a strong resemblance to his son. On the desk in front of me were two plaques; one had J. P. Watterson Jr.'s name and title, while the other held the quote: "What's good for General Motors is good for America."

"It looks like you do some sailing?" I asked.

"Popeye did some sailing," he snapped. "I'm Commodore of the Los Angeles Yacht Club. We're having our big Catalina race this week. I plan to win it again."

"Oh," I said, considering whether I should mention Vlatko, since he also belonged to the club. "Do you know my Cousin Vlatko, he's a member?"

"Vlatko Petrovich is your cousin?" he said, with a surprised look.

I nodded yes.

"That man has no propriety, restraint, or decency. I can't tell you how many marriages he's ruined in the club."

"That sounds like my cousin alright."

"I've been trying to remove him from the club for years, but he has some special membership that was grandfathered in."

"He's always been very resourceful."

He gave me a long look. "And what does your father do?"

"He's a fisherman."

"What boat?"

"*Neptune's Prize*, the skipper is Augie Ancich. My dad's worked with him for years."

"He doesn't own his own boat?"

"No, but he's the first mate, and Augie calls him the best one in Pedro."

"So, he's just a working man, probably belongs to the Fisherman's Union?"

"Yes, I think so."

"I don't like the unions, never have and never will. Neither did my Father," pointing to the photograph of J.P. Watterson Sr. "And he built this peninsula."

"No disrespect to your father," I said, bluntly. "He might have financed the building, but someone else had to roll up their sleeves and do the actual work. Those people probably had to join a union just to get a fair wage and safe working conditions. Being a good business man, I'm sure your father probably pinched every penny to maximize his own profits."

Watterson just glared at me. I probably shouldn't have said that to him, but I didn't like him calling my dad "just a working man."

"Now I see your true color," he said, pointing to my bag of books. "Red, just like your hero Louis Adamic there."

"I have no idea what you're talking about."

"What's happening to this country is terrible," he said. "The American free enterprise system is under attack. Government regulations, consumer protections, and trade unions are making life difficult for business."

"Okay," I said, wondering why he was telling me this.

"The business executive has been the forgotten man," he paused. "But that's about to change."

He picked up a few sheets of paper that were stapled together. "This memo is a call to arms." He held it so that I could see the front page. It read:

CONFIDENTIAL MEMORANDUM
ATTACK ON THE FREE ENTERPRISE SYSTEM

"It was written by new Supreme Court justice Lewis Powell, two months before Nixon nominated him to the Supreme Court. It's a manifesto."

The only two manifestos I'd ever heard of were *The Communist Manifesto* by Karl Marx and *Mein Kampf* by Adolf Hitler. And I wasn't really interested in reading any of those either.

"This is a blueprint," he said. "A long-term game plan for corporations to use their money and political clout to do battle with their enemies. The Chamber of Commerce will lead the way."

"Why are you telling me this?"

"Because you young people need to understand that your views are all wrong. It's like the Beacon Street Redevelopment, the old must be torn down first, so that the new can flourish."

It sounded to me like he was saying that everything had to be destroyed first so that it could be rebuilt later in a more acceptable form for people like him. After a while, I politely thanked him for his lecture, wished him good luck on his upcoming yacht race, then grabbed my books and headed out the door.

"You young people don't understand!" he shouted.

As I walked away from the Chamber of Commerce, I couldn't help thinking about what Watterson had said. He saw himself and other millionaires as a persecuted minority. As if they all had to conspire together in order to fix things and make them right.

When I reached the nearby Beacon Street Redevelopment office I stopped. I realized how little I knew about it, so I decided to go inside. The young woman I saw earlier was still at her desk. She was a shapely; blue eyed and blond, but obviously several years older than I was. She wore a proper blouse and skirt.

"Can I help you?" she asked.

"I just wanted to see what I could learn about the redevelopment project."

"If there was someone you wanted to see, they've all gone home."

"No, that's okay."

In the center of the room was a large tabletop model of the current Beacon Street redevelopment area. The buildings on the model represented what was there now. She walked over to me as I studied everything.

"After the demolition, we'll remove the buildings from the model," she said. "Later, we can add the new buildings as they're built."

"To reflect the progress."

"If that's what you want to call it," she said with a frown.

"What do you mean?" I asked, a little surprised

by her response.

"I shouldn't say anything," she said, apologetically. "It's not really my place."

"What do you do here?

"I'm only an intern," she smiled, revealing two perfect dimples. "This is my first taste of how things really work."

"And how do they work?" I asked, laying my books down on a nearby desk.

"Well, everybody is on board with this project." She said with a scowl. "The feds are providing funding through local banks, business leaders welcome the opportunities, the workers and unions are happy about construction jobs, and the citizens look at it as an easy way to eliminate urban blight. It all seems like a win, win."

"But you don't think it is?"

She hesitated for a moment. "No."

"Why?"

"I'm getting my master's degree in Architecture and Urban Planning, and I've learned that most of these large redevelopment projects usually don't succeed. The current thinking is going away from this type of redevelopment."

"Why don't they succeed?"

"The new buildings usually aren't built on a human scale, and they aren't pedestrian friendly. Cities are for people, they should be low-rise, mixed use, and the sidewalks should be inviting. It should have a neighborhood feel, which makes people want to get out and mingle. This whole

Beacon Street area should be renovated instead of torn down. That would make so much more sense for the town."

"But the area is old, dirty, and tired."

"So, clean it up. If it needs earthquake reinforcement, do that. The buildings are all similar in scale and style. It could be a model community that preserves the town's history. That's what's succeeding now all around the country."

I thought for a moment about what she was saying.

"My name's Niko," I said, extending my hand.

"Carol," she said, shaking my hand.

We stood and talked for a while. Carol told me that she was almost finished with college, and after that she was planning to join an architecture firm that specialized in historic preservation. She also told me about several successful preservation projects around the country that would be good examples for what could be done here on Beacon Street. As she spoke, I couldn't believe how smart she was, and how pretty she was. And I noticed that she wasn't wearing a wedding ring. I was out of my league and I knew it, but what the hell.

"Would you like to go out for coffee sometime?" I asked.

"Coffee?" she smiled. "I usually go out for drinks."

"Oh," I stammered. "I'm not old enough for that."

"Yeah, I figured. Anyway, I have a boyfriend, and I don't think he'd like me having coffee with a cute guy, even if he is a little young."

"I understand," I said, grabbing my books off the desk. I moved toward the door.

"It was nice meeting you, Niko." She smiled.

"Thanks for all the information," I said, opening the door. I smiled then closed the door behind me.

After dinner with my parents, I called the number that I had for Nancy McClay. She seemed happy to hear from me.

"I was looking over April's Playboy," she said. "The centerfold is the prettiest black girl, what a body."

"All of the Playmates are pretty," I said, trying not to speak too loudly since my parents were both in the next room.

"As I looked at the pictures, I kept imagining what I would look like in the magazine," she sighed. "What time can you be over here tomorrow?"

"When will everyone be gone?"

"They usually all leave by eight."

"So, how about nine o'clock?"

"That's perfect," she said, with obvious joy.

145

"Today, a friend and I drove up to the Playboy Building in West Hollywood. I got a Playmate application form with some photo suggestions."

"Really?"

"Yeah. I couldn't have it mailed to the house, my parents would have flipped out."

"Oh, right."

"It was so exciting just being in the building. It's right there on the Sunset Strip."

"How appropriate."

"I'll see you tomorrow morning," she said. "I'll be the one wearing a smile and not much else." She hung up the phone.

"Oh my God!" I thought to myself as I laid down my phone. "This is going to happen!" I nervously grabbed the school's 35mm camera and put in a new roll of film.

My mom came in my room with a handful of folded laundry. She laid it on my bed. "It's so nice that you have a hobby," she said, smiling as she walked away.

"Yeah," I smiled. "Hobbies can be fun."

Tuesday

▽

Nancy McClay's home was on a pretty, tree-lined street up near Weymouth Avenue. I double checked the address on my piece of paper with the address on the house. They matched. It was a beautiful home, two story, and done in the Spanish Revival style. It reminded me of the house in that old movie, *Double Indemnity*, which I watched last month on TV. It was a good movie, but things sure didn't turn out so well for the main characters. I thought about that as I walked up to the door.

Nancy answered the door wearing a silk, Oriental robe. The robe barely reached her knees, and it didn't look like she was wearing anything underneath. I tried not to stare, but there was a lot of jiggle going on beneath that silk.

"Hello," she said, smiling and motioning for me to come in.

"Hi," I said, stepping inside.

The front entryway had a Spanish tile floor and an archway that led into the home. On the walls, were family photos, a large cross with a figure of Jesus, and a large portrait of Monsignor McClay.

"You're right on time," she said.

"I didn't want to be late."

Through the archway on the left was a library type den. The hallway continued straight ahead past a Spanish tile staircase. A high ceilinged living room with hardwood floors and Persian rugs was to the right. All of the furniture fit with the Spanish theme.

"Where do you want to shoot these pictures?" she asked.

"I don't know," I said. "Can I see those photo suggestions?"

"Sure, we have to get them." She grabbed my hand. "They're in my bedroom." She led me up the stairs.

This was too good to be true. Nancy was beautiful and sexy. And all I had to do was say the word, and she would drop her robe for me. Life was good.

Her bedroom was a vision in pink. The bedspread was pink, the walls were pink, the carpet was pink, and the chair and pillows were also pink. She had teen idol posters on the walls, and plenty of photos of herself and her family. There were a whole section of pictures from her first communion. She looked quite angelic in those, very innocent, a good Catholic girl.

On one wall, there were some beauty contest photos and newspaper clippings. There was a large photo of Nancy being crowned while holding a bouquet of flowers.

"That's when I won the Miss San Pedro beauty contest," she said, proudly.

"Really?"

"Now, I'll be competing in the Miss Los Angeles contest, and if I win that, the Miss California, then Miss USA, and finally Miss Universe."

"I didn't know you were interested in that stuff."

"I want to do that while I'm in college."

Suddenly, I started to feel ill. I looked again at Nancy's first communion pictures on the wall. My stomach was now in a knot. If I let Nancy pose nude for me, then sent the photos to Playboy, that would ruin things for her other ambitions. No beauty contest will accept anyone that's posed for Playboy.

"Look, Nancy, I don't think Playboy is a good idea for you right now."

"Why?" she asked, confused. "Don't you think I'm pretty enough?"

"You're plenty pretty," I said. "That's not the problem."

"Maybe I'm not exactly the girl next door?"

"No. If any guy were lucky enough to live next door to you, you would certainly qualify as the girl next door."

"Then what's the problem?"

"The problem is that you don't need to do this. A lot of these girls probably do it for the money. You don't need the money."

"Niko, I'm only young once."

"Well, that's true, you are young now," I said. "But these photographs will never go away. Some day, you'll be a mom, with kids in school, and someone will bring out an old magazine with your pictures in it. Don't you think your husband and kids will be a little embarrassed?"

"Wow," she said. "I never thought of that. I never considered what could happen in the future."

"Most people don't. They hardly look at the past, much less the future."

"Niko," she said, after a pause. "You know what, I think you'd make a great priest."

"Oh, please don't say that." I begged. "I just want to be a regular guy. I hardly go to church anymore. I didn't even do my confirmation. But here I am, telling a beautiful girl to keep her clothes on. There must be something terribly wrong with me." I hung my head in shame.

Nancy walked over to me. She lifted my head with her hands, and kissed me on both cheeks, very gently and sweetly. Then she backed up a step, and dropped her robe on the ground, revealing herself to me in all her glory. She was the most beautiful thing I'd ever seen.

"Well, do you think I'd have looked good in Playboy," she asked.

I didn't answer right away because I couldn't speak. "Yes," I finally said. "Definitely, yes."

"I know it's probably hard to believe," she said, "but I'm still a virgin, and I'd like to stay one for at least a while."

"So am I," I confessed. "And the way it's going, I'll probably die one."

"Don't say that," she frowned. "You just need to meet the right girl."

She picked up the Oriental robe and put it back on. "Have you had any breakfast?" She asked.

"No, not really."

"I could make us some scrabbled eggs and toast."

"Sure, I'd like that."

She took my hand and led me down the stairs to the kitchen. We talked as I watched her make us breakfast. After breakfast, I left. Nancy was lovely and sweet. She did look like the girl next door. "Poor Hugh Hefner," I thought. "This was one beauty that he would never see."

On Weymouth, I caught a bus traveling through town. I looked sadly at the 32mm camera that lay on my lap, and thought about Nancy and my damn conscience. I was glad that I talked her out of any Playboy pictures, but frustrated that nothing happened between us. She was so beautiful. If it had been Jake or Randy instead of me, then the outcome would have been different. I know it would have been different with Cousin Vlatko. Maybe he could give me some advice as to what I was doing wrong.

When I got to Vlatko's boat, he was just getting it ready for sailing and invited me along. I told him the story of what had happened with Nancy McClay.

"You're a better man than I, Niko. I wouldn't have been such a gentleman."

"I don't want to be a gentleman, I want to be like you!"

Vlatko let out a hearty laugh. "Niko, you can only be what you are. You shouldn't try to be something you're not. Me? I know I'm no gentleman." He pointed to a spot down the wharf. "You see that boat slip?"

I nodded yes.

"Bogart used to keep his boat right there."

"You mean the movie star, Humphrey Bogart?

"Yes, Bogey, the actor. He was also a member of the L.A. Yacht Club. We would often drink together, and sometimes we even sailed together."

"Really?"

"His boat was named the Santana, and he spent every weekend he could on her. He was a real sailor, not like some of those Hollywood pretty boys who just liked to pose for pictures."

"Was it a nice boat?"

"She was a beauty, and fast, too. He beat me in the Catalina race one year, and I asked him, what makes the Santana so fast? He looked at me with a cocktail glass in his hand, and says: 'Scotch.'"

"He sounds like fun."

"He was, sometimes. But sometimes he could be an angry drunk. Once he got upset with me just because I flirted with his wife, Betty. "

"Betty?"

"Lauren Bacall, but we all called her Betty."

"Oh."

"She was a dish. I think I almost had her under my charms. But then Bogey wouldn't let her come sailing with us anymore. He claimed that he didn't like women on board because then men couldn't pee over the side. That wasn't it at all; he just didn't trust me with his wife. But who could blame him, I'm a real son of a bitch."

"Nancy said she was a virgin."

"That can be cured."

"She wanted it to stay that way."

"She's eighteen, right?"

"Yeah."

"What's she waiting for, a rainy day?"

"I don't know?"

"Beautiful women don't grow on trees. They aren't like fruit in that way. But they are like fruit in that when they are ripe, they need to be picked, or else they rot on the vine."

"I don't think she's going to be rotting anytime soon."

"No, but why take the chance?" he smiled wickedly.

Vlatko's advice just made me even more confused about the opposite sex.

We finished preparing the Illyrian Queen and then cast off with Vlatko motoring the boat away from the marina.

"Before we leave the harbor," said Vlatko, "I want to show you a little history over on Terminal Island. You seem to be interested in history these days."

"Sure. Why not?"

We moved from the West Channel into the outer harbor.

"If you had been out here in the 1930s," said Vlatko, "you would have seen the Pan Am China Clipper flying boats using these waters as their runway for trips to Hawaii and Asia. It was a glorious way to travel.

"I'll bet."

"That all ended after the Japanese bombed Pearl Harbor in 1941. Then the Pacific became a war zone."

"Yeah, I know."

"Did you also know that the U.S. Pacific Fleet had been stationed right here in San Pedro until 1940?"

"No, I didn't."

"Yes. Military Intelligence thought it would be a good idea to move the Fleet to Pearl Harbor instead."

"Not a great move."

"You can say that again."

The six-story, concrete Warehouse Number One stood at the mouth of the main channel. At its base, sat Louis Adamic's Port Pilot's Office, with its Pilot boat docked nearby.

"How is your research on Louis Adamic going?" asked Vlatko.

"Good. I've read his first two books, and that might be enough. I liked his stuff on Pedro."

Once in the main channel, we passed the Terminal Island Federal Penitentiary on our right. "Club Fed," they called it, the seaside residence for such inmates as Al Capone, Salvatore Bonanno, and Charles Manson.

On our left, was the Southern Pacific slip, home to our dwindling fishing fleet, and probably where my dad was right now, mending the nets and preparing the boat for tomorrow's fishing.

Next to that, on Berth 76, was the former home to the E.K. Lumber dock. Long schooners once unloaded Pacific Northwest cedar, used to build the young city of Los Angeles. At that time, San Pedro was the busiest lumber port in the world.

We finally arrived at the old Municipal Ferry Building, closed since 1964 when the Vincent Thomas Bridge was completed. The ferry,

Islander, once departed every ten minutes for its short trip over to Terminal Island. Vlatko turned our boat and followed the same route as the ferry once had.

When we arrived at the island, Vlatko turned his motor to an idle and the boat just floated. This was where the twin of the mainland Ferry Building had once stood, but now there was no sign that it had ever even existed.

"What's your address?" Vlatko asked, lighting a cigarette.

"You know what it is," I smiled. "615 West Thirteenth Street."

"Have you ever wondered why there is no East Thirteenth Street?"

"No, not really," I paused. "But now that you mention it, that is odd."

"Right over there," he pointed. "By the canneries and the Fish Harbor was a city, or part of a city anyway."

"Where?" I said, looking to where he pointed. There was nothing there except bare streets and vast emptiness.

"It was called East San Pedro, and there were probably 3,000 Japanese who lived there. They had businesses, churches, and schools. The men owned fishing boats, and the women worked in the canneries. A horn would blow, day or night, and the women had to go in to clean and prepare the fish. They didn't return home until the job was done. The men were wonderful fishermen, excellent at catching tuna."

"I had no idea."

"The kids went to elementary school on the island, but then they went to Junior High and High School in San Pedro. As I got to know them, I made many good friends because we played a lot of baseball together."

"What happened?"

"After Pearl Harbor, everyone was afraid that these Japanese were going to become spies. So the FBI came and rounded up all of the first generation fishermen. They were mostly not U.S. citizens, and they just took them away. Then, later, they took the rest of the men away; most of them were U.S. citizens. Finally, they gave the women and children 48 hours to evacuate their town. It was a mess, they tried to pack what they could, but there was so much that they had to leave behind. We knew the Hiyashi family, and we came over with a truck. We moved whatever we could into our garage for them, but we had to come back later for their piano. When we came back, it was gone. Someone had stolen it. There was a lot of that going around, since no one was allowed to stay and guard their things."

"That's terrible."

"Then they were all sent to different relocation camps. The Hiyashi family was sent to Manzanar. We didn't see them again until after the war."

"What about their fishing boats?"

"They tried to sell them, but most ended up practically giving them away. Before Pearl Harbor, seventy-five percent of the fishermen were Japanese, after that, zero. While they were in the camps, East San Pedro was torn down, every last house and business. After the war, there was really nothing for them to come home to. Their history was erased."

"I'm really surprised that I never heard about this."

"Sometimes history's events aren't always tidy, and they don't fit neatly into the mythology. You need to read some more Louis Adamic. He wrote some good stuff. There's no excuse for ignorance. Most of the important things that happened, they don't teach you in school."

Vlatko tossed his cigarette into the water, put the motor in gear, and pointed us toward the harbor's exit. After we passed through the Angel's Gate and lighthouse, we hoisted our sails and caught the wind. It was a good strong wind.

After the sailing, we made it back to the dock before dusk. I thanked Vlatko for everything, grabbed my camera, and headed up Twenty Second Street. I had to get home for dinner, because I didn't want to hear an earful from my mom if I was late.

At Pacific Avenue, I noticed Miss Martin coming out of Pacific Central Market, loaded down with two heavy bags of groceries. She noticed me across the street and called me with a loud whistle. I guess I was helping her.

"Thank you," she said, handing me a bag.

"You're welcome," I said.

"What happened to your car?"

I didn't want to tell her about Father Jason. "It's in the shop for some work."

We continued up Twenty-Second Street to Grand Avenue where we turned north.

"How's your report coming?" she asked. "Did you decide on an author to write about?"

"I took your advice and chose Louis Adamic."

"Oh, how wonderful."

"I've read his first two books, but I might read more.

"Good. The more you read, the more you'll have to write about."

"How is your vacation going?" I asked, adjusting the bag of groceries in my arms.

"Well, to tell you the truth, I'm a little troubled by this whole Beacon Street situation."

"What do you mean?"

"Well, you know the Beacon Light Mission?"

"Yeah," I said. "A little bit."

The Beacon Light Mission was a Christian charity that had been on Beacon Street since 1905. It's provided comfort to sailors and seamen for almost seventy years. Its motto was, "soup, soap, and salvation." It was originally called The Sailor's Rest Mission.

"When I was a nun, I used to spend a lot of time there, tending to the poor and less fortunate. The building is going to be torn down as part of the redevelopment."

I didn't want to say anything to Miss Martin, but honestly, it was difficult for me to feel sorry to see The Beacon Light Mission go. The crowd of broken and disheveled men that gathered there daily was one of the reasons why Beacon Street was going to be torn down and redeveloped.

"I think they're moving the mission to Wilmington," I said.

"Yes, but the new facility won't be as large or as accessible." She adjusted the grocery bag in her arms. "The test of a moral society is how it treats its most vulnerable citizens."

She thought for a moment, and then remembered something.

"There was this homeless man, Gerald. He would come in to the mission almost daily. He had lice, snot running down his mustache and beard, matted hair, and he wore four or five layers of clothing. He smelled like the city dump. He wasn't interested in our soap and salvation, only our soup. One day, Gerald notices me hug another man there, who had asked for a hug. Human touch is really important you know. People long to feel a human touch. So, Gerald comes over to me, and says, Can I get a hug? I need a hug."

I cringed at the thought of Miss Martin having to hug this disgusting man.

Miss Martin began to tear up.

"I couldn't do it, I couldn't hug him." She started to cry. "I told him, tomorrow maybe. I went home and I cried my eyes out, because I couldn't hug him." Still crying. "Everyday when he'd see me, he'd ask for a hug, and I'd tell him, no, maybe tomorrow."

"It's okay," I said, putting my hand on her shoulder.

"Finally, through much prayer, something opened inside my heart, like a window. I came into The Beacon Light Mission and found Gerald. I hugged him for the first time." She smiled broadly. "I didn't need to make anymore excuses about tomorrow. From that day on, I never had a problem hugging anyone."

Miss Martin seemed to glow now from some inner light, as if she'd swallowed a 100-watt bulb. I didn't know anything about saints, but to me at that moment, she was a saint. I didn't need the Catholic Church to proclaim her one. Hell, they already booted her and her sisters out of the church, what did they know anyway?

"You're amazing," I said, shaking my head.

"Nonsense, that's just what we nuns do." She stopped herself. "Or did anyway."

"And they're tearing the old Beacon Light Mission down."

"Yes." She said, drying her eyes. "The Mission is where Joe Hill wrote his songs. There was a nice pastor there who let him come in and use their piano. I don't know how many songs he wrote there, but quite a few."

"Joe Hill, why do I know that name?"

"He wrote songs for the IWW, the Wobblies. He became a member right here in San Pedro."

Now I remembered. I read about Joe Hill in one of Adamic's books. At Fourteenth Street, I handed Miss Martin back her groceries, said goodbye, and headed home. I made it there just in time for dinner. My dad told me that Pacific Body Shop called, and my car was ready to be picked up.

After dinner, I called the number that I had for Carissa Johansson, hoping that she hadn't changed her mind about the prom. Also, I thought I'd invite her to Vic's Big Blowout on Saturday. I was feeling lucky. Carissa's mom answered the phone. She seemed a little irritated that someone was calling, but she brought Carissa to the phone anyway.

"Hello," she said, in that lovely voice.

"Hi, Carissa, this is Niko."

"Oh, hi, Niko," she paused. "I forgot that you'd be calling."

"Is this a bad time?"

"No," she said with a sigh. "It's just that Dad's not better. We finally took him to the doctor and they scheduled some tests."

"Oh, I'm sorry. Maybe I should call back later."

"No, it's okay. We can talk."

"I just wanted to make sure that we're still going to the prom?"

"I've been so busy taking care of Dad that I haven't had a chance to think about the prom. But sure, I'd still like to go with you."

"Good," I said, hesitating. "I was also wondering, but maybe this isn't such a good time."

"What?"

"My friend Vic is throwing a party on Saturday, and I was wondering if you'd like to go?"

There was a pause on the other end of the phone. Maybe I was asking too much. She had a boyfriend after all, and her dad was sick.

"Sure," she said. "My older sister will be here this weekend with my mom. It'll be nice to take a break."

She gave me her address and I wrote it down. "I'll pick you up at eight o'clock."

"That sounds fine."

"Tell your dad to get well soon. We all want to see him back at school."

"I'll tell him."

After I hung up the phone, I just sat there for a moment, feeling like the lucky guy who'd just won the jackpot in Las Vegas. Not only was I taking the prettiest girl in school to the prom, but I was also bringing her to my friend's party on Saturday. Things were starting to look up. Then I noticed the stack of books by Louis Adamic on my dresser. They reminded me that I still had a report to write. Now I didn't feel quite so lucky.

I turned on my stereo and put both records of Cream's double album, *Wheels of Fire*, onto the record changer spindle of my turntable. The song "White Room" began to play. I sat up on the bed with my back against the headboard. My open, three-ring binder rested on my knees; my notes from my earlier reading were beside me, and Adamic's books were stacked nearby.

Using my notes from reading "Dynamite," and "Laughing in the Jungle," I wrote an introduction about Adamic and his early life. It wasn't very long, but it was a good beginning. Then I quickly realized that I needed to do more reading.

I started with Adamic's next book, *A Native's Return*. It was about his trip back to the "Old Country," and his reconnecting with his family and heritage. I could see why the book had been a best seller. So many people could relate with his desire to return and reconnect with his heritage. I became so involved with the book that I finished it in just one sitting. With my eyelids starting to droop, I set my books and papers on the floor, and reached over and turned off the lights. I was asleep in seconds.

Wednesday

APRIL 18

"You have to get up," said my dad, pulling at my covers. "Coffee's on the table."

"Just let me sleep a little longer," I pleaded, my eyes not adjusting well to the bright light.

"No, we've got to get to the boat." He managed to yank the covers right off my bed, exposing me to the chill of the morning.

"Okay," I said, reluctantly, wondering why I had ever agreed to go fishing.

I threw on an old flannel shirt and a pair of worn jeans, had some coffee and toast, and said goodbye to my mom, who was just getting up. We grabbed two sack lunches that my dad had prepared.

"Be careful!" she yelled as we stepped out into the cold morning.

"I will," I answered, realizing that I really didn't know what I was getting myself into.

We had to walk down to the boat, since I hadn't picked up my car yet. As we walked, I mentioned to Dad what Vlatko had said about the Japanese fishermen and East San Pedro.

"It was a shame, no spies were ever found. Those poor people lost everything."

"So why did it happen?"

"Unfortunately, the Japanese looked different than most Americans. You see, no German-Americans were ever rounded up, because the Germans looked like everyone else."

"And the Italians too?"

"Yes, and the Italians were the largest group here in San Pedro for a while. The ones from Genoa, settled in the area between Sixth and Ninth Street. We called the area "Vinegar Hill," because of the smell of them pouring out their soured wine."

"I remember your wine making in our cellar on Centre Street."

"Yes, good Dalmatian Wine."

We crossed Pacific Avenue and continued down Thirteenth Street. My dad continued talking.

"Between Ninth and Twelfth, were Italians from the island of Ischia, by Naples. And from Thirteenth to Seventeenth Street were the Sicilians," he smiled. "You have to keep an eye on those Sicilians."

We crossed Mesa Street, still heading east.

"How about the Croatians?" I asked.

"We lived right here among the Italians. After awhile, we had more fisherman than the Japanese and Italians put together. We built the largest and best canneries and designed the best fishing boats."

"Of course," I said with some pride.

"But that's all changing now. I don't know what's going on anymore."

The Italian Fisherman's Social Club stood at the corner of Thirteenth and Centre Street, where retired Italian fisherman played Bocce Ball and cards. Down the street, was our old house, right next door to the Yugoslav Fisherman's Social Club. The two clubs were only a block apart, but it might as well have been the Adriatic Sea. The two groups never mingled.

"I miss that little house," I said. "Besides the wine cellar, I liked the backyard with the fruit trees. If we were still living there, you could go next door for a card game."

"It would be nice. That hall has been around forever. In the 1920s it was the union hall for the IWW."

"The IWW, really?"

"It was before my time, but one night, the Ku Klux Klan actually paraded past the hall, trying to intimidate the immigrants that were its members. Many of them left town, fearing for their lives."

"But San Pedro is a town of immigrants."

"It wasn't so much back then, and the natives didn't like the trend. We were loud, mostly Catholics, and we ate strange food. You were okay if you landed on Plymouth Rock, but not so much if you landed on Ellis Island."

We walked along the viaduct bridge to the stairs that led down to the fishing boats. Neptune's Prize, a white Purse Seiner, was floating there at the dock waiting for us. A large black net was piled up near the stern of the boat, with a skiff behind that. The cabin and wheelhouse were toward the boat's front. Most of the crew was just arriving. My dad had already given me a run down of everyone. Mike, one of the fishermen, spoke up.

"Hey, Nick, is that your boy?"

"Yes," answered my dad. "This is Niko. It's his first time out."

"Ah, shark bait." laughed Joe, another fisherman.

Some of the others laughed, too.

"He doesn't look like he's that much," said Frank, an older fisherman. "More like guppy bait."

Oh boy, I thought to myself. So this was going to be "pick on the new kid day." Well, what did I expect. I was green, and these guys were all grizzled veterans. I just hoped I could hold my own. Augie Ancich, the skipper, came over to me.

"Niko, I want you to know that I'm doing this

as a favor to your father. I can't give you a full share of the catch, or even a half share. But if we do well, I'll give you something."

"That's okay," I said. "I'm just trying to get some experience."

"Fair enough. But if you think you want to start doing more of this, let me know and I'll help you get into the union."

"Thanks."

Augie was in his late fifties, and my dad had worked with him forever. He was tall and commanding and had fingers like sausages. No one would dare to mutiny on his boat. Several years ago, another boat he'd owned, the Gypsy Princess, sank in a violent storm off of Mexico. Fortunately, my dad hadn't been on that one, several fishermen died.

I never thought about my dad as being particularly brave or reckless, but being a fisherman is one of the most dangerous jobs to have. We always heard about boats going down, and crews being lost. It was just part of our culture. Fishermen were a tough group. Most of them worked hard, played hard, and cursed up a storm. But my dad was different, he hardly drank, didn't curse, and he was usually home by dark. Augie loved that my dad was reliable; he could always count on him.

Joe Vitalich and Mike Bebich were both about forty. Joe was a large guy, very thick. He was also gregarious and loud. His family had a Yugoslav restaurant in town, where you could get roasted lamb, seafood, and pasta. Some of the Vitalich family worked there, while others were fishermen like Joe.

Mike was Joe's friend, and he was tall and lean. He was usually quiet, but he had a devilish sense of humor. His father owned a fishing boat, but he didn't like working for him because of his dad's awful temper. Once at the Fisherman's Social Club, he broke a chair over a guy's head when he caught him cheating at cards. Augie was much easier to deal with.

Frank Lucich was about my dad's age, with skin so tan and weathered that it looked more like leather. Frank had all the fisherman traits that my dad didn't have. Every other word was profanity, and he could often be found at the bars and bordellos on Beacon Street. Frank was a typical San Pedro fisherman.

Everyman knew his job, and they got right to it. Joe and Mike put the hatch lids on top to close the refrigerated hold. Augie went into the wheelhouse to check all of the instruments and the radio. My dad and I climbed the ladder to the boat's upper controls on the bridge above the wheelhouse.

"You stay with me," he said.

"Sure," I replied, happy to be out of the way.

My dad fired up the diesel engine and checked all of the gauges. It's funny, my dad never learned to drive a car, but he's been piloting boats since he was little. He had seen the world and had friends and probably girlfriends in every port.

Frank untied the lines from the large cleats on the dock and then jumped back into the boat. The water behind the boat churned white from the spinning of the propellers. Dad steered us toward the breakwater's opening as the sun was just coming up in the east. We passed a fleet of merchant ships anchored in the outer harbor. They were all waiting to load or unload their cargo at the crowded port.

Today was the start of the Los Angeles Yacht Club's annual Catalina Island race. Vlatko wasn't participating this year, but he had in the past and did well. There was already a large fleet of boats preparing for the race.

Our skipper's plan was for us to spend about 24 hours fishing for skipjack tuna over by Catalina Island. The Neptune's Prize had good luck there last week and caught its limit. Augie was confident that he could fill the hold in just 24 hours. I was hoping that he was right, since I was scheduled to work lunch tomorrow at the Hungry Fisherman. They wouldn't like it if I cancelled. Especially since I told them I couldn't work today.

We motored for a couple of hours over to Catalina Island. Off the southern tip of the island, we stopped the boat near where we thought there would be fish. Mike grabbed the binoculars and climbed up into the crow's nest, while Augie studied the instruments in the wheelhouse. They shouted directions to my dad, who was on the helm. Dad maneuvered the boat as instructed. This went on for about an hour.

"Fish!" Mike shouted, as he pointed ahead toward the horizon.

Dad moved the boat in the direction that Mike pointed. When we got close enough, we could see the foamy water and the flock of seagulls circling overhead.

"Skipjack!" shouted Dad.

Mike climbed down from the crow's nest, as everyone was getting into place to set the net. After Frank had gotten into the skiff, Augie signaled for the skiff's release, and it splashed into the water, dragging the end of the net with it. My dad steered the boat carefully around the school of tuna, encircling it with the net. The cork line, with its yellow floats rested on the ocean's surface. The net was successfully connected by returning the boat with the other end of the net back to the skiff. Once the net had encircled the fish, the chain line was closed below, trapping the fish as in a purse.

The power block at the end of the largest boom began to pull up the net, as the deck's winch brought up the purse rings. I grabbed a pair of thick rubber gloves and helped Joe and Mike gather the cork line, the netting, and the chain line all into neat piles on the deck, making it ready for the next set. Once enough of the net was on board, and the fish were crowded into

one small area, then Augie started operating the
brailing scoop and bringing the fish out of the
water and into the boat's refrigerated hold. After
the brailing was complete, the rest of the net
was hoisted up, and then everything was neatly
arranged for the next set of the day. This all took
a couple of hours.

It was a good morning. Dad estimated that
we pulled in over 100 tons of Skipjack tuna. The
skipper suggested that we have lunch before we
go looking for another school of fish.

We all grabbed our lunches and scattered out
on the deck. I sat on an overturned bucket by my
dad.

"Hey Petrovich," said Joe, to me. "For a punk
kid, you didn't do so bad."

"Yeah," said Mike. "We've seen worse."

"Hell yes," said Frank. "You didn't shit your
pants yet, that's good."

"Well, thanks," I answered, biting into my
salami sandwich.

"Your dad said you work over at the Hungry Fisherman," said Joe, shoving food into his
mouth.

"Yeah."

"I know money is money, but how can you
work with those damn Italians?"

"They're not so bad, Tommy's a good guy."

"Yeah, but that Galasso bastard," said Mike. "I
would kick that wop's ass just for fun."

"He's not my favorite."

"I once screwed a dago whore in the Colonial Hotel on Beacon Street," said Frank. "She was okay," he paused. "Except I think she gave me the clap. It was either her or one of the other girls."

"You should probably figure out which one it was," said Mike.

"Yeah," said Joe.

"What does it matter now," said Frank. "They're tearing down all the whore houses, all of the bars, all the pool halls. This town is trying to be goddamn respectable."

"We'll never be respectable," said Mike.

"Hell no," said Joe. "You can dress us up, put a new suit of clothes on us, but we're still who we are."

Everyone sat and ate their lunches.

"I think Frank is going to miss Beacon Street," said Dad.

"You bet your ass I will. What other town our size can you go into a different dive bar every night for three weeks and not repeat yourself?"

"A man likes variety," said Joe.

"I was in the White Swan the other night," said Frank, "I got shit-faced drunk, got in two fights, and I had a great time."

"Beacon Street just has a bad reputation," said Mike.

"Did you ever go into Shanghai Red?" I asked Frank.

"Oh, hell yes! Now that was a bar!"

Shanghai Red was named after its proprietor, Charles "Red" Eisenberg. Red was born and raised on San Francisco's Barbary Coast. Then as a teenager he shipped out as a sailor, finding himself in Shanghai, China, where he stayed for a while and ran a saloon. With the money he earned there, he came to San Pedro just as prohibition was ending, and opened his now famous bar on Beacon Street.

"Shanghai Red was the toughest waterfront bar in the whole world," said my dad. "I knew some sailors that got rolled there."

"Rolled?" I asked.

"They got beat up," answered Joe. "And all of their money was taken."

"Red would tell you that he could flatten any man in the joint!" said Frank.

"Did he kick your ass?" asked Joe.

"No, he liked me. But his bouncer, Cairo Mary, once threw me out on my butt."

"Cairo Mary?" I asked.

"Yeah," she was something," said Frank. "She was a big dame, with a tattoo on her right bicep of a heart, and she was tougher than any man."

"Wow," I said, shaking my head.

The skipper finally announced that it was time to get back to work, so everyone took their places. My dad fired up the engine and Mike climbed back up into the crow's nest. Augie went back to his instruments in the wheelhouse. We looked and looked for about an hour before we found our next school of Skipjack. There was even more fish in this school than the first one. We repeated the same procedure for setting the net, everyone working together.

I had to admit it, I kind of liked this fisherman thing. I liked the teamwork, and I liked bringing in the catch, and I loved being out on the ocean. But the work was hard. After several hours, we finished up. Most of us were spent. The sun was almost setting as we all went inside and sat around the galley's table. Dad and Augie were frying up some steaks on the stove. A cold six-pack of Eastside Beer was being passed around.

"None for you, kid," said Joe, to me. "You're not legal."

"It wouldn't be my first beer," I said.

"Still, it's contributing to the delinquency of a minor."

"He can have a beer," said my dad, from the stove. "He's been drinking wine since he was a baby."

"Okay," said Joe. "Papa knows best."

"Thanks," I said, grabbing a cold beer.

"What's that old fisherman's saying?" asked Mike. "You know, about the fish biting."

"Why don't you ask that old fisherman over there," said Joe, pointing to Frank.

Frank swallowed a large gulp of beer, and then spoke.

"When the wind is in the east, then the fishes bite the least. When the wind is in the west, then the fishes bite the best. When the wind is in the north, then the fishes do come forth. When the wind is in the south, it blows the bait in their mouth."

"And if you're too stupid to figure out the wind," said Joe, "then you're screwed."

"That doesn't rhyme," said Mike.

"Who gives a shit?" said Joe. "I'm a fisherman, not a poet."

When the steaks were done, we all sat around the table, having salad, French bread, and the steaks. We washed it all down with some red Dalmatian Wine.

"What happened to your boat, the Gypsy Princess?" I asked Augie.

"Kid," said Joe, giving me a disapproving look. "Don't you know it's bad luck to talk about that crap?"

"You're just asking for trouble," said Mike.

"No," said Augie. "That's okay, I can talk about it now, I couldn't for the longest time."

"You don't have to, Skipper," said my dad. "It was a terrible thing."

"That's okay," said Augie, clearing his throat. "We were down in Mexico, not too far from Cabo San Lucas, in international waters. We had a full load of Albacore, 1,000 ton of fish. We were coming home, but there was a tropical storm coming up from the south. It wasn't supposed to hit for another day, so we thought we had time. Also, reports were that it wasn't going to be that bad. So, there was no urgency." He clears his throat again, taking a sip of wine. "But then all hell broke loose. The daytime sky turned black, the winds kicked up, rain came down in sheets, and the swells became ten to fifteen foot. Now, the boat's loaded down, we're low in the water already, and we're starting to flood. Andy Ferkich is down working the bilge pumps trying to get the water out, but it can't work fast enough. John Kostrencich is down there trying to keep the engine running, and Paul Zupanich is trying to help both of them." He takes another drink. "I was in the wheelhouse and Frank here, is on the deck. I put out a distress call on the radio. Then, that's it. The boat starts sinking. It just goes under. Frank had tossed out a lifeboat just as the boat was going down. He and I found the lifeboat, but three good men were gone, and my boat, all gone." He finishes the glass of wine. "We didn't get picked up for a whole day."

"Two days," said Frank.

"Yes, you're right, two days."

"Those poor men," said my dad.

"Yeah," said Augie.

I shouldn't have asked the question about the Gypsy Princess. It made everyone feel awful, Augie and Frank especially. I ruined the mood, because nobody wants to be reminded of how fast things can go from good to bad.

"Alright," said Augie. "We've got to find some more fish before we can go home."

The sun was finally setting, so we had to hurry

if we wanted to use what was left of the daylight. After we cleaned up from the meal, we took our places again. Before we got too far, Mike, in the crow's nest, spotted something in the water.

"Over there, starboard side," he yelled, pointing. "It looks like a piece of something."

Dad turned our boat and headed in that direction. When we got there, we could see that it was part of a boat, the rear section of what looked like a large sailboat. Frank grabbed a pole with a hook on the end. He turned the section over, so we could read the boat's name. It read:

"*Carpé Diem*"
　　"Los Angeles Harbor"

"*Carpé Diem*, I thought. That was the name of J. P. Watterson's boat from the Chamber of Commerce, the Commodore of the L.A. Yacht Club. He must have been out here today competing in their Catalina Race.

"I know whose boat that is," I told everyone.

"What?" asked Frank. "You do?"

"Who?" asked Joe.

"J. P. Watterson. He's a big shot in town."

"I know who you're talking about," said Augie.

"Yeah," said Joe. "He owns that big construction company. He's a cheap bastard, won't even hire union workers."

"I remember his father," said Augie. "Now there was a piece of work."

"He didn't like anybody," said Frank. "Unless you were protestant and lily white. We fisherman sure didn't count."

"Well, that's Watterson's boat. I'm sure of it."

"I'll radio it in to the Coast Guard," said Augie. "There's not much else we can do."

We used the winch and hauled the section of the *Carpé Diem* out of the water, and then we shoved it out of the way. I looked out at the vast ocean, scanning it. Hoping that I would see Watterson out there, safe and floating in a lifeboat, but all I saw was water. The sun was just about down, when Augie turned on the boat's safety lights, running lights, and work lights. Everybody took their places once again, looking for fish.

We were lucky, just before the last bit of daylight was gone, we found another school of skipjack. Using our lights, we managed to set the net and bring in our catch. It was harder working in the dark and much more dangerous, but we got it all done. We secured everything then headed back to San Pedro. The work lights were turned off, with only the running lights and a few safety lights on.

As we were heading home, Dad heard something. It was very faint, but it sounded like a voice.

He quickly switched off the engine.

"Listen!" he shouted. "Everybody be quiet and listen!"

We all stopped what we were doing and got quiet. For a moment we didn't hear anything, but then we heard a faint voice. "Help," then again, "Help... help."

Mike pointed to our boat's port side, and Joe shouted, "Over there! It's coming from over there!" Frank grabbed the boat's spotlight as Dad turned on the engine and pointed the boat toward the sound, moving the vessel as gently as he could. The spotlight swept slowly across the water as we all followed it with our eyes.

"There!" I shouted. "Right there!"

The light stopped on a man floating in the water. He was wearing an orange life jacket, and he began waving his arms frantically.

"We see you," said Augie. "Relax, we're going to pull you in."

Frank threw the man a life preserver attached to a rope. The throw was perfect, and the man grabbed hold. Mike helped Frank pull in the rope. Joe climbed over the side and stood on a small ledge near the water line. He held onto the boat with one hand, and then extended the other hand out to the man. I went over and grabbed hold of Joe, trying to make sure he didn't fall in. The man in the water pulled himself up and grabbed Joe's hand. With my help, Joe pulled the man onto the deck, where he collapsed. Everyone gathered around him. It was J. P. Watterson, and he was cold, wet, and exhausted.

"That's Watterson," I said.

We got him into the cabin and helped him take off his wet clothes. We then wrapped him in a warm blanket, and Dad poured him a glass of Old Crow Whiskey.

"Here," said Dad, handing him the glass, "It'll warm you up."

Watterson took the glass in his shaky hands and took a sip. He choked on the whiskey, coughing several times.

"Smooth, huh?" said Frank.

"No," Watterson said, "I've had better."

"You're a lucky man," said Augie. "The chances of us running into you were a million to one."

"Yeah," he said, glumly. "I'm so lucky."

"Where's your crew?" asked Frank, handing him a towel.

"I don't know."

"What happened to your boat?" asked Mike.

"We were leading the Catalina race and way ahead. Then out of nowhere, something hit my boat, smashing it to pieces. I must have passed out, because when I came to, I was all alone, floating in the water, debris all around me."

"You're lucky you didn't drown," I said.

"Or freeze to death," said Frank.

"Yeah," he agreed.

Everyone thought for a moment about how lucky Watterson really was. The fact that he was alive and well was a miracle.

"I'll bet you hit a submarine," said Mike. "U.S. subs are always practicing in these waters."

"Yeah," said Joe. "Didn't Eddie DeMeglio once claim that he lost his fishing net to a submarine?"

"Eddie DeMeglio is an asshole," said Frank. "I'm surprised he didn't claim it was Moby Dick."

The truth was, that many U.S. submarines had been spotted in these waters, and there have been several instances where they actually sank boats. But the U.S. Government was always reluctant to claim responsibility, using national security as a reason.

"How many crewmen did you have?" asked Augie.

"I had three. They were all well paid professional sailors, hired for the race. I barely knew them."

"And now they're gone," said Augie.

"Yes, but fortunately, I had them all sign a standard legal waiver, absolving me of any harm that might come to them. Their families won't be able to sue me. "

"That's thinking ahead," said Mike, with a glare.

"I wouldn't be a very good captain if I didn't consider my men."

I could tell by looking at them, that our crew didn't like Watterson. Frank looked like he wanted to throw him back in the water, while Joe and Mike just shook their heads. They left the cabin before they said something that they might regret later.

"How about your boat?" I asked. "Was it insured?"

"Of course," he said. "Well insured."

Augie's former boat, the Gypsy Princess, hadn't been insured when it sank. In fact none of the fishing boats were insured anymore. No company would insure them.

"I'd better get us home," said Augie. "It's getting late."

He left the cabin for the wheelhouse, and then the boat was headed home. Watterson looked over to my dad.

"Are all of you fishermen in the union?"

"Yes, except the boy."

"That's too bad," said Watterson. "Men who join unions are weak."

"Excuse me," I said. "Are you calling my dad weak?"

"Niko," said Dad, "The man is a guest on our boat."

Dad looked over to Watterson.

"How is a worker joining a union any different than a businessman joining a business association, or the Chamber of Commerce, or even a private club, where business is discussed over lunch?"

"It just is, that's all," said Watterson.

"And why is it okay for the bosses to meet and plan together, but not the workers? What's wrong with a level playing field?"

"Business men have to take back our country."

"From whom," I asked. "Working people?"

"Working people are okay, it's their unions that are the problem," he said "They have too much power."

"Before unions, workers had no power," I argued.

"Maybe that's how God meant for it to be," said Watterson.

I don't think he wanted to, but I think my dad felt like he had to say something.

"Too bad Mr. Watterson studied all of that business and no history."

"You have your history," said Watterson. "And I have mine."

"Only if you distort the actual facts," I said.

Dad finally decided to speak up.

"Recently, our country has had a shared prosperity. People, who work hard, are rewarded for their labor. They earn a piece of the pie. They can buy homes, and they can send their children to college. This wasn't always so. There was a time, when only a few men got rich, and nobody but the rich profited. Everybody else had to settle for their scraps."

"I didn't know I was rescued by the world's only Fisherman Economist."

Dad pointed his finger right in Watterson's face.

"You are lucky that there are still working

people out here who can rescue you. There will come a day, that you will destroy everything with your greed, and there will be no one left to rescue you.

Dad glared at Watterson for a moment, and then walked out. Watterson watched him go without saying a word. At that moment, I was so proud of my father; I'd never even seen him raise his voice before.

Augie radioed the Coast Guard to tell them about J.P. Watterson's boat. They would let his family know, so that they could meet us at Fisherman's Wharf. When we finally docked at the wharf, Watterson's wife was there with dry clothes for him. While he was putting them on, she tearfully thanked all of us for saving his life. She seemed truly grateful. They then got into their red Cadillac and drove off. It was past midnight, but we still had to get Neptune's Prize over to the fish cannery on Terminal Island to unload the Skipjack.

"Nick," said Augie, "Take Niko and go home."

"But Skipper," said Dad. "There's more to do."

"That's okay. Get the boy home, he's had a full day." He then looked over at me. "And Niko, I'm giving you a half share of the catch.

"Thanks, Augie. I really appreciate it."

"And if you want to go up to Alaska this summer, there might be a place for you on the crew." He smiled. "Think about it."

"I will."

I waved goodbye to the crew and they each returned the wave.

"I was wrong about you, kid," shouted Frank. "You would make some good shark bait."

"Thanks," I said, smiling.

They were a good bunch of guys, but I still didn't know whether I wanted to spend the whole summer with them in Alaska. One day was okay though.

As Dad and I walked over to the viaduct stairs, Augie steered Neptune's Prize over to Terminal Island to unload the catch.

Thursday

APRIL 19

▼

The next morning, on my way to the Hungry Fisherman, I stopped at Pacific Body Shop to pick up my car. It looked great, and I couldn't even tell that it had been in an accident. Having my Chevy back, I now felt complete. Unfortunately, stopping to pick up my car made me a few minutes late for work.

Everyone was busy preparing for lunch when I finally arrived at the restaurant. Dean and Diana were settings the tables, Vince Galasso was working in the kitchen, and Tommy and Marie were at the back table having one of their usual arguments. Tommy stopped arguing when he noticed me trying to sneak in.

"You're late," he shouted.

"Sorry," I said, "I had to pick up my car at the shop."

"So, it had nothing to do with you going fishing yesterday?"

"No," I said, wondering how he knew about that.

"You said you weren't available to work here yesterday because you were sick, but you could go out fishing on Augie Ancich's boat, eh?"

"I had to get some experience, in case I wanted to go to fishing in Alaska this summer."

"Augie's a good skipper," said Marie. "You could do a lot worse."

"What the hell do you know about fishing?" asked Tommy, to his sister. "You've never even been out on a boat."

"Papa said Augie was a good fisherman. That's all I need to know."

"Oh, Papa said," sneered Tommy. "You must be Papa's little girl."

"Tommy, you need to get over this thing with Paulie. Papa put him in charge of everything when you were in Vietnam. But he was never going to put a hot head in charge of anything."

Tommy gathered a load of spit in his mouth, then leaned over and spat directly in Marie's face. She was stunned for a moment, but then grabbed a napkin from the table and wiped the spit from her face.

"You're an animal!" she shouted.

"And you're a brat!" he shouted back, storming off into the kitchen and then right out the back door. Vince followed him out. Marie shook her head in disgust, and then went in the restroom to wash her face.

Dean and Diana came over to me.

"That was terrible," said Dean.

"He was never like this before Vietnam," said Diana.

"Really?" I asked.

"No." She looked at me for a moment. "Nancy told me what happened with her Playboy pictures."

"I didn't want to be responsible for helping her mess up her life."

It seemed that Diana had more to say.

"What?" I asked, curious.

"After you left, Nancy called Jim Pallente. He came right over with his camera and took the pictures for her."

"No way." I said.

"I know it's crazy, but being in Playboy Magazine has always been one of her dreams."

"I thought she agreed with what I was telling her."

"She did," said Diana. "But dreams aren't always logical."

"I guess we weren't on the same page."

"No," said Dean, wide eyed. "I think her page was a centerfold."

Tommy and Vince came back into the kitchen from outside as Marie came back into the dining room from the bathroom. Nothing more was said between them, but we could all feel the tension in the room. Somehow we managed to make it through lunch without another incident.

I'd worn out my dad's rubber work gloves while fishing, so I'd decided to stop at Union War Surplus to get him a new pair. Like Seaside Books, Union War Surplus had recently moved up Sixth Street to their new location. Their old location, which had started as a place for surplus military gear, was also to be demolished as part of the Beacon Street Redevelopment.

Like the old store, walking into the new Union War was a true spectacle. As kids, we just loved exploring the place, touching everything that had a unique feel, and even smelling everything that had a interesting smell. When we actually had money, we bought sporting goods, camping equipment, and fishing gear. The place was also stocked to the rafters with aisles of work clothes and shoes. Working men and women loved the place. Shipyard workers, cannery workers, long-shoremen, and fishermen all knew that whatever they needed could be found right here. The sign out front read:

"If you need a battleship or a hunting knife we have it or will get it."

I parked my car on the other side of the street and then crossed over to the store.

"Cheerful" Al Kaye, the bearded proprietor, was there at the cash register. Al looked less like a small business owner, and more like a 1849 California gold prospector.

"You know what you need?" he asked.

"Yeah," I answered. "But I might also do some browsing."

"You go right ahead, but just let me know if you need help."

"I will, Al. Thanks."

Making my way down a center aisle, I passed stacks of yellow rain slickers that fishermen wore out at sea. If I did go up to Alaska, I'd have to do quite a bit of shopping here. I finally found the gloves, and picked out the best pair I could find.

"Niko," a voice called out from behind me.

I turned to find Solomon Jefferson standing there with a big smile on his face. He was wearing a blue chambray work shirt and a pair of faded, black Frisco Jeans. He had a stevedore's hook sticking out from his back pocket. This was the uniform of sorts for the working longshoremen.

"Hi Mr. Jefferson," I said, shaking his hand. "You look like a real longshoreman now."

"That's me," he said. "A real longshoreman."

I told Mr. Jefferson all about going out fishing with my dad, and what an experience it had been for me. I finally got around to telling him about how we rescued J.P. Watterson.

"No offense," he said, shaking his head. "But you should have let that man drown, he's no better than his daddy."

"We sure felt like throwing him back in. What a jerk."

Mr. Jefferson then told me all about his first week as a full-time longshoreman. With every detail, the smile on his face grew bigger and bigger. He couldn't have been happier with his new job.

"I'm getting these gloves for my dad. What are you getting?" I asked.

"A cap."

"Like a baseball cap?" Wondering if he was going to be doing some more coaching.

"No, a different kind of cap." He started walking and motioned me to join him.

I followed him over to the huge hat area, where an entire wall was covered with all types of headgear. Solomon found what he was looking for. He pulled the round, white cotton cap from the shelf. It was flat, and had a snap over the bill, which attached the bill to the upper part of the cap. He found his size.

"It's called a West Coast Stetson, the historic cap of the longshoremen," he said, putting it on. He found a mirror, admiring how it looked on him.

"Do you mind if I ask you another question about the IWW?" I asked.

"No, go right ahead."

"My dad told me that the Yugoslav Fisher-man's Social Club on Centre Street was once the IWW Union Hall."

"That's right," he said. "The KKK held a huge parade right past it one night. Klansmen from all over Southern California showed up. Another day, they stormed into that hall one day while Wobblies were having a social for the families. I'll bet you daddy Watterson was leading the mob. They busted up the place, threw chairs around, and dumped a big pot of hot coffee on two little kids. They were burned so badly that they had to go to the hospital."

"With tactics like that, no wonder the strike didn't work."

"Some people were so scared, they just left town after that, just gave up."

"So how did things finally improve for the longshoremen?"

"It took an act of congress; The National Industrial Recovery Act of 1933 passed ten years after the IWW strike. It gave longshoreman the right to organize and to join what later became the ILWU."

"And that solved everything?"

"No," he laughed. "We still had to fight and scratch, which led to the general strike of 1934."

"How did that strike succeed, when the 1923 strike didn't?"

"For one thing, the ILWU had a real leader,

a smart Australian fella named Harry Bridges. He organized the entire west coast, not just San Pedro, but also Seattle, San Francisco, Portland, and San Diego."

"Amazing."

"Yeah, they succeeded, but only after some good men died. Then the public finally embraced their cause."

"But somebody had to die first."

"Unfortunately, somebody always has to die. Every year, we commemorate the loss of those brave men on "Bloody Thursday." We never want anyone to forget the struggle." He paused for a moment, and then smiled.

"Well, what do you think?" referring to the cap.

"It looks great."

"My daddy would be so proud." Solomon beamed.

His father, who was a Wobbly back during the failed strike of 1923, might also look back on the struggles of 1934, and then the success of Solomon's lawsuit here in the 1970s, and realize that all of the efforts were finally worth it.

Driving by the hand car wash on Pacific Avenue, I notice Randy there washing his van. I hadn't seen Randy since I had helped him rescue the van from the police impound. I pulled into the car wash and parked. Melissa was nowhere around.

"Where's Melissa?" I asked.

"I don't know, Man," he answered. "I have no idea what she's doing anymore." He turned away.

I should never have promised Melissa that I wouldn't tell Randy about her and Pancho. Obviously, she hadn't told him herself.

"Are you working today?" I asked.

Randy had a job pumping gas at Sam Bodine's Union 76 service station. Sam, who owned the place, was an old southern redneck, who had Confederate flags displayed all over the place. It looked like he was ready to refight the Civil War.

"Sam fired me."

"Why?'

"He says that some money was missing and I must be the one who took it."

"Are you?"

"He can't prove shit."

"But did you take it?"

"Hell, yes I took it! He doesn't pay me squat."

As Randy finished rinsing the soapsuds from his van, I told him all about Carissa, and how I was bringing her to Vic's party on Saturday.

"Holy shit." He smiled.

"I know she has a boyfriend, but she said she'd go."

"Melissa is supposed to go with me, but she's been canceling a lot lately."

"I'm sure she'll go."

Randy looked deeply troubled. I could tell that this whole thing with Melissa was really bothering him.

"Hey, man," he said, looking right at me. "You know Melissa pretty well, you two are friends."

"Yeah?"

"I need you to talk to her, find out what's going on. I know something's going on, but she won't tell me anything."

This is exactly what I was afraid of. How do I tell him that I already know that she's seeing another guy behind his back?

"Would you do that for me, man?" he started to tear up. "Something's going on, I know it. I feel like I'm losing her."

Randy choked up and couldn't speak.

"I'll talk to her. That's all I can promise."

"Thanks," he said, wiping his eyes with his shirtsleeves. "You're a good friend."

Right then I didn't feel like a good friend. I felt like a truly crappy friend. I felt like I was stuck right in the middle between Randy and Melissa. So far, I've been honoring Melissa's wishes. But that's obviously not working anymore. If I couldn't talk Melissa into telling Randy about Pancho, I would just have to tell him myself.

Melissa was working the counter at our local Crunchy Chicken franchise. Her brother, Sam, a fry cook there, had gotten her the job. She was wearing her tan colored uniform. The uniform made her look like a Girl Scout. I thought she looked awfully cute. A couple of tables had people seated eating their fried chicken. I said "hi" to Melissa's brother, Sammy, through the kitchen pass through window. A customer was paying Melissa for her takeout, and then left carrying a large tub of chicken. Now there was no one else at the counter but me.

"Are you hungry?" she asked.

"I'm always hungry."

Melissa fixed up two plates of chicken from the heat lamp warmed basket of chicken. She added mashed potatoes and two small ears of corn to the plates. I poured us two cokes from the machine, and we put everything on an orange tray. She let Sammy know that she was taking her lunch break. He came out of the kitchen to watch the counter as we went over to a small table in the far corner of the dining area. We both talked for a while about work, and then I got to the point of my visit.

"I just saw Randy," I said, taking a bite of chicken.

"Oh," she said.

"He's really in a bad way."

"He's not the only one."

"I was hoping you would have told him by

now."

"What am I supposed to say? Randy, I'm screwing somebody else."

"If that's what's going on, then yes."

Melissa put down her food and wiped her hands.

"My period is late."

"What does that mean?"

"Boy, you are a virgin aren't you?"

"Sadly, yes."

"It means that I might be pregnant."

I was stunned, and Melissa looked worried.

"Oh, shit," I said.

"Yeah, oh shit."

We both just stared at our food, having lost our appetites.

"Is it Randy's baby?"

"I don't know. It might be Pancho's."

"Oh, shit."

"Yeah, oh shit."

This was really serious now. Melissa had a real dilemma, not just some high school romance stuff.

"What are you going to do?" I asked.

"I have no idea."

We talked for a while about her options. None of them were very good. But she did realize that if she were pregnant, she would have to tell both of the possible fathers. She had already decided that she wasn't going to have an abortion. After that, she wasn't so sure what would happen.

"Deciding to date Pancho has really complicated things. But now I really like him. I don't know who I would pick."

"Sometimes you can't put the genie back in the bottle."

"No."

She told me that tomorrow she was going to the Free Clinic on Sixth Street for a pregnancy test. After that, she would decide what to do. I offered her a ride there, or any other help that she might need. She thanked me, but said that she would be fine. Then her brother called her back to work. I gave Melissa a hug, said goodbye, and left.

I turned left out of the Crunchy Chicken parking lot, then steered my Chevy east on Sixth Street. A baby, I thought to myself. Melissa wasn't even out of high school. She was practically a baby herself. I passed the Free Clinic, where she was going tomorrow for her pregnancy test. Across the street, were Mabel's Seaside Books, and Al's Union War Surplus, which was a little further down the road. Finally, I drove past all of the closed and boarded up businesses of the Beacon Street Redevelopment area. Except for a couple of businesses that stubbornly remained open, the area looked like a ghost town, bleak and forlorn. Then for some reason, I suddenly had a revelation. What if Carol, the intern, was right? What if the town was making a huge mistake by tearing everything down? Once it was gone, it was gone. Maybe they could just postpone the demolition for a while, just until everyone was sure that they were doing the right thing. Maybe there was still time. I drove over to the Beacon Street Redevelopment office.

Carol wasn't there, unfortunately, but a man and a woman that I'd never seen before were. The two looked like they were just getting ready to leave for the day. The man was middle-aged, and wore a blue business suit. The woman looked business like as well.

"Is Carol here?" I asked the woman, who was grabbing her coat as I entered the office.

"No," she answered. "She's not in today. Can I help you?"

"I don't know, but is there any way we can stop this demolition from happening? Just until we're sure it's the right thing to do."

Her eyes opened wide, and she looked at me puzzled, as if it's something she'd never heard before. I'd also gotten the man's attention.

"Why would you want to stop the demolition?" she asked, slightly tilting her head as she looked at me.

"Just so we can make sure, because after everything's torn down, then it's too late."

The man grabbed his briefcase and walked over to us.

"It's already too late," he said. "This is happening, this is progress, this is what the future looks like." He pointed to the large model of the Beacon Street area. "All of these buildings are going to come down starting Monday."

"Everybody wants this," said the woman. "The whole community is on board."

"But what if it's the wrong thing to do?" I said. "What if we're all making a terrible mistake?"

"It's no mistake," the man said. "Haven't you seen the pictures in the front window? Everything will be new and beautiful."

"It's not like there are any architecturally important buildings to save," the woman said. "No famous architects or anything." She went over to her desk and picked up an envelope, taking one tickets out of it. She brought the ticket over to me. "Here, this is a ticket to Saturday night's Last Night on Beacon Street Celebration." She handed it to me. "The Chamber of Commerce is throwing quite a party."

"The Chamber of Commerce, eh?" I asked, taking the ticket.

"Yes," she said. "They have a great night planned." She pointed toward the door, as if to say it's time to go.

The man opened the door, and we all step outside onto the sidewalk.

"We'll see you at the celebration," said the

man. They said their goodbyes, then walked over to their cars.

The Chamber of Commerce to me meant J.P. Watterson. Maybe he had the clout to delay this whole project. Our fishing boat had just saved his life; maybe he had the power to save Beacon Street. I got in my car and drove the short distance over to his office.

Watterson's red Cadillac sat parked in front of the Chamber of Commerce offices. I parked my '54 Chevy behind it, and then went into the building. There was no one in the front office and it was dark, but Watterson's office door was open and the lights were on inside.

"Hello," I called out, shutting the front door behind me.

I heard a chair move inside Watterson's office, and then heard someone walk over to the door. It was Watterson. He was in his shirtsleeves.

"Oh," he said, "the fisherman's son."

"Yeah, one of the fishermen who saved your life."

"My wife thanked you for that, I believe."

"Yes, she was very nice."

"Then what, are you expecting a reward or something?"

"I don't want your money."

"Then what do you want?"

At first I hesitated, questioning my decision to ask him for help. But finally I just let him know why I was here.

"Mr. Watterson, I need you to help me postpone this Beacon Street demolition, or even just delay it for a while."

He let out a small laugh. "Even if I could, why in the world would I want to do that?"

"To give everybody time to make sure it's what's best for the town."

"What's best for the town's businessmen is what's best for the town."

"As long as somebody makes money off of it, right?"

"That's right."

"Like that manifesto you showed me last time?"

"Things are going to change, you'll see."

"Did the KKK change things when they marched in San Pedro back in the 1920s?"

He paused, giving me a cold stare.

"Yes, they did. That march was a year after the 1923 IWW strike. Do you know how much money businessmen lost during that strike? Millions! They weren't going to let that happen again."

"Did your father lose money?"

"A lot of money."

"So he had to do something about it."

"Do you know how difficult it was for him

to gather thousands of Klansmen from all over Southern California?"

"Why couldn't he just look in the Yellow Pages?" I smirked.

"Very funny."

"What category would he look under, secret societies or masked vigilantes?"

"That year, the government made a law where the Klansmen could no longer wear masks. But they had nothing to hide anyway. Some of these 100% Americans were leaders in their communities, bankers, businessmen, and even law enforcement officers. These weren't some kind of rabble."

"100% Americans?"

"That's right."

"Well," I paused. "I guess I made a mistake. I thought that someone with so much history in this town might not want the town to lose theirs."

"If some old buildings have to fall, well, somebody has to make money tearing them down. It might as well be me."

This was like what Gary Gabelich said about Lion's Drag Strip. A whole group of people had to lose out so a few people could make some money.

"I don't know why I thought you might help me," I said. "This is your baby, this is something you've probably wanted to do for a long time."

"You're right. How can you put up new buildings, when there's no place to build? First, you have to find some space."

"Even if that space is the town's historic center?"

"What did your hero Karl Marx say? Oh, yeah. You can't make an omelet without breaking some eggs."

Obviously, I had come to the wrong place. Watterson was going to do things his way. The way his father had done things before him. Probably the way things got done in most towns.

I just turned and walked out. It was time for dinner, and after that, I had to work on my report on Louis Adamic. Maybe that's all I could really control.

"There's someone on the telephone for you," my mother called out.

I'd heard the phone ring, but I was so busy working on my Adamic report that I tried to ignore it. My mom handed me the phone in the hallway.

"It sounds like an American woman," she said, frowning.

I grabbed the phone and pulled the cord inside my bedroom, closing the door behind me.

"Hello."

"Hi, Niko, this is Nancy."

"Oh. Hi, Nancy," I said, surprised to hear from her.

"I really messed up," she said, choking up.

"What happened?"

"Jim Pallente," she said, starting to cry. "After you left, I called him to come over and take my Playboy pictures. He came right over with his camera. I should have listened to you."

"Did he take the pictures?"

"Yes. But afterwards he started acting like a jerk. He wanted me to do things that I didn't want to do. I told him I wasn't interested."

"Did he stop when you asked him to?

"Yes, finally, but it wasn't easy, he was all hands."

"I'm sorry you had to go through that."

"He has the undeveloped film, and he wouldn't give it to me. He threatened that he would get the photos developed and plaster them all over town, unless I did what he wanted."

Nancy had picked about the worst guy she could to take her pictures. Jim Pallente was arrogant, and had absolutely no respect for anyone. At school, he would grope girls in the crowded hallways and just laugh. He was a bully. Even on the school football team, he had a reputation as a dirty player. Usually after one date, girls never wanted a second.

"What are you going to do?" I asked.

"I don't know," she said, trying to regain her composure. "Could you ask him for the film? Maybe he'll just give it to you."

"Nancy, I hardly know him, he's not a friend."

"Please, Niko, could you just try to get my film back."

"Then what?" I asked, hoping that she wasn't still thinking about Playboy.

"I just want to destroy it. You were right about everything."

If only Nancy had listened to me in the first place, then this wouldn't have happened. Now she needed someone to rescue her. I didn't really didn't want to be her "White Knight." But she sounded desperate.

"Okay," I said. "I'll talk to him."

"Thanks, Niko," she said. "I can't thank you enough."

I said goodbye to Nancy and put the phone back in the hallway.

I had no idea what I'd do to get Jim Pallente to give Nancy back her film. I couldn't threaten him. He'd just laugh at me. He was bigger, stronger, and definitely meaner. I had to try and reason with him. But how do you reason with a bully? I'd have to figure that out by tomorrow, but right now I had my report to work on. I went back to work.

In one of Adamic's books, I found his article on Harry Bridges, the man who Solomon Jefferson said had led the successful 1934 longshoreman's strike. This is what he wrote about his success on the San Francisco waterfront:

"The whole spirit of the waterfront changed. Competition for jobs at pierheads gave way to cooperation and solidarity. The longshoreman union membership increased from below two thousand to over four thousand... and the average wage was raised from about $20 to $37 a week, with opportunities to make, under greatly improved working conditions, as much as $200 a month. As one of the longshoremen put it to me: We experienced the unaccustomed luxury of being men."

As I read through Adamic's books chronologically, I took many notes. Based on my reading, it seemed that during the 1930s and until World War II, Adamic became an important champion for something called *cultural pluralism*. He wrote:

"Ellis Island must become as much the symbol of the United States as Plymouth Rock."

He advocated for a united American society that respected the ethnic and racial differences of various groups. He also wrote:

"In the past there has been entirely too much giving up, too much melting away and shattering of the various cultural values of the new groups."

Adamic used Walt Whitman's phrase, "A Nation of Nations," as the title for his four book series on *multiculturalism*. His first book in the series, *From Many Lands*, won him a prestigious award for the most significant book on race that year.

In 1940, he became the editor of the journal, *Common Ground*, which was the first American journal to focus on ethic and intercultural issues. In it, he wanted to change the story that America told about itself. He wanted the story to include all of the ethnic contributions and experiences. He demanded that American history textbooks acknowledge the contributions of all the different national and racial groups. He also declared that American fiction should not perpetuate the false notion that we are solely a white, Protestant, and Anglo-Saxon country. *Common Ground*'s most frequent contributor was the writer, Langston Hughes.

But with the situation in Europe worsening, "The Next War," as Adamic called it was becoming much more of his concern, especially with how it affected his native Slovenia and Yugoslavia. Hitler was on the rise, and war seemed certain. Adamic resigned from *Common Ground* in 1941, giving him more time to devote to his other concerns.

I had so many notes on Adamic, I just needed to finish everything up. If I get this done, my teacher, Mrs. Colman, will faint.

Good Friday

▼

Jim Pallente transferred to San Pedro High for just his senior year after the boy's Catholic High School closed. Because he had gone to parochial schools, while I had gone to public schools, I didn't really know him very well. But we had mutual friends. Recently, we had played some pickup basketball together at the high school. He played basketball like a football player. His idea of playing defense was to knock you down whenever you got the ball. If you called a foul, then he'd call you a wimp or worse. I knew he had a part-time job at the McCowan's Market, where he was learning how to be a butcher, so I thought it would be best to try to catch him in the morning before he went to work.

I drove over to his family's white stucco house up on Nineteenth and Walker. After I'd knocked on the door, he opened it. When he saw me he looked confused.

"Petrovich?" he asked. He looked bigger and more muscular than I remembered. "What are you doing here?"

"Are your folks home?"

"No," he said. "My mom just stepped out for a minute, and my dad's at work."

I knew his dad worked over on Terminal Island for Bethlehem Steel.

"Can I come in?"

"Sure," he said, motioning me inside.

His home was small and tidy, with hardwood floors, white plaster walls, and built-in cabinets. It was similar to most of the older homes in town.

"What do you need?" he asked, standing in the center of his living room.

"Nancy McClay," I answered. "You took some pictures of her and she wants them back."

He started to laugh.

"She does, eh? Did she tell you what kind of pictures they were?"

"Yeah, I know all about them. I'd been there earlier, before you, but I refused to take them."

He stopped laughing.

"Are you some kind of homo?" he asked me, sneering. "Or are you her boyfriend?"

"I'm neither, just a friend."

He stepped right up to me and looked me right

in the eye.

"She has a great bod," he grinned. "And I plan to have some fun with it."

"You make her sound like a piece of meat," I said, not flinching.

"You better get out of here," he said, coldly.

"Not without that film."

Before I knew it, he'd punched me right in the face. I saw stars, and felt the blood gush down from my nose. I grabbed my nose with both hands. I knew it was broken.

"I'm not leaving," I said, as the blood dripped from between my fingers.

He went to the kitchen and grabbed a towel, handing it to me.

"You're crazy!" he said.

I put the towel under my nose and held it tight.

"Yeah, I'm sure you're right," I managed to say.

"You got to get out of here, my mom's coming back any minute."

"Not until I get that film, or I might have to tell her all about Nancy's pictures."

"Oh, man," he said, pacing nervously.

"I'm sure she'll appreciate knowing that her son's blackmailing a girl."

He just glared at me for a moment, and then stormed out of the room. He came back with his 32mm camera. He quickly wound the film up, popped the back open, and then pulled out the little yellow canister. He handed it to me.

"Here!" he shouted, and then opened the front

door and stood there waiting. "Now, get lost!"

As I was leaving, I offered him back the bloody kitchen towel.

"Keep it," he said, looking away.

I held it back on my still bleeding nose and walked out.

My nose had stopped bleeding by the time I'd gotten over to Nancy's house. But it was swollen and blood had dripped down the front of my white t-shirt. When she answered the door, her face told me all I needed to know about how I looked.

"Oh, my God! Are you alright?"

"Well, it stopped bleeding."

"Come in," she said, taking my hand and guiding me inside. She was wearing a t-shirt and shorts.

"I have your film," I said, pulling the little yellow canister from my pocket and handing it to her.

"Oh, I'm so sorry," she said, taking the film. "What happened?"

"He was being difficult, so I smashed my nose into his fist."

She let out a small laugh, but quickly stopped herself.

"I hope I didn't break his knuckles."

She laughed again, but again tried to stop herself.

"Poor Jim," I said, "he had no idea who he was messing with."

"Thank you," she said, "and again, I'm so sorry."

"I have one small request, well, actually two."

"What?" she asked, curiously.

I took the film canister from her hand, grabbed the tab at the end of the film, and started pulling out all of the film, exposing every frame to the light and ruining it. When I was finished, the entire roll of exposed film lay in a pile at our feet.

"What's your second request?" she asked.

I reached over and gently held her by the waist then pulled her close to me. She put her arms around me and looked warmly into my eyes. I kissed her on the lips, careful not to bump her nose with mine. It was a long kiss. When we finished, we just looked at each other.

"That wasn't my second request," I said. "I just thought that a knight deserved a kiss."

"What?"

"Never mind," I said, as I released her.

"Then what's your second request?"

"I didn't get a chance to have breakfast, so I was hoping that you could make us some eggs again, they were good last time."

"Sure," she said, smiling, "That's the least I could do." She grabbed my hand and led me into the kitchen. We had a nice breakfast. We talked and we laughed, and I made her promise that I would not have to come to come to her rescue ever again.

I decided to drive over and visit Cousin Vlatko. Maybe he was taking his boat out, that's always fun. I used the rear view mirror to look at my face. It looked like I was developing two black eyes, and I could also tell that my nose was probably broken.

As I approached Vlatko's boat, I noticed that he had a guest on board. He was a tall, older man, with a gray, medium-length beard. They were both drinking red wine and were in the middle of a boisterous conversation.

"Niko, hello," said Vlatko, noticing me.

"Hi, Vlatko," I said.

The other man looked over to me. He reminded me a little of the author Ernest Hemingway.

"Come aboard," said Vlatko.

I climbed up onto the boat.

"What happened to your face?" Vlatko asked, noticing my swollen nose.

"I was trying to be a knight in shinning armor," I said, with a frown.

The man let out a small laugh. "I was a knight

once, didn't turn out that well for me either."

Vlatko stepped over to the man. "This is my old friend, eh, John Hamilton," said Vlatko, hesitantly. "John, this is my cousin, Niko Petrovich."

I shook hands with him. He had a handshake like a vise. And for some reason he looked familiar, like I'd seen him somewhere before.

"Good to know you, Niko." He said, with his booming voice. "I met your father the other day I think, good man. We have a hell of a lot in common, a hell of a lot."

"Are you a fisherman?" I asked.

"I was a fisherman, yeah, I was a fisherman. I was also a merchant seaman, and a stevedore, among other things."

"Oh, really?" I said, "just like my dad."

"John's done a lot in his life," said Vlatko. "I met him when we were in World War II together."

I hadn't even known that Vlatko had been in the war. "You never said you'd been in the military?" I asked.

"Technically, I was in the Marines," said Vlatko, slyly, looking at Hamilton. "John was a Marine, right?"

"Yeah, a Marine, officially."

What was this technically and officially stuff? It all sounded a little vague. "So, did you serve in the Pacific?" I asked John, curiously. "Most Marines were in the Pacific, right?"

"That's right," he said. "But I was in the European theater, I never made it to the Pacific."

Boy, did he look familiar. I could swear that I'd seen him somewhere before.

"John and I were in the O.S.S. during the war," said Vlatko. "We both worked for 'Wild Bill" Donovan.'

"'Wild Bill'" Donovan?" I asked. Why did that name sound familiar?

"Bill Donovan created the O.S.S.," said Vlatko, "modeled after British intelligence. It later became the C.I.A."

"You guys were spies?" I asked, somewhat amazed.

They both laughed. "I was a seaman, actually," said Hamilton. "I ran arms and supplies to Tito's Partisans in Yugoslavia while they were under Nazi occupation."

"I was his radio operator and interpreter," said Vlatko.

Hamilton raised his wine glass. "*Smrt Facizmu — Sloboda Narodu*!" he shouted.

I knew this translated to "Death to fascism — freedom to the people!"

Vlatko and Hamilton both downed their wine in one gulp.

"It was a hell of a time, a hell of a time," shouted Hamilton.

Vlatko looked over to me. "John knew your Uncle Ante, who was a Partisan."

I really didn't know much about my Uncle Ante, my mom's older brother. All I really knew was that he had died fighting the Nazi's during the war.

"Ante Katnich! Ante Katnich!" Hamilton shouted, grimacing. "Damn it! Damn it!" looking right at me. "He was one of the finest men I ever knew."

I'd heard some stories growing up about the Partisans. My friend, Marko's dad had been one. He was the toughest guy I'd ever met. He was always angry, and he had the most menacing glare. He kept a small pistol in his pocket, and a knife strapped to his calf. Evidently, he'd killed a dozen Nazi's with that knife. Mostly, he said he preferred strangling them with his bare hands.

"I hear the Partisans were tough." I said.

Hamilton looked over to me. "I went through basic training as a United States Marine. I trained in Scotland with British Commandos, the only American there. I learned to parachute in Manchester, made a dozen jumps. Broke my ankle on the last one, lucky it wasn't worse. All those guys were good soldiers, but you give me a handful of Yugoslav Partisans, and I could defeat an entire company of other soldiers, there was nothing like them. The Nazi's found out, boy did they find out!"

Vlatko took a wine bottle and filled John's and his glass. He looked over to me, as if to ask if I wanted any. I shook my head no.

"So, tell me about my Uncle Ante, I really don't know much about him."

"The damn British," said Vlatko, " they were always getting in the way, making everything worse."

"It was Christmas day," said John, looking toward me. "Vlatko and I had arrived on the Island of Hvar aboard a British LCI. From there we crossed to Korcula the following night in a Partisan launch. At this time there were approximately 3,500 German troops there. They were all well equipped, and with four tanks and air cover. They were trying to push 1,500 ill-equipped Partisans off the island. The Partisans, led by your Uncle Ante, were managing to hold on. I don't know how they did it. There was constant dive-bombing by Stukas and ME-109's." He took a sip of wine. "On the night of the twenty-ninth, Ante led a complete evacuation off the island, got everyone off safely to Hvar." He takes another drink. "On the thirty-first, New Year's eve, Ante grabbed a car, and asks us if we wanted to all go along to inspect the Partisan defenses. When he was done, he said we could have a drink to celebrate the New Year." He finishes his wine. "On the road, four Stukas attacked our car, the rest of us dove out to find cover, but Ante was killed behind the wheel. Terrible, very sad for everyone."

"That night we buried him with full honors," said Vlatko. "You only bury the dead at night, because of the Nazi planes."

"That night was as black as coal," continued John. "They had this little band that played a funeral dirge. We all walked behind them in a procession. My God, that music, it was hypnotic and so damn sad. Then everyone spoke, one at a time, all through tears, about your Uncle, what a fine man he was, what a fine leader."

"There's a memorial with a plaque in Zlarin," said Vlatko, "his village, our village, that honors him."

"I had no idea."

John looked over to me. "Niko, you don't come from timid people. They don't put up with disrespect, turn the other cheek, and let someone trample them. No, they fight back. I'm not saying that people from the Balkans are rational; they can be crazy as hell. But they pushed the Nazis out of their country, all while fighting their own civil war."

"Because Tito and the Partisans were communists," said Vlatko, "they didn't get too much help from the allied forces, especially the British."

"Excuse me, John," I said, "but there's something really familiar about you, like I've seen you somewhere before."

John let out a laugh. "Do you go to the movies?" he asked me.

"Yeah," I said.

"John Hamilton is the name I know him by," said Vlatko, "the name he had in the O.S.S."

"Among other things," John said, "I've been an actor. Right now I have a movie out with Elliot Gould, called *The Long Goodbye*."

"I haven't seen it," I admitted.

"Well, have you seen *The Godfather*?" John

asked.

"Yeah," I said, "who hasn't?"

"I played Captain McCluskey, the corrupt police captain that gets shot in the restaurant. I didn't have my beard or this longer hair. My real name's Hayden, Sterling Hayden."

Sterling Hayden? *The Godfather*? Of, course. He was the guy who punches the Michael Corleone character outside of the hospital, and then later at an Italian restaurant, Michael grabs a pistol hidden in the bathroom and blows him and another character away. It was a great scene, blood and bodies everywhere, if you like that kind of stuff.

"Let's go eat," said Hayden, "I'm hungry and thirsty."

Vlatko invited me to come along with them for lunch, and Hayden insisted that I join them. They were headed to Cigo's Restaurant on Pacific Avenue and Ninth Street.

"I can't go like this," I said, referring to my bloody t-shirt.

"I have a clean t-shirt you can wear," said Vlatko. He went down into the cabin and came back with a white t-shirt. "Here," he handed it to me.

I noticed the writing on the front. It read:

"You're only as old as the women you feel."

And it had a picture of a dirty old man, and a gorgeous young girl.

"I can't wear this," I said.

"Why the hell not?" asked Hayden.

"It's embarrassing."

"You'll be fine," Hayden insisted.

"Errol Flynn would be proud," said Vlatko.

"Oh, why not?" I finally agreed, taking off the old t-shirt off and putting the new one on. I offered to drive, since Vlatko had a two-seat Fiat 124 Spider roadster, and Hayden had a two-seat Karmen Ghia.

It took us only a couple of minutes to get to Cigo's, which was in a free standing windowless building in the middle of the block. The restaurant was a Croatian fish house, and a good one. We parked in the busy parking lot next door.

It was dark and moody inside, and they had a pretty good crowd for lunch, so I was hoping that we could get a table. Cigo, a well-dressed Croatian man, greeted us as we entered. He immediately embraced Hayden. Evidently, they were old friends, because we were quickly seated in the best booth in the place. There was a man playing the accordion while strolling the room. He finished the tune he was playing, and then started playing the theme from *The Godfather*. Everyone in the place looked around to see if any Mafioso had entered the place. I don't think anyone recognized Sterling Hayden, with his beard, and longer hair.

"I Love this place," said Hayden, "really do. The food reminds me of the Tadich Grill in San Francisco. I live in Sausalito part of the year."

He started telling us about his other home in Connecticut, where his wife and kids live, and the barge that he sometimes lives on in Paris.

"How'd you become an actor?" I asked him, as the waitress came over for our drink order.

"Starting out, I wasn't so much an actor as I was a male starlet," he replied. "Black Label, make it a double," he told the waitress.

"The Beautiful Blond Viking God," said Vlako, with a chuckle, ordering some red wine.

"I was in a fisherman's race in Gloucester, Massachusetts.

"He was young," said Vlatko, "just twenty-two?"

"Yeah," said Hayden, "twenty-two. I got my picture taken for a magazine. Beneath the photo, it said: 'Gloucester Sailor Like Movie Idol.'"

"But instead of going to Hollywood," said Vlatko, "this genius captain's a schooner around the world instead."

"That was the first time," said Hayden, "then while working as a stevedore in Brooklyn, I did a screen test, and was offered a seven-year-contract with Paramount Pictures, making $250 a week."

"That was really good money then," said Vlatko.

"Were you any good?" I asked.

"Hell no, I didn't know anything, not a thing" he admitted. "I'm with all these people who had years of experience and talent, and I didn't have a clue."

The waitress delivered the drinks to the table.

"What I wanted," said Hayden, "was to earn five thousand dollars, so I could buy my own schooner and get the hell out of there."

"But then the war happened," said Vlatko, "and the next thing he knows, he's sailing the Adriatic with me, dodging Nazis, and delivering supplies to the Partisans."

Hayden raises his glass. "*Zivili!*" he shouts, which means "to life."

Hayden spent the afternoon philosophizing about everything. He had led an incredible life, and he had a passion for living. He had written an autobiography back in 1963, called *Wanderer*, which he said was well received. And he was now working on a sailing novel set in the 1800s. Making movies for him was just a means to an end. It paid the bills with minimum effort. There were only a few films that he made that he was actually proud of, the rest were just for a paycheck. He was staying on Vlatko's boat for a few days while he was doing publicity for his latest movie. After that, he was gone with the wind, so to speak.

After lunch, I was anxious to get back to work on my report. Listening to Sterling Hayden talk about his love for books inspired me.

As soon as I got home, I cracked open another book. As I read, I noticed that Adamic's writings during World War II had a much more nervous tone, maybe because no one knew how the war would turn out. Like Sterling Hayden, Adamic supported Tito's Partisans, over other non-Communist factions. This caused him problems with some critics, who felt that his politics had become too radical. But also like Hayden, Adamic believed that Tito and his cause was the best hope for Yugoslavia.

Adamic's book, *Two-Way Passage*, earned him a dinner meeting at the White House. President Roosevelt seemed to like some of his post war ideas very much. Winston Churchill was also at that dinner.

"Hey," said my dad, at my bedroom door, "aren't you working at the restaurant tonight?"

"Yeah, thanks for reminding me," I answered, "I have to be there soon."

I put down my books and gathered my papers. Earlier, I had told my parents that an errant elbow during a basketball game had caused my broken nose. They believed me, but they were still suspicious. My mom was now sitting on the sofa when

I entered the living room. She was doing some sewing, a needle and thread in one hand, and a thimble on the other. I sat down beside her.

"How come you never told me about my Uncle Ante?" I asked her.

"What was I going to say?" she replied, hardly looking up from her sewing. "He died."

"Yeah, but he was a hero, and a leader during the war."

She finally looked at me. "So, would you want to be a great leader, like him, a great soldier?"

"I don't know," I said, "but it was good to learn about him."

"When the Vietnam draft ended last month, I was so happy," she said, with a slight grin. "I had prayed everyday, and God finally answered my prayers."

"God, or maybe Richard Nixon," I said, with a smartass grin.

"You don't understand what war is," she said, becoming sad. "I lost my brother, and I lost my fiancé. I lost so many friends." She put down her sewing. "They bombed our village, skies filled with big airplanes, dropping bombs on us to kill the Germans. They killed more of us than them." She looked at me, with sadness. "After the war, I volunteered in an orphanage. There were so many babies, so many motherless and fatherless babies, but no food," fighting back tears. "I took care of them, too many to count." She wiped her eyes. " Then I met your father, and I had my own baby," smiling, "you. I was not going to let another war have my baby."

"So you prayed?"

"Yes, I prayed," wiping her eyes. "So that God would tap Richard Nixon on the shoulder and tell him enough! Enough boys have died already in this war, save some boys for next war."

My poor mother, I thought. She didn't tell me about my uncle, because she didn't want me to glamorize him. She didn't want me to develop some romantic notion of what war was. She'd seen war, lived through it, survived it. She knew that war wasn't glamorous or romantic; it was just about dying and suffering and not much else.

Before I'd headed over to the Hungry Fisherman, Randy called me. He told me that one of the old pool halls on Beacon Street was still open, and that the owner was letting anyone come in to play pool and drink beer. The owner wasn't worried about getting in trouble for selling beer to minors, since his business was going to be torn down in a couple of days anyway. I told Randy that I would join them there after work.

When I got to work, Vince noticed my broken nose and made a crack about it, and he just wouldn't stop. During dinner, I was bussing tables for Diana, while Dean was bussing tables for Marie. Every chance Vince had, he poked fun at my injury and me. I couldn't even pick up food at the kitchen without him making some smart remark.

"Why don't you just give me a break?" I said. "And let me do my job."

"It looks like somebody already gave you a break!" said Vince, chuckling, and bringing his fist to his nose. "Ka-boom!"

"That's it!" I said, dropping the plates of food hard on the counter and charging right into the kitchen. I didn't even know what I was doing; it was like something had possessed me, I was so angry. Tommy tried to stop me, but I just brushed him aside and grabbed Vince by the collar. I actually picked him up and slammed him hard against the refrigerator.

"Are you going to stop?" I asked him. I could see the fear in his eyes. He tried to get loose, but I just clamped down even harder. "I'm going to ask you again," I said. "Are you going to stop?"

"Niko," said Tommy, "Put down that dumb dago!"

I kept pressing Vince against the refrigerator.

"Okay," said Vince, "I'll stop bothering you."

I finally released my grip and let him go. He straightened his collar and shirt.

"Now," said Tommy, to Vince, "tell Niko you're sorry for being an asshole."

"No," said Vince.

233

Tommy slapped Vince across the back of the head. "Come on, tell him, we got dinner to serve, look." He pointed out at the dining room.

We turned and noticed that all of the customers had stopped eating, and they were just standing there watching us.

"Alright," said Vince, reluctantly, "I'm sorry."

"Okay," I said, calming down, "forget it."

The customers all applauded politely and then sat back down to finish their dinners.

The Seven Sea's Pool Hall had been on the corner of Sixth and Beacon Street for over eighty years. The three-story building that housed it was once white limestone, but over time the soot and grim made it now look more like a dingy gray. I don't know what was upstairs exactly, maybe old offices. It looked like some 1940s private investigator might have had his office there. All of the other buildings on the same block were boarded up. There was a large sign for "Watterson Construction and Demolition" pasted on some plywood.

The pool hall had two large picture windows on either side of a double door. On one window was painted the word "Pool," on the other "Hall." The double doors had screen doors on them, so that the actual doors could stay open. Both screen doors had old advertisement signs for "7up."

I could see all of my friends' cars parked on both sides of the street. I managed to find a spot myself.

It took a moment for my eyes to adjust to the darkness inside the pool hall. I could see four pool tables, and a long mahogany bar, with a brass foot rail running its length. There was a mirrored wall behind the bar, and various liquor bottles were displayed. A pair of beer taps was right at the bar. Over near the back wall, I saw my friends. As I walked toward them, the Oak floor creaked under my feet. Randy and Dean were engaged in a game of 8-ball. A couple of half-full pitchers rested on a shelf against the wall.

"Man," said Randy, holding a half-empty glass in one hand and a pool cue in the other, "isn't this great?"

Hank and Jake were also drinking beer while sitting on bar stools. When Hank saw me, he got up and came over.

"Let me see your nose," said Hank, "Dean told us all about it."

Hank gave my nose a good look. "That Pallente, I never liked that guy."

"I didn't tell them about Vince Galasso," said Dean.

"What about Galasso?" asked Jake.

"Nothing really," I said, "he's been on my case forever, I just finally had enough."

"Niko jacked him up against the wall," said Dean. "You should have seen Vince's face, he was ready to crap his pants."

"You should have smacked him," said Jake. "You know I would have."

"I know," I said, "but I have to work with the guy. It's going to be hard enough now."

Casey Boyle, the owner of the place, walked over to us. Casey was a short, stocky, Irishman, with a mop of red hair. He looked to be about seventy, but he still looked like he could throw a punch. I had first met him while playing Little League with two of his sons.

"No fighting in here, boys," barked Casey. "I'm the only one allowed to knock heads." He poured one of the half-full pitchers of beer into the other half-full pitcher, consolidating them. "Another pitcher?" he asked us.

"Sure," said Hank, "keep them coming."

"I'll be back," said Jake, setting down his empty beer glass on the shelf. He headed over to the door labeled "Gentlemen." I wondered when was the last time a real gentleman actually came in this place? I didn't see a door labeled "Ladies," I wondered if they even had one.

"I'll buy the next pitcher," I said, loudly.

"Way to go, Niko!" said Randy, already showing signs that the beer was starting to affect him.

Casey was already filling the pitcher from one of the taps at the bar. As I walked over to him, I couldn't help but notice what a great bar it was, it was truly beautiful. The wood looked old, but it was clear and smooth. It was so much nicer than anything else in this place.

"Nice bar," I said to Casey, running my hand along the top.

"It's older than me," said Casey, "probably one hundred years old."

"Really?"

"Grandpa Boyle told me it was made in Philadelphia, and shipped here around Cape Horn, because the Panama Canal hadn't been built yet."

"No kidding?"

"Three generations of saloon keepers, and I'll be the last one."

Casey started to reminisce about all of the soldiers and sailors that had been through the place, about the B-girls, who hustled them for drinks, and how during prohibition they had to hide the booze. Then he just stopped, as if he'd had a revelation.

"After they've torn everything down," said Casey, "there'll be no place for my memories to go, there'll be nothing in my past that I can touch. I'll be lost."

Casey looked truly worried, as if he was going to lose a piece of himself.

"Yeah," I said, "but what can you do?"

"How long do you think it will take," he asked, "for everyone to forget what was here?"

"I don't know."

"You know, in Europe they cherish old buildings, they have some respect for things."

"I know."

Randy and Dean had finished their game, and Hank and Jake were up next. Hank was starting to rack up the balls, as Dean came over to the bar.

"I'll take that fresh pitcher," he said.

Casey slid the pitcher over to Dean, who grabbed it and took it over to the group. I paid Casey and he gave me back my change.

"You know," said Casey, "the Wobblies use to meet in this place."

"The IWW?" I asked.

"Yeah," he said. "Have you ever heard of Joe Hill?"

"I have," I said. "He wrote the songs that they sang."

"That's right, songs like 'There's Power in the Union,' 'Rebel Girl,' and 'The Preacher and the Slave'."

Then Casey started to tell me more about Joe Hill. He said that Joe had become a Wobbly here in 1910, when he was working on the docks. He'd been up in San Francisco during the 1906 Earthquake, and he was glad to be down here in San Pedro. He would have stayed here, but he was blacklisted for being in the union, and couldn't get work. That's why he left for Salt Lake City. In 1914, two masked intruders murdered a grocer and his son there. Joe was tried and convicted of the murder. Many people believed he'd been framed and they tried to overturn the conviction. But finally, he was executed on November 19, 1915, by firing squad, and then he became a martyr for the labor movement.

"He wrote his songs over at the Beacon Light Mission down the street," said Casey.

"That's what I heard."

"His body was sent to Chicago," said Casey "where it was cremated. He joked, that he wouldn't be caught dead in Salt Lake City."

We both chuckled.

"According to Wobbly legend," he said, "his ashes were placed in 600 small envelopes and mailed to IWW locals around the world."

"Really?"

Casey reached under his counter and pulled up an ancient cigar box. From it, he pulled out a little red book, which he handed to me. The book looked older than the cigar box. On the cover, it had "IWW Song Book," at the top, and "Price ten cents," in the middle.

"His songs," I said, carefully looking through it.

"He'd coined the phrase 'Pie in the sky'," said Gene. "Referring to some form of heaven that you'll never reach."

Then Casey brought out a piece of folded and yellowed paper. He unfolded it and handed it to me. "It's Joe Hill's will," he said. I read it.

My will is easy to decide
For there is nothing to divide

My kin don't need to fuss and moan
"Moss does not cling to a rolling stone"

My body? Oh, if I could choose
I would to ashes it reduce
And let the merry breezes blow
My dust to where some flowers grow

Perhaps some fading flower then
Would come to life and bloom again.
This is my last and final Will
Good Luck to All of you
Joe Hill

Then Casey pulled out one last item from the cigar box, a battered old envelope that had actually turned brown. "Here," he offered me it with one hand, while taking back the songbook and will with the other.

"What is it?" I asked, carefully peeling it open.

"Joe Hill's ashes," said Casey.

I froze for a moment, and then finally looked inside the envelope. Inside, was a fine gray powder, only about a half-inch deep, the ashes of Joe Hill.

"My father had given them to me," said Casey, "and his father had given them to him."

I didn't know what to say. Here I was, holding the ashes of a man who died almost sixty years ago, a martyr.

"I don't know what to do with them," he said.

"I don't know either," I said, carefully handing the envelope back to him. "But they should be saved."

He put everything back into the cigar box, and put the cigar box back under the bar. "They will be, somehow," said Casey.

I really didn't know what else to say to Casey about Joe Hill's ashes, so I changed the subject. "It really is a nice bar," I said, admiring it. "Too bad it's going to face the wreaking ball."

"It won't," said Casey. "Some fancy private club in Beverly Hills offered me a lot of money for it. They're bringing in a crew and taking it out of here tomorrow."

That figures, I thought to myself. Here, the working class people of San Pedro didn't want it, didn't see its value, but some "rich man's club" in Beverly Hills did. That made me almost as sad as holding the ashes of Joe Hill in my hands.

My friends and I played pool and drank beer long into the night. The Seven Seas Pool Hall provided one last night of comfort and hospitality to its clientele. Tomorrow, the beautiful bar would be gone, and a few days after that, the whole building. I wondered about the answer to Casey's question: How long do you think it will take for everyone to forget what was here?

Black Saturday

APRIL 21

"**D**id you see yesterday's *News Pilot*?" asked my dad, as I sat having my breakfast.

"No," I mumbled, with a piece of toast in my mouth. I actually felt pretty good this morning, considering last night's beer and pool. Maybe it was the ice that I'd put on my nose when I got home.

"You need to look at the second page," said my dad.

"Why?"

"It says something about an anti-cruising ordinance, you kids can be pulled over and get a ticket."

"What? No way."

"Here," he said, handing me the paper already turned to page two.

The title read: "City to Begin Enforcing New Anti-Cruising Ordinance."

I couldn't believe it, but there it was in black and white:

Prompted by concerns over traffic control and safety, the city council's new anti-cruising ordinance will go into effect this Saturday night at 7:00 P.M. LAPD officers will begin enforcing it citywide.

"You can always tell the difference between a normal motorist in the community, and a cruiser," said one council member. "The general public shouldn't worry about traveling to the store, restaurant, or to the movies. This is to stop certain teenage behavior such as loud music, underage drinking, and fights between teens."

Police officers will be setting up checkpoints on some of the city's busiest streets and most popular cruising routes.

"We will be recording license plate numbers," said an LAPD spokesman, "and if a car passes by more than twice in a three-hour period, that driver can be cited, and fined $100 for the first offense, and $250 for any second violation."

Not everyone likes the new law, including the local chapter of the American Civil Liberties Union.

"This anti-cruising ordinance is fraught with problems," said the local ACLU director, "including the simple right to just travel as you wish."

But local authorities claim that the new law is based on other successful anti-cruising ordinances that have worked elsewhere around the state.

"I don't get it," I said, after reading the article. "$100 fines?"

"$250 if it happens twice," said my dad.

"Are kids supposed to stop cruising, just like that? What are we supposed to do on Saturday nights?"

"You can still go to the movies, or out to eat," he said.

"But what do we do after that?"

"Come home, I guess."

Why was the city doing this? All of these people were young once, weren't they? If they'd grown up here, then they all did the same thing when they were kids. Why would they want to deny us our fun? I wondered if my friends knew the situation. I'd better let them know. First, I called up Jake. He'd been asleep, but when I told him the news, he quickly woke up."

"This sounds bad," he said, "like when they closed down Lion's Drag Strip."

"I know," I said, "but even worse."

After Jake, I called Randy. He was up and arguing with his sister.

"Man," he said, "we're becoming the Soviet Union! Next we're going to all be arrested by the no-fun police!"

Then, I called Hank.

"I still have a one-way plane ticket to Canada," said Hank. "I never used it, because they ended the draft. Maybe things are better up there?"

"I don't really know if they have cruising in Canada," I said.

"I don't know either," he admitted.

Finally, I called Dean. Evidently, he had known all about the new anti-cruising ordinance because his dad was a member of the Elks Club, and they were involved with getting the ordinance passed. Many of the town's business leaders had lobbied for the new law.

"Why didn't you tell me?" I asked him.

"I thought you knew," he said, defensively. "Anyway, there's nothing any of us could have done to stop it. The city wanted what they wanted."

"Yeah, like the Beacon Street Redevelopment," I added.

Dean told me he was bringing Diana to Vic's party and he'd see me there. He still couldn't believe that I was bringing Carissa. I put the phone back in the hallway and went out to the living room. My dad was sitting in his favorite chair reading another book on world history by author Will Durant.

"Thanks for the head's up on the cruising," I said, "I just told all of my friends."

"Yes," he said, putting down his book. "I thought you would want to know."

"Hey," I said, sitting on the sofa, "I met Sterling Hayden on Vlatko's boat."

"Vlatko told me."

"Is he really a big movie star?"

"He's a movie star. I don't know how big," he said, "When I met him, we just talked about sailing, and fishing, and being merchant seamen. I shared some sailing stories, that he said he liked, and asked if he could use them in the novel he's writing."

I couldn't believe that Sterling Hayden was interested in my dad's sailing stories. I've never even asked him about his past, as if what he'd done in his life didn't really matter to me.

"How old were you when you first went sailing?" I asked.

"My father, your grandfather, took me out on a boat when I was five or six."

"That's young."

"When I was a little older, he made me a small sailboat so I could sail around the island."

"Your own boat, how fun."

"At your age, I was on the crew of my uncle's yacht, 'Nirvana.' We sailed the Adriatic as a charter for rich Europeans, a lot of British, French, and Germans. That was my first time on a crew. That was my education, my high school."

I knew that my father hadn't had much formal schooling, he'd only finished the eighth grade, but he spoke five languages and knew more about world history than any of my high school teachers. Evidently, he managed to learn something.

"What did you do after that?" I asked.

"I didn't want to leave home, but we were poor, and there was no work. So I signed up as a merchant seaman and saw the world. That was my college."

"The whole world?" I asked, sarcastically.

"Just about, wherever there were people. We didn't need to deliver cargo to penguins, they didn't need anything."

He started to tell me all of the countries he'd been to, and all of the ports he'd visited. It was a long list. It all sounded very romantic to me, my dad, the world traveler.

"Did you ever go through the Panama Canal?" I asked.

"Of course," he said, "many times. I piloted cargo ships into the canal; I was the helmsman."

"You piloted ships into the Panama Canal?" I said, in amazement.

"That's what a helmsman does," he said, in a matter of fact way.

Here was my dad, who I always thought of as just an old fisherman, who actually had led an interesting life. No wonder he and Sterling Hayden had things to talk about.

The San Pedro Library called to let me know that my Louis Adamic books had finally arrived from Los Angeles. It was a little after the fact, since I'd already read most of them, but since I'd requested the books, I thought I would at least go and look them over. I considered walking there, but if I had to bring home any books, it would be easier in my car.

The librarian gave me a strange look when I asked for my books. She pointed to one of the tables.

"She has them," said the librarian, with a scowl.

There at one of the tables was Miss Martin, my teacher. She was seated there with my stack of Adamic books, which now looked like they'd all been bookmarked with small bits of paper.

"Hi Miss Martin, doing a little reading?"

"Oh, hello, Niko." she said. "Yes, I've been marking some pages for you." She placed another bookmark between two pages. "I hope you don't mind, I saw the books there with your name on them."

"How'd you get them?"

"I told them I was your teacher and that I'm helping you with your research."

"I'm surprised they gave them to you."

"I mentioned I'd been a nun, and if they didn't hand over the books, I'd rap them across the knuckles," she said, with a chuckle.

I grabbed a seat across from her. "Thanks for

your help."

"It's the least I could do, since I got you into all this reading."

I've never read so many books in my life."

"The good news is that they won't kill you," she said, "they might even make you smarter."

"I don't know if I want to get too smart," I said. "All the really smart people are usually full of themselves."

"But you already realize that, so that makes you even smarter than they are," she said, smiling. "Tell me something interesting you've learned during your research."

"Adamic had dinner at the White House with the President and Mrs. Roosevelt, and Winston Churchill was there, too."

"Yes," she said, frowning, "Churchill ended up suing Adamic over something he wrote about that dinner."

"Churchill sued him?"

"And won, it was the beginning of some very difficult years," she said, sadly. "Where are you in your reading?

"I'm in the middle of World War II. Adamic was supporting Tito's Partisans."

"That caused him even more problems."

"Why, because Tito was a communist?"

"Yes," she said. "You should talk to Mabel over at Seaside Books, she knew Adamic well, and kept in touch with him during that time."

"I spoke to her," I said, "but she never said that

they were close."

"I don't know why, but she and I have talked about him often."

I thanked her again for her help, piled all of the books into my trunk, and headed over to Seaside Books.

Steinbeck, the cat, greeted me with an annoyed hiss as I stepped up to the bookstore's counter. Henry was just bagging a book for a female customer, who was also trying not to provoke Steinbeck's wraith.

"Where's your mom?" I asked Henry.

"She's back in the used book area," he said, "sorting books or something."

When I found Mabel in the back, she was pulling books from a box and putting them onto a shelf.

"Hi, Mabel," I said, stepping into the room. It took her a moment, but then she finally recognized me.

"You're the one who was looking for the Adamic books, aren't you?" she asked, looking at me through her glasses and cataracts. "They're over there," she said, pointing to the shelf where I'd found my Adamic books days ago.

"I don't need anymore books right now, but

Miss Martin, my teacher, said I should talk to you about Adamic."

"Oh, she did, eh?"

"Yeah, she said you stayed in touch with him."

Mabel just looked at me for a moment, trying to decide how much to say.

"I loved Louis," she said, stopping what she was doing. "But not much happened."

"Tell me about him," I asked.

"He barely spoke English when I met him. I was a pretty, young girl back then, when he'd come into my father's store."

"That was in 1923 right?"

"Yes. But I actually remember seeing him even earlier, when he was a soldier stationed at Fort MacArthur."

"How did he ever improve his English?"

"The old-fashioned way," she smiled, "he got an American girlfriend."

"Was that you?"

She didn't answer my question.

"He had a stutter also," she said, "which only made his thick accent even worse. But he was so adorable, like a big puppy dog, and so damn smart."

"I didn't know he had a stutter."

"Yes, which he worked hard his whole life to overcome."

How did he overcome so much? I thought to myself. He came here at fourteen with nothing, through Ellis Island, into the U.S. Army, worked as a laborer, and finally became an important American writer. He must have been more than just smart.

"What did you two talk about?"

"Everything," she said, "and he was a voracious reader. Father was always ordering books for him, and not just one or two at a time, but six or seven, whatever he couldn't find over at the Carnegie Library."

"So he was always reading?"

"And writing, he hardly ever stopped to breathe."

"He left San Pedro for New York in what year?"

"1929, I think, yes, 1929, the year of the stock market crash. His timing was perfect," she frowned.

"I read that he moved there to be closer to the publishing world."

"That's a lot of baloney," she barked. "He met a girl."

"Really?"

"Yes," she admitted, "her name was Stella, and she eventually became his wife."

"Oh," I said. "How did that make you feel?"

"I was happy for him," she hesitated, "she was beautiful, intelligent, and a perfect partner for a young writer."

"But you might have been a good partner too?"

"We'll never know now, will we?" she stepped over to the shelf of Adamic's old books. She closed her eyes, as she gently rubbed her hand over the book's spines, as if to try to feel something more than just the covers. I gave her a moment before I continued.

"Miss Martin said that his support for Tito led to problems."

"It was the beginning of the end," she said, opening her eyes and looking back toward me. "You have to understand the times, the anti-communist sentiment in this country."

"The Cold-War," I said, remembering the term that Miss Martin had used in class for the post-war period. "But didn't Tito break with the Soviet Union?"

"It didn't matter. Louis' support for Tito's communists caused Americans to label him a communist. Louis had never been one. But being labeled a communist, true or not, was the worst thing that you could have been called during that time."

"Did it hurt his career?"

"It destroyed it," she paused, "before he finally decided to destroy himself."

"What do you mean?" I asked.

"He killed himself," she said, "evidently."

I had no idea that Adamic had committed suicide. If that's the case, then he must have felt that things were hopeless. It really saddened me, that this young immigrant, completely in love with his strange new country, could have gotten to the point later in life, where he felt that all was lost.

"What do you mean, evidently?" I asked.

"He hadn't left a note, and there was some evidence that he'd actually been murdered. But there was nothing definitive. And it wouldn't have changed the outcome though, Louis was gone."

"So, he died mysteriously?"

"Yes," she said, "and Stella completed the unfinished book he had been working on. It was about Tito and Yugoslavia, and it was published after his death."

Mabel and I talked for a few minutes more, but after I learned that Adamic had killed himself, I really don't think I heard much else. I thanked her for answering my questions, and then left.

When I arrived at The Hungry Fisherman to prepare for lunch, Paulie Russo, the owner, was actually there. He was seated at his favorite table, looking out at everyone else, like a judge presiding over a packed courtroom. Big Sal stood next to the table, as if he were his bailiff. I realized that if Paulie had Steinbeck, the cat, on his lap, this would look like the opening scene from *The God-father*, although Paulie was certainly no Marlon Brando.

"So, that's what you're going to do, Tommy," said Paulie.

"I don't need to go to the V.A. Hospital," said

Tommy.

"You can't go around spitting in your sister's face, it's not okay. If you have problems with me, you need to deal with me, not your sister."

"You have no idea what I went through in Vietnam."

"No we don't," said Marie. "But we do know that you haven't been the same since you got back."

"You'll get some counseling," said Paulie, "they'll help you."

"Marie," said Tommy, contritely. "I'm sorry, okay?"

"I accept your apology, Tommy, but I'm still worried about you."

"You're not sleeping because of your back pain," said Vince, "and you're not eating because of the pain killers."

"You've been jumpy and tense," said Diana, "when I tapped you on the shoulder yesterday, you almost punched me."

Tommy hung his head in resignation. "Okay," he said, "maybe I do need some help."

"We just want what's best for you," said Paulie, "we're all family here."

"I know," said Tommy, "I know."

With that problem handled, Paulie then looked around the room.

"Vince and Niko, come up here where I can see you."

Big Sal motioned for us to step up in front of

Paulie, like we were both being summoned before the judge.

"Both of you are like family," said Paulie."

"Yeah," said Vince, "You make me feel like a cousin."

"I don't have any complaints," I said, "the Russo family has been great to me."

"I'm glad to hear that, Niko," said Paulie, "But do you have anything against Italians?"

"No," I said, honestly, "of course not."

"That's what I thought," said Paulie. "Now, Vince, do you have anything against Slavs?"

Vince hesitated, but finally spoke. "No."

Paulie glared at Vince for a moment, then spoke. "Vince, tell me the truth."

"Okay," said Vince, "I don't really like them."

"That's what I thought," said Paulie. "You're going to have to get over it. You can't dislike Niko for his nationality. He can't help it if he's not Italian, poor guy."

"I understand," said Vince.

"Now, both of you shake hands," said Paulie, "and no more hostility."

We shook hands.

"Alright," said Paulie, "Sal, give me your pocketknife."

Big Sal dug into his pocket and pulled out a large pocketknife. He opened its blade, and carefully handed the knife to Paulie.

"Now, it's time for the blood oath."

"The what?" I asked.

"Both of you step up here and give me your right hand."

Vince and I looked at each other and hesitated, but then reluctantly stepped up and stuck out our right hands. For a long moment, Paulie just held the blade up and looked at us. Finally, he smiled broadly, and then burst out laughing. Everyone else did the same.

"You guys watch too many movies," said Paulie, closing the blade and handing Sal back his knife. "Now, get to work, we have to get ready for lunch."

Vince and I were greatly relieved that we didn't have to spill any of our blood. As we prepared for lunch, Vince actually tried to be nice to me, and I tried to do the same. Evidently we didn't need to become blood brothers for that to happen. A few minutes into lunch, Augie Ancich walked in with a small group. I wasn't surprised to see Frank Lucich, his longtime crewman with him, but I was surprised to see Gary Gabelich there, with another man whom I didn't recognize. I grabbed four menus and greeted them at the door.

"Hi Augie," I said. "Four for lunch?"

"Yeah," he said.

"Hi kid," said Frank. "Does the Hungry Fisherman have food for some hungry fishermen?"

"I think we do," I said.

Gabelich gave me a look of recognition. "I know you," he said, "from Lion's the other day, right?"

"Right," I answered, smiling.

This is my cousin John Gabelich," said Gary. "He's a fisherman,"

"Hi," I said, as I led the group over to one of Marie's tables. She came over as I was filling their water glasses.

"Hi Augie," she said, and then greeted everyone at the table.

"Hi, Marie," Augie replied, opening his menu. "What's good today?"

"The Red Snapper and the Sand Dabs are really fresh," she said, "but everything's good."

"As always," said Augie.

They all chatted for a while, and then Marie took their orders. As I was picking up food at the kitchen for another table, I stopped to talk to Vince. I knew that he had been a big drag racing fan.

"You used to go to Lion's Drag Strip didn't you?" I asked.

"All the time," he replied, "I was really pissed off when it closed."

"That's Gary Gabelich over at Augie's table."

Vince looked over to the table and recognized Gabelich immediately.

"That's him," said Vince, in amazement, "the fastest man in the world."

"Let me go deliver this food," I said, "then I'll introduce you."

"You know Gary Gabelich?" he asked, surprised.

"Oh, wait," I said, "he's Croatian, you probably don't want to meet him."

"I'm trying to be open-minded," he said.

I took Vince over to meet Gary Gabelich, who was very gracious. Vince acted like a star struck kid meeting his hero. Tommy brought out a camera, and got a picture of Vince and Gary together, and then got Gary to sign an autograph for Vince. Gary wrote:

"To my pal Vince Galasso,
Thanks for being such a great fan.
Your friend,
Gary Gabelich"

Gary just stared at the autograph, like he'd just been handed a precious stone. He thanked Gary and went back into the kitchen. I followed him there.

"I guess you Croatians are okay after all," said Vince.

"I'm glad you think so," I said.

After Augie's group finished their lunch, I went over to clear their table.

"I saw the News Pilot," said Gary. "I can't believe what they're doing to you kids. I used to cruise all the time."

"It's terrible," I said, as I cleared off their table.

As I walked to my car after working lunch, I noticed a female leaning up against it. I realized that it was Melissa; she looked so somber I almost didn't recognize her. She was supposed to get a pregnancy test yesterday, so I wondered if she'd gotten her results.

"Hi," I said, approaching her. "Are you okay?"

"Define okay," she said. "Actually, I've been better."

"How'd your pregnancy test go?" I asked, opening the car door for her.

"I passed the test," she said, sarcastically, "with flying colors."

"What does that mean?" I asked, getting in the car beside her.

"I got an 'A,'" she paused, "I'm pregnant."

I didn't know what to say to that. I couldn't say that everything was going to be all right, because I didn't know if it would be. "Oh boy," I said, exhaling.

"Well, it could be a boy," she added, "or a girl, I don't know yet. In fact, I don't even know who the father is. Delivery day is going to be one big surprise."

"I don't like surprises," I said.

"You know," she admitted, "neither do I." She sat there for a silent moment, and then big tears welled up and started to flow. "Could you just drive us somewhere, please, anywhere?"

"Sure," I said, starting up the car.

The Cat Stevens song, "Trouble," began to play

on my 8-Track, as I drove up the hill to Friendship Park's observation point. I parked in a spot that overlooked the city. I handed Melissa a tissue from the glove box.

"Thanks," she said, wiping her eyes. "You could get me out of this mess, Niko, if you wanted to."

"How could I do that?" I asked, puzzled.

"You could marry me."

I looked at her for a moment and smiled. "You're not serious?"

"I am serious," she said, "my mom's always told me that when I look for a husband, I should make sure he's a friend."

Melissa was my best female friend, but she was also Randy's girlfriend. Now, she's complicated things even more with Pancho, and the pregnancy. I couldn't be the simple fix to all her problems.

"You need to talk to Randy, tell him the truth. If you still care about him, tell him that. Say you're sorry and explain what happened. This might be his baby."

"What if it's not?" she said, "I'm too embarrassed."

"You're going to be even more embarrassed if you don't deal with this."

Just then, we heard the loud roar of a high performance car engine, and we saw Dragan Mosich's baby blue Corvette make a fishtail stop right behind us. Chad Wagner's navy blue Chevelle then came to a screeching halt behind him, both drivers quickly got out of their cars. Chad pointed angrily at Dragan, who just seemed annoyed.

"What's the matter with you?" shouted Chad.

Melissa and I got out to see what was going on.

"You need to learn how to drive, little boy," laughed Dragan.

"And you need to learn the rules of the road, asshole!"

"What happened?" I asked, getting between the two.

"He almost ran me off the road!" complained Chad.

"You're so sensitive," chuckled Dragan, "like a little girl."

"I was going up Ninth Street, where it narrows into one lane," said Chad, "and this fool passes me on the right, sending me into oncoming traffic!"

"You need to retake driver's training," said Dragan, with a sneer. "I can't believe you passed it."

"I'll show you who can drive, idiot!'

"Yeah, how?" asked Dragan, "By calling me names? You need to race me, or you're a coward."

"You don't need to prove anything to Dragan," I told Chad. "He's the most reckless driver in town.

"You're a South Shores boy," sneered Dragan to Chad, "nice and soft, like Pillsbury dough."

"Okay, fool, let's race!" shouted Chad. "Tonight,

Westmont Avenue, midnight."

"You shouldn't do this," I warned Chad. "He's just trying to provoke you."

"It's okay, Niko, I can handle this."

I'd seen Chad race on Wednesday nights at Lion's, but I don't remember him ever street racing. He's always been too cautious for that.

"Make sure you wear your big boys pants, little man," said Dragan, getting back into his car.

"See you tonight, asshole!" shouted Chad.

Dragan burned a cloud of rubber as he left the scene.

"He's crazy," I said, as Chad appeared to be calming down. "And he'll do anything to win."

"I've seen him race," said Chad, "and I've seen him lose."

I didn't want to tell Chad that Jake was the only one I'd ever seen beat Dragan in a drag race.

"Yeah," I said, "I've seen him lose too, but when he races, he's reckless."

"I'm not afraid of him," said Chad, steely-eyed.

He got back into his Chevelle to leave. I wished him luck and told him that I'd be there tonight at his race.

As I drove Melissa home, we continued to talk, but she still didn't know how she would tell Randy her news. She was seeing him tonight, and they were planning to go to Vic's Big Blowout together. Maybe when they were both good and drunk, she thought, she could tell Randy about Pancho and the baby. Somehow I didn't think that was the best time to tell him.

On my way home, I noticed the police already preparing to enforce the new anti-cruising ordinance. At Pacific Avenue and Sixth Street, officers were dropping off the white wooden street barriers and the yellow traffic cones. Everything was stacked neatly on the curb for tonight. I also saw signs that read: "Police Checkpoint," and "Caution, Prepare to Stop." I still couldn't believe that they were going through with this.

Besides the Fisherman's Fiesta, which used to be enormous and well attended, the Last Night on Beacon Street celebration had to be the largest event I'd seen in San Pedro. Temporary "No Parking" signs were hung from Fifth Street on the north, to Seventh Street on the south, from Harbor Boulevard on the east, to Centre Street on the west, pretty much the whole area slated for demolition and redevelopment. Temporary street barriers were placed at the ends of the streets. Parked nearby, were large construction vehicles labeled with Watterson Construction and Demolition, just waiting for Monday. The Chamber of Commerce had even reopened a few of the old historic bars that had recently closed just for tonight's festivities. I guess the bums and the winos weren't going to be the only ones having one last drink.

I had to pick Carissa up at eight o'clock for Vic's party, so I couldn't really stay long. I don't really know why I came, except that I didn't want to waste a ticket, and I just had to see things with my own eyes.

It looked like the town's best people were here to commemorate this occasion. There were banners displaying the names of their service organizations, The Jaycees, the Rotary, The Kiwanis, The Elks, and the Masons. There was even a banner for the Loyal Order of Redmen. Dean's uncle was their treasurer or "Great Keeper of the Wampum," as he called himself. He once told us proudly of the organization. The local unit, he said, was called a "tribe," and their meeting hall was called a "wigwam." The state level was referred to as the "reservation." When I asked why real American Indians weren't allowed to join, he made some excuse about how the tradition started with "white men" dressing up as Indians at the Boston Tea Party. He didn't like it when I suggested that maybe after 200 years, it was time for a new tradition.

There was a stage set up for a band to perform, and a microphone for someone to make speeches. The band looked like the type our parents would enjoy. It was more like Lawrence Welk, and less like Jimi Hendrix. That was appropriate, since I didn't really see anyone here near my own age.

There was a whole group of people wandering around in costume. Some of them wore little signs that identified what character they were portraying. There were soldiers and sailors, merchant seamen, fishermen, longshoremen, shipyard workers, bartenders, and old-time police officers. As for women, there were cigarette girls, taxi dancers, and B-girls. I didn't notice anyone playing the roles of drunks and prostitutes; I guess nobody was willing to play those parts.

When the streets were almost full, J.P. Watterson took the stage to make a speech. He first thanked the City Council, even introducing some of its members, and then he thanked the Community Redevelopment staff, introducing some of them as well. I noticed Carol, the intern, up on the stage. She didn't seem as joyful as they were; I even noticed her checking her watch. Finally, Watterson introduced the entire Chamber of Commerce, and explained how they had been working since 1958 to tear down Beacon Street. When he exclaimed, "And now we're finally going to tear it down!" the entire crowd let out a huge cheer and applauded enthusiastically.

With that, Watterson instructed the band to play. Several couples began to dance ballroom style across the asphalt. Several more joined them, and then several more. Pretty soon most of the people in the street were dancing. Many others just stood on the side, talking and laughing. Some of the historic bar's patrons spilled out onto the street and join in the merriment. I managed to find Carol in all this excitement. She seemed happy to see me.

"Did you come back to the office the other day?" she asked.

"Yes," I said, "I was hoping that I could convince them to wait on the demolition."

"That's what I heard. They told me that some nut came by looking for me, he had some crazy idea about postponing the redevelopment."

"That nut was me," I smiled.

"That was pretty ballsy."

"I guess that would describe me, sometimes."

"I'm done with my internship," she boasted. "Now I can get to work trying to restore old building, instead of knocking them down."

"Congratulations."

"I've got an entry-level position at an architecture firm that specializes in historic restoration, I start Monday." She handed me her business card.

"Wow," I said, looking over the card. "You're really doing it."

"I'm trying to," she said, glancing out at the revelers. "Look at them."

I looked over at the celebrating crowd.

"They could be on the deck of the Titanic," she said, "and the band is playing."

"Are you saying that they're all about to get wet?"

She smiled. "I don't know, and we won't know for years, but it didn't need to happen."

Carol was several years older than me, but she was so beautiful, and so damn smart. She was a woman, not a girl.

"You're really something," I said, looking at her with admiration.

"Thanks, so are you," she said, starting to walk away. "Look me up when you get a little older."

"Okay," I smiled, "but won't you also be older too?"

"Maybe," she grinned, "but you might be ready for that then."

Something told me that I was ready for that now, but I understood what she was saying. I hadn't even finished high school, and she had just finished college. "Okay, I'll keep the number."

"Good luck, Niko," she said, starting to turn away.

"You too," I said, watching her disappear into the crowd.

At Pacific Avenue and Sixth Street, I was stopped at my first anti-cruising checkpoint.

"Pull over!" said the police officer, as he guided my car, and several other cars into a tunnel of yellow traffic cones.

It was obvious what type of cars the officer

was pulling over. Besides my '54 Chevy, there was a lowered '57 Chevy and '64 Impala, and a supped-up '67 Camaro and '68 Firebird. All of these cars were driven by teenagers my age, while contemporary sedans and station wagons, driven by older drivers, were just allowed to bypass the checkpoint. The officers wrote down our license plate numbers, and gave us a warning, that if they saw us more than once more, we would be issued a citation. The citation would include a $100 fine. We were then allowed to leave.

Before I picked up Carissa, I decided to see where the other checkpoints might be. It was better to know the situation, then to be surprised later. I continued on Pacific Avenue to Cabrillo Beach, where we all liked to park, and watch the bonfires and the waves come in. Unfortunately, there was a police barricade closing the beach off to us, and another anti-cruising checkpoint. Those officers recorded my license plate number again, along with several other cars that also tried to park at Cabrillo Beach.

From there, I headed west on Paseo Del Mar toward Royal Palms beach, traveling on my normal cruising route. Unfortunately, this wasn't a normal cruising night. Another barricade closed off the beach there, and yet another police checkpoint stopped me and recorded my license plate number. This was awful, the police knew our cruising route, and they were shutting it down.

Carissa opened her front door to greet me. She looked lovely, but her eyes appeared red, and I thought her smile seemed forced.

"Are you okay?" I asked.

"Yeah," she said, with little enthusiasm, "I'd introduce you to my mom, but she's busy." She stepped outside, quickly closing the door behind her.

"Alright," I said, following her down the steps.

She frowned when she noticed my '54 Chevy. "This funny old car again."

"Yeah," I said, opening the car door for her. "I don't know what to do with it."

"Thanks," she said, sliding into the front seat.

I got in on the other side. There was a Rod Stewart 8-Track in the player just for this moment, but now I didn't feel good about playing it.

"Do we have to go right to the party?" she asked.

"No," I said, "but it's going to be difficult to drive around because of all the police checkpoints."

"Is there somewhere we can go to just talk?"

I thought for a moment, "How about Averill Park?"

"Sure, that's fine."

The park was only a few blocks away. It was dark and deserted there. I stopped the car by the same picnic area where I went to with Dean the other night. In fact, I still had some firewood in my trunk. I got out the firewood and a beach blanket, and then used the Bic lighter that Tommy had given me to start a fire in the barbeque. The fire gave off just enough light that allowed us to see each other. Even in this dim light, there was no mistaking Carissa's beauty; she looked great in any light.

"It's really bad out there on the streets," I said, "I was stopped three times, and they've closed Cabrillo Beach and Royal Palms."

"I saw the article in the *News Pilot*. It just doesn't seem right."

"No, it's not."

Carissa looked like she was getting cold, so I wrapped the beach blanket around her. She pulled me next to her inside the blanket. Oh my God! Can it get any better than this? Here I was, wrapped in a blanket with the girl of my dreams. I put my arm around her lovely shoulders. We just watched the fire for a time before she finally spoke.

"My father died this morning," she said, with almost no emotion.

I was stunned by her announcement.

"I'm so sorry," I stammered.

"I thought about calling you to cancel, but I just had to get out of the house. It's such a sad place right now."

"I really liked your father," I managed to say.

"He was a really good guy."

"He died peacefully," she said, "with us all around him. There was something wrong with his heart. Can you believe it? I just thought he had the best heart of anyone I knew."

She broke down crying, really sobbing, and I just held her. This poor creature, I thought. She lost her father, and there was nothing that I could do to help her. After a while, she stopped crying and dried her eyes. She then looked into my eyes, curiously, and then kissed me. It was the best kiss I'd ever had. It was like all the other kisses I'd had were like the warm-up band at a concert, and this kiss was the Rolling Stones.

She reached down and started to unbuckle my belt. This was exactly what I wanted, but not like this. Not with her father dying this morning. It wasn't right. I reached down and stopped her hand.

"Carissa, I really like you, but you've been through a lot today. Why don't we just take it easy?"

"Are you stopping me?" she asked, surprised. "Are you serious?"

"You're really emotional right now, and I don't want you to do something that you'll regret later."

I watched as her beautiful face turn into a scowl and her blue eyes narrowed.

"Right now," she said, "what I regret, is being out here with you."

She tossed the blanket off of herself and moved away. She folded her arms in front of her and just glared at me.

"I didn't mean to upset you," I tried to say.

"You know, I never really liked the sports stories you wrote. They weren't very good."

"I'm sorry, I just wrote the best I could."

"Yeah, but they were stupid, you were lucky that I even allowed them in the paper."

"Well, then I appreciate you giving me a chance."

"You don't know what to do with a chance!" she shouted.

"You're upset," I said, "maybe we should do this some other time?"

"I don't think so," she sneered, "you're not that much fun."

I couldn't blame her for being upset, but this was getting uncomfortable.

"I should get you home."

"Oh, and the prom next month," she announced. "I'll be going with my boyfriend, Tony. He might have a broken leg, but all of his other parts work."

She gave me a long glare, then turned toward the path that led out of the park.

"Carissa, let me give you a ride."

"I can walk."

As she moved further away from the fire, the darkness enveloped her.

Victor Hofmeister inherited his house back in high school when both of his parents died in a plane crash. After high school, Victor didn't go to college or get a job and go to work. Instead he just sat in his house, smoked grass, and drank liquor. When he ran out of milk, he occasionally poured beer over his morning cereal. Sometimes he threw parties. His parties were usually large, noisy events. His neighbors dreaded Saturday nights. He called his parties blowouts. Tonight was billed as "Vic's Big Blowout."

Vic was originally Hank Pilsner's friend, but eventually we all became friends with him. He had the appearance of someone who never exercised, unless you count playing golf. But Victor was the world's worst golfer, and he topped that off, with having the worst temper regarding his bad golfing abilities. He became frustrated often; sometimes using his putter as a garden hoe to mercilessly destroy whatever green he had missed his putt on. But these were his shortcomings; Victor owned the "party house." This simple fact, made him very popular.

After Carissa left me at Averill Park, all I could think of was getting to Victor's party and having a drink, or two, or three, or four. Hell, why limit myself? Not only did I mess up my evening with Carissa, but also now I'm without a date again for my prom. And, except for some future possibilities with Carol, whom I might never see again, this whole night has been completely screwed up.

It has to get better, I thought.

I got to Victor's house before nine, when everyone was supposed to start arriving. Victor was still trying to get things cleaned up for the party. Hank Pilsner was there helping Vic by picking up the many old newspapers that were scattered across the living room floor.

"Here," said Victor, handing me a large trash bag, "pick up all of the old beer cans and bottles lying around."

"Yeah," added Hank, "people will need a place to throw their new ones."

I managed to fill the bag quickly and I brought it into the kitchen, where Hank and Victor were looking at a sink full of dirty dishes.

"Do you really want me to wash them?" asked Hank, in disgust.

"Hell no," said Vic, handing Hank a box, "just throw them in here and put them in the garage."

I carried the bag of empty beer cans and bottles with me as I followed Hank to Vic's garage. I set the bag by his trashcans, which were near the garage door. Inside the garage, were a dozen more boxes of dirty dishes. Hank set his box next to the others, and then looked at me.

"I guess it's easier to buy new dishes than wash the old ones."

"For Vic, anyway," I said.

One item Victor didn't cut corners on was his sound system. He had the best, and an enormous collection of records that he'd purchased at the

Tower Records on Sunset Boulevard, and the Licorice Pizza in Long Beach. But for parties, instead of records, Vic always played his reel-to-reel tape player with his own personal party mix of songs. He also had speakers everywhere. The song "La Grange" by ZZ Top was currently playing.

Dean and Diana were some of the first to arrive. I was pleasantly surprised to see that they brought Nancy McClay along with them. They also brought some beer and food, which I had neglected to bring. The four of us quickly became a group for the night.

After awhile, Jake showed up with Marisol Rodriguez, Melissa's best friend. Marisol was an attractive and sexy Mexican-American girl, and also Pancho Rodriguez's sister. I didn't even know that Jake was seeing her, but just like his driving and his track, Jake moved fast.

Chad Wagner and Cheryl Patterson were the next of my friends to arrive. I asked Chad if his race with Dragan Mosich was still on for midnight, and he assured me that it was. Evidently, he hadn't told Cheryl, who wasn't exactly happy to hear about the race, and thought that the whole thing was dumb and very dangerous. Jake was particularly interested in Chad's race, and told him that he'd definitely be there to watch it.

Bobby Jefferson and his best friend Clifford Brown arrived with their dates, Althea Hamilton, and Odessa Porter. It was great to see Bobby, and I congratulated him on his dad's longshoreman success. Clifford was a good student, and quite an athlete. He was on the varsity football team, and his brother was a star fullback at U.S.C.

The last of my friends to get there were Randy and Melissa. They must have been arguing, since they both had resentful looks on their faces. It didn't appear that she'd told him anything yet about her pregnancy.

So much liquor, beer, and wine was being consumed, that you would have thought that at least someone there had to be 21 years old, but that wasn't the case. Every teenager here had his or her own favorite method for acquiring booze. Some had an older brother or sister that would buy for them, some had fake I.D.s, and others just frequented various mom and pop markets that never cared about their age. Teenagers rarely let something as trivial as laws get in their way. It was just another challenge to overcome.

The song "Born on the Bayou" by Credence Clearwater Revival began to play. Several couples started to dance, and several couples joined them. Bobby and Althea, and Clifford and Odessa, were definitely the best dancers. They were also the best dressed.

Between dances, there was a lot of discussion about the new anti-cruising ordinance and the $100 and $250 fines. Everyone was also angry that Cabrillo Beach and Royal Palms were now closed to us at night. Most of these kids had been born here. We were locals. This was our town as much as anyone else's, but we certainly weren't being treated that way.

As the night wore on, the booze flowed and the music played. Dean, filled with liquid courage, acquired the arrogance of someone twice his size. He went around puffing out his chest and almost daring anyone to pick a fight with him. This was comical, and most everyone just laughed at him. But Howard Stevens, a big football player, didn't get the joke. Howard got angry and just snapped. His two wide swings at Dean missed their mark, but landed right on the faces of two other guys. They went down like lead weights into water. Hank and I jumped on Howard and managed to grab both his arms. Dean was now cowering with fear and couldn't believe that his bravado had caused this aggression. He apologized profusely and loudly, and this finally subdued Howard, who then calmed down and even apologized to the two guys he'd hit in the face. They reluctantly accepted his apologies.

After so many drinks, Nancy started to look really good to me. I don't know why it had taken so long. I already knew what she looked like without any clothes on. Now, with a little liquor in me, maybe I could get something going.

The song "Oh! Darling" by the Beatles played over Vic's stereo as Nancy and I began to slow dance to it. I kept sliding my right hand from her waist to her butt. But she kept sliding it back up to her waist.

"What do you think you're doing?" she asked.

"Uh," I mumbled, bleary-eyed, "I don't know."

Between dances, Hank had been sampling a little bit of everyone's booze. I saw him taking sips of Bacardi rum, Seagram's whiskey, Popov vodka, and some stuff that was simply labeled "Fire Water." Because of his size, Hank was usually able to hold his liquor, but I'd never seen him drink this much or such a variety.

I managed to get Nancy to follow me to the hallway that led to the bedrooms. I cracked open the door to Vic's spare bedroom just enough to see Jake and Marisol making out. Jake had his shirt off, and he was starting to unbutton Marisol's top. I quickly closed the door.

"What's going on in there?" asked Nancy, trying to take a peek.

"Nothing," I said, "the room's just too messy."

I then opened the door to Victor's bedroom to see if it was occupied. It was empty, so I pulled Nancy inside. I started to kiss her and she kissed me back. Then suddenly the door swung open and in staggered a drunken Hank Pilsner. He dove right onto Vic's bed and landed across it with a thud. He then started to throw up violently, his puke covering the floor near the bed.

"Oh, gross," said Nancy, trying not to gag.

"Never mind him," I said, hardly noticing the mess and going back to kissing her.

She stopped me, and then dragged me out of the room. We left Hank lying on the bed. He had finally stopped vomiting.

In the living room, I saw that Pancho had arrived at the party with his two friends, Luis and Chuy. Pancho noticed Melissa standing with Randy on the other side of the room. Pancho and his friends walked over to them.

"You haven't returned my phone calls," said Pancho, to Melissa. "What's up with that?"

Randy looked at Melissa. "Why would Marisol's brother be calling you?"

"Stay out of this *homes*," said Pancho, "This is between me and my woman."

"Your what?" asked Randy.

"Both of you, stop!" pleaded Melissa. "I can't deal with this!"

She hurried across the crowded living room, through the front door, and out to the front yard. Everyone involved followed her out.

Several partygoers were drinking out on the front lawn, and some guy was passed out and laying on the grass. He didn't look like he was going to be doing anymore drinking that night.

Randy followed close behind Melissa. "Why is Pancho calling you his woman?" he asked.

"I don't know," she said, defensively.

"I'll tell you," said Pancho, "because we've

been seeing each other, that's why."

Randy looked at Melissa. "Is this true?"

Melissa stood silently for a moment, and then spoke. "I'm going to have a baby, and I don't know which one of you is the father."

The two were both stunned and neither knew what to say.

"That's what I thought," said Melissa, looking to Randy. "Give me my car keys."

Randy pulled the keys from his pocket and handed them to Melissa. Everyone watched as she walked to her car and then drove off.

"Man," said Pancho to his friends, "let's get out of here, I need some Tequila." He looked over to the guy who was passed out on the lawn. "I want to get like that guy, *mucho barracho.*"

Pancho and Chuy started to leave, but Luis stopped to talk to me.

"Remember, *vato,*" he said. "I want to buy your car. I'll even throw in an extra hundred dollars."

"Wow," I thought, $700. If I wanted to sell it, I'd never get a better price. "I still have your phone number," I said.

"Good, don't lose it."

The three got into Pancho's '64 Impala. He started up the car, and "Black Magic Woman" by Santana started to play on his stereo.

"Come on," I said, as I led Nancy over to my Chevy, which was parked just across the street from Victor's house. I still had a pretty good buzz on.

"Why are we going to your car?" she asked, "We're not leaving, are we?"

"No," I said, thinking maybe that my car would give us a more private place to neck. Who knows how far we could get from there?

Randy had gone back inside the party to find a drink. Like Pancho, he also said he wanted to get drunk.

I had Alice Cooper's *Billion Dollar Babies* 8-Track in my car stereo. When I turned it on, "No More Mr. Nice Guy" started to play.

I had this one chance with Nancy. If I didn't take advantage of it, then I'd be a loser. I started kissing Nancy and I even tried to feel her up. She was kissing me back, but she was also fighting me off. I didn't quite understand it. I thought she wanted the same thing I did. Hell, she wanted to be a Playboy Playmate. Those girls don't stay virgins for the rest of their lives.

"What is wrong with you!" she shouted, as she shoved me to the other side of the bench seat. "When I say stop, I mean stop!"

"Huh, what?"

"This is not the Niko I know!" She turned off the music. "You are acting like a Jerk!

"I thought you liked me?"

"I liked the sober Niko, not this guy!"

"What am I doing wrong?" I asked.

"Everything!" she shouted. "When a girl asks you to stop, it doesn't mean try harder, it means stop!"

I immediately felt terrible, but my head was still cloudy. "I'm sorry," is all that I could say.

"Before today, you treated me with respect, probably more than I deserved. You were the kind of guy any girl would like to know better."

"I'm drunk," I said.

"That's just an excuse." She kissed me on the lips. "And you need to sober up before you drive anywhere."

"Yeah," I agreed, rubbing my eyes.

We both noticed someone tapping on my fogged up driver's side window. I rolled down the window and found Randy standing there.

"Hey, man," he said. "Victor's pissed off because Hank threw up in his bedroom."

"Yeah," I said, "we watched him puke."

"Vic wants him out of there. Can you give me a hand?"

"Sure."

Randy and I headed towards Vic's front door. Inside, the party was still going strong. Nancy decided that she wanted to stay outside and get some fresh air. I turned to Randy as we were going inside.

"What are you going to do about Melissa?"

"I don't know, man," he said. "I feel like she was cheating on me."

"Well, she was. But she still might be carrying your baby."

"Yeah, but she might not be." He paused for a moment. "I loved her, man."

"I believe you," I said, putting my hand on his shoulder.

"I just knew there was something going on. She'd changed."

"Maybe she had."

We made our way inside the door, past the living room, and to Victor's bedroom. Vic stood outside the door, pointing at Hank who was passed-out on his bed.

"You guys need to get him out of there."

"He's heavy," I said to Vic. "Can you help us?"

"I've got a bad back," he said. "It got me out of Nam."

"Okay," said Randy to me. "Then I guess it's just me and you."

We managed to step around all of the puke and get to Hank on the bed. This wasn't going to be easy, Hank had to weigh at least 300 lbs. Randy was able to get his left arm up, and I was able to get my arm under his right arm. At the count of "three" we both picked him up. It was a real struggle to get him out of there and into the hall. Once in the hallway, we carried him toward the living room, with his legs dragging on the floor.

In the living room, Black Sabbath's song "Iron Man" played over Vic's sound system. It felt like we were carrying an "iron man." Some of the partygoers moved out of our way, while others were just oblivious, and we had to yell at them to move. Right by Victor's glass coffee table, Randy lost his grip, and Hank slipped out of my hands too. His limp body came crashing down on the glass table, smashing it to bits, with shards of glass flying everywhere.

"My table!" hollered Victor. "Look what you guys did to my table!"

"You wanted him out of your bedroom, man," said Randy. "Well, now he's out of your bedroom."

"Get him outside!" yelled Vic.

Falling on the table had somehow woken Hank up. He looked around the room in a daze.

"Hey," I said, "he's awake."

"Hank," said Randy, "we need your help, man. We're going to get you to your feet, and then we need you to walk outside."

Randy and I were able to pick Hank up and onto his feet. He was really out of it, but he still managed to walk. We were finally able to get him out the door and onto the front lawn. He collapsed right by the other guy who had already been lying there. Nancy had been examining this other guy. She stood up and looked at us.

"This guy is dead," said Nancy.

"What?" I asked.

"He's not breathing and he has no pulse."

Victor had come out with us and was standing by his front door.

"Hey Victor," said Randy, "Nancy said that this guy next to Hank is dead."

"Are you sure?" asked Victor.

"He has no pulse, and he's not breathing," said Nancy.

"Oh crap!" said Vic, "I guess the party's over."

"Well," I said, "for him, it certainly is."

Someone at the party knew the dead guy, and said that he had graduated from San Pedro High just last year. That would have put him in Hank's class. It seems that he'd been taking some pills earlier in the evening, and washing those down with whiskey. Obviously the combination hadn't agreed with him. Most everyone had left the party by the time the police had arrived. We had some difficulty convincing the cops that Hank wasn't also dead. But the officers managed to revive him, and his dad was called to take him home. The coroner finally came and took the dead guy away. Vic's front lawn now looked kind of empty without the two bodies lying there.

Most of us had sobered up by the time we needed to get over to Westmont Avenue for Chad Wagner's drag race with Dragan Mosich. It wasn't exactly a good omen that some guy had died tonight, but that wasn't going to stop this street race. Dragan had challenged Chad, and Chad accepted the challenge. If he backed out now, he would have looked like a coward. Chad didn't want to look like a coward.

It was almost midnight on Westmont Avenue. Unlike last Saturday night when Jake and Gene raced under a full moon, tonight there was barely any moon at all. It was quite dark, and you could barely see the long stretch of four-lane road. If it weren't for the headlights of all the cars arriving for the race, you wouldn't have been able to see anything.

Dragan's baby blue Corvette was there already and he was talking to some of his friends who were there to watch. He looked pretty confident, and he was doing his usual boasting. Chad's navy blue Chevelle was there also, and he was talking to some of his friends as well. Cheryl Patterson, his girlfriend, stood off to the side and couldn't conceal her displeasure with him participating in this race.

Just before the drivers were to get into their positions, a Harley Davidson motorcycle pulled up to the curb. It was Gary Gabelich. He dropped his kickstand, removed his helmet, and got off his bike. I quickly went over to him. He recognized me immediately.

"I was headed home," he said. "When I saw all of the cars coming here, I knew that it had to be a street race."

"Yeah," I said, pointing. "My friend Chad is

racing this guy Dragan."

"They're crazy," said Gary, "this is way too dangerous."

I was surprised that Gary Gabelich, who made a living out of doing dangerous things, would have a problem with a street race. Chad and Dragan both recognized Gabelich and came over to meet him. I introduced the two of them.

"You guys shouldn't be doing this," Gary scolded, "you should be racing on a track, not on the street."

"They took our race track away," said Dragan. "What are we supposed to do?"

Gary knew kids were always going to race. If they had a track to race on safely, well that would be better, but if you took that track away, then unfortunately that just meant that the races would have to be more dangerous.

"Maybe you can drive down to Orange County," said Gary, "They still have a track there."

"I'm not driving all the way down there," said Dragan. "It's too damn far."

"Yeah," said Chad. "Let's just get this thing over with."

They both returned to their cars and friends. Gary shook his head in resignation.

"I can barely use my hand anymore," he said, flexing his gloved hand, "and a metal rod holds my leg together," slapping his leg, "so maybe I'm not the best one to judge, but street racing is really stupid."

"Hopefully," I said, "nothing bad happens."

"When you're putting your life on the line, you don't just want to just hope that nothing bad happens," he said. "I'm not going to be a part of it."

Gary slid his helmet back on, started up his motorcycle, and drove off toward Western Avenue.

As Chad and Dragan positioned their cars on the starting line, everyone found good spots to watch the quarter-mile race. Chad would be in the middle lane and Dragan would be in the lane by the curb. Jake would be the starter.

Looking at both of their cars, I thought back about how long I'd known both of them. I'd gotten to know Dragan for a summer when I was about 12 years old, and he had shown me the ropes as a newspaper boy in town. But Chad had been a good friend for a long time. Before he'd moved to South Shores, we were inseparable. He had only lived a couple of blocks away, and we were always playing sports or just riding our bikes together. His dad had managed the Sea Scout camp at Cabrillo Beach, and we learned all about the ocean there. Chad even talked me in to ushering Catholic Mass over at the small chapel at Fort MacArthur. That was the most I'd gone to church in my life. Then he moved away, but we never stopped being friends.

When everything was ready, Jake got between the two cars and looked toward the two drivers. He looked at Chad, and he nodded. Then he looked at Dragan, and he did the same.

Finally, Jake raised the white t-shirt in the air and held it there. When he dropped his arm, both cars started off the line. Immediately, Dragan's engine exploded, sending shards of metal, plastic, and rubber flying. It was like a bomb going off. His hood crunched up and smashed into his windshield, blocking his view.

Chad, who was next to him, saw the explosion, and tried to get out of his way, but couldn't. Dragan veered left, directly into him, forcing his car onto the opposite side of the street and then right into a telephone pole. Chad's car hit sideways, tearing the car in half and snapping the pole right in the middle.

The Corvette rolled for a distance until Dragan could stop it. He then climbed out of the vehicle and stumble away, just as the car went up in an enormous fireball.

Everyone ran over to the mangled wreckage that once was Chad's car. Cheryl, his girlfriend, was right beside me as we ran there together. At first we couldn't find him, because he wasn't in the mess. But then someone noticed him; he was laid out on the ground, several feet away, and face down. He wasn't moving. Cheryl became hysterical, I grabbed her and tried to hold her, but she fought me off. Jake kneeled at Chad's side, looking him over. Jake looked over at me with tears in his eyes and shook his head.

"He's gone."

Cheryl heard Jake's words and became even more hysterical.

In the distance, we could see the red lights and hear the siren of a police car approaching. Last time, we all ran off to escape, this time, there was no escaping.

Easter Sunday

APRIL 22

▼

The Easter Mass at Our Lady of the Harbor Church was crowded. It looked like half of San Pedro was there, and it was difficult to find a seat. After several deaths the night before, a morning about resurrection seemed more ironic than appropriate. At one pew, I saw Carissa and her family, seated stoically, having just lost their father. At another pew, I noticed Chad Wagner's family, surprisingly there as well, maybe looking for some comforting words over the loss of their son. They sat tearfully beside Cheryl Patterson and her family. I didn't know the guy who had died on Victor's lawn, but I hoped that his family was there also, to share in the mutual grief.

My mom sat between my dad and myself. She was drying her

eyes with a handkerchief. Mom had always liked Chad, and remembered him as my little friend, before he'd moved off to South Shores. Even though she hadn't seen him in years, she still remembered him as that little boy.

Last night, Officer Barberi and Officer Hanson had been in that first police car that arrived to the scene of Chad's accident. They agreed with Jake's initial assessment of Chad's condition, but they quickly radioed in for an ambulance anyway. He was pronounced dead on arrival at the hospital. Matt Barberi was now seated there at the church with Randy's family.

As I glanced around the crowded pews, I could also see Melissa's family, Marisol and Pancho's family, and Jake seated there with his grandparents. Nancy and her family sat up front in a prime spot. Monsignor McClay, Nancy's uncle, sat up by the altar, bedecked in the fine robes that signified his position in the church.

Hank and his family were also present. Fortunately, Hank looked better this morning than he did last night. But he was obviously hung over and still looked a bit queasy.

After the choir had sung their hymns, Father Jason approached the podium for his Easter sermon. I noticed that he gave a quick wink to the red-headed woman from my car accident of the other day. She was seated in one of the front pews with friends. Father Jason certainly looked quite different sober and wearing his priestly robes.

After speaking first about the true meaning of Easter, and Christ's resurrection, Father Jason began his homily:

"Monsignor McClay and I share a love for good wine. Fortunately, here in San Pedro there's never a shortage of that."

There were a few chuckles in the audience and Monsignor McClay smiled. Father Jason continued:

"We both make wine, another local tradition. Sometimes we even enter into a friendly competition to see who can make the best bottle. As you might know, it's all about the grapes. The quality of the grapes determines the quality of the wine. The right grapes can make all the difference."

I started to tune Father Jason out. I didn't know where he was going with his story, but I really didn't care. I wasn't very good at sitting in church and listening to sermons. Maybe if I went to church more than just Easter and Christmas, I would be better at paying attention. Instead of listening though, I started admiring the stained glass windows of Our Lady of the Harbor Church. The windows depicted Christ's life, death on the cross, and his resurrection.

There seemed to be so many things dying, I thought. Not just my friend Chad, and my teacher, Mr. Johansson, but Beacon Street, and our town's history. How can you know where you are, if you don't know where you've been? How can you know who you are, if you're not aware of your people's struggles and accomplishments? Why do we always have to lose the things that connect us with our past?

I looked over to Chad's family again and Cheryl Patterson, who sat nearby. Then I looked over to Carissa and her family, who were trying their best to hold it together. It was just all so sad.

After the Easter service, I returned home with my parents, changed out of my Sunday best, and grabbed the 35mm camera that I'd borrowed from school. I stopped at Thrifty Drugs to pick up a few rolls of film and then headed down to the Beacon Street area.

The place was almost deserted, except for the street sweepers and cleanup crews that were still picking up after last night's celebration. All the revelers were now long gone, and the last of the businesses were finally shuttered. The demolition equipment rested nearby, prepared to do their work starting tomorrow.

I parked on Harbor Boulevard and began taking random pictures: the Mission Smoke House, Hirschman's Drugs, the Criterion Café, the Ocean Club, the Silver Dollar Café, and The White Swan Café, where Frank Lucich had always enjoyed a good drink and a fight.

I turned up Sixth Street, and took a picture of the old Seaside Books, which had recently had its signage removed. I thought about Mabel as a pretty young woman, with a young Louis Adamic there buying books to improve his English and to learn about his new country. I wondered what books Jack London might have purchased when he visited the place.

A few doors down was Casey Boyle's Seven Seas Pool Hall, where my friends and I had played pool into the evening. I guess it was good that the bar had been rescued from the demolition.

Across the street, was Slim Harrison's Bank Café, the Old Bank of San Pedro, which had long ago been repurposed as a restaurant. Further up the street, was the Globe Theater, which in its final days, had been reduced to showing X-rated movies.

On Beacon Street itself, I captured images of the Beacon Light Mission, where Miss Martin had volunteered her time, and Joe Hill had written his union songs. Then I got a picture of Shanghai Red's, where Cairo Mary would throw drunks out on their ass.

That's all I did for about an hour, just took pictures, up and down those lonely streets. Some buildings I tried to just document their existence, while others I focused on a particular architectural detail. I was trying to capture one last view of the town's history, my feeble attempt at preservation.

I parked on Thirteenth and Centre, right behind Danny Sanchez's '54 Chevy with the gray primer spots. I took a screwdriver from my trunk and removed his four hubcaps from my car. I carried them over to the apartment building where I thought Danny lived. Looking at the mailboxes, I was able to find his unit. I knocked on the door and Danny answered it.

"These are yours," I said, handing the hubcaps to him.

He took them and then turned them over to find the driver's license number that he had engraved.

"Where did you get these?"

"A friend of mine thought he was doing me a favor by stealing them from you. I'd had mine stolen, so he thought they would make good replacements."

He glanced over at my car and noticed that my wheels were now bare.

"Did you have these on your car when I met you over at Point Fermin Park?"

"Yeah," I said, with some embarrassment.

"This guy, Pancho Rodriguez, has some money and he wants me to do some work on his '64 Impala. He said you gave him my number."

"Yeah, I did."

"Good. He likes my ideas, and I think I can

help him out."

"Great."

He looked at the hubcaps in his hands. "You want to help me put these back on my car?"

"Sure."

He handed me two of the hubcaps and we walked over to his car on the street. He put his two hubcaps on the street side wheels and I put mine on the two wheels nearest the curb.

"If I were you," I said, "I would take these off at night or even during the day sometimes."

"I plan to be a lot more careful, believe me."

He then looked over to my car, which now looked incomplete without its hubcaps.

"What are you going to do now with your car?"

"Can I borrow your phone?" I asked, "I need to make a call."

"Yeah, no problem."

Luis was very happy to hear from me, and since I knew where Pancho lived, he asked me to meet him there. Before I went, I took all of my personal things out of my car at home and found the car's pink slip, its ownership papers. I then met Luis out on the curb in front of Pancho's. Luis was standing there with Pancho.

Luis and I shook hands, and using the hood of my car as a writing surface, I signed over the ownership. After Luis handed me seven one hundred dollar bills, I handed him the keys.

"I've wanted this car for a long time," said Luis.

"How long?" I asked.

"Before you even bought it," he said. "But that old man sold it to you first, I missed out."

"I guess I was lucky."

"Yeah, you were."

I'd had the car all through high school, about three years. I'd never had any major repairs, only maintenance. It had served me well: all of the cruising, all of the trips to the beach, all of the good times.

Pancho patted Luis on the back to congratulate him on his purchase; then Pancho looked over to me.

"Melissa and I are getting married, *vato*."

"Really?" I asked, a little surprised.

"Yeah," he said, "I love her, and I just know it's my baby. And if it's not, well, then we'll have a half dozen more of our own."

I was glad that Melissa's baby was going to have a father, even though it wasn't going to be Randy. I hoped that Pancho could make her happy.

"Congratulations," I said.

"She wants you to be in the wedding, *homes*." He said, looking at me.

"I'd be honored," I said. "She's a good friend."

"Luis is the best man, *vato*, maybe he'll let you ride with him in the procession after the wedding, your old car and all."

"Yeah, sure," said Luis. "It's only right."

I looked down at the car, noticing its bare wheels. I wondered why Luis hadn't said anything about the car's missing hubcaps.

"You never asked me about the car's hubcaps?" I asked.

"It's no problem," said Luis. "I've got my own."

"You do?"

"Yeah, last week, when it was parked up by the school, I stole them from you."

"You're kidding?"

"No. I planned to own this car some day, and I wanted to protect them from everybody else. You can call it a little insurance policy."

I shook my head and laughed.

Pancho smiled. "Yeah, *homes*, you should have known that a Mexican stole your hubcaps."

Of all the people that I could have sold my car to, I'm glad that it was Luis, because he's wanted the car for a long time, and I knew that he'd take care of it. But then I thought about the anti-cruising checkpoints of last night, and how difficult it was going to be to cruise anymore.

"What are you going to do about the police checkpoints? Are you still planning to cruise?"

"Hell yeah!" said Luis. "They might stop you white boys, but they're not going to stop us. If we can't cruise in Pedro, then we'll go to East L.A., or somewhere else. It's in our blood."

"Yeah, vato," said Pancho. "We've got a long history of cruising, and we don't plan to stop."

Pancho let me use his phone so that I could call Hank Pilsner. I asked him if he felt well enough to give me a ride home. He said he'd be right over. Luis and Pancho stayed in the house and talked, while I went outside to wait for Hank. While I was out by the curb, I gave my '54 Chevy one last look. I thought about all of the times I'd washed it, all of the nights I'd cruised Pacific Avenue, all of the trips to Hermosa Beach during the summers, and all of the dates I'd been on with it. The car was made the year I was born, which made us the same age. We were linked in everyone's mind, Niko and his '54 Chevy. My first car, just like a first girlfriend, inevitably, you always break up. For some reason, sadness suddenly enveloped me and I started to cry. This was silly, I thought, it's just a car, just transportation. But as I dried my eyes, I realized that it had been so much more.

Hank arrived after a few minutes. I got into his Pinto and we drove off. Of course, the 8-Track of *After the Gold Rush* played on his stereo.

"I didn't even know you were thinking about selling your car."

"Luis made me a good offer."

"What are you going to do now?"

"I have no idea, probably look for another car."

Hank rubbed his swollen eyes.

"I was really sick last night," he said. "All I can remember is drinking everything that was handed to me, and then, somehow I found myself lying out on the lawn."

"You puked in Victor's bedroom."

"Really?"

"Yeah, then Randy and I dropped you through a glass coffee table."

Hank held up his right arm to reveal a long gash that had already scabbed over. "That must be how I got this."

"Probably."

"When my dad woke me up on the grass, the police were checking out some guy lying there next to me."

"Yeah, he was probably dead when Randy and I laid you there."

"You guys laid me next to a dead guy?"

"Well, at the time, he actually looked in better shape than you did."

Just then, Hank's 8-Track started to garble Neil Young's music. Hank quickly popped out the tape, shook it, hit it against his leg, and then put it back in. But that didn't correct the problem, and the music was still coming out garbled.

"Crap!" said Hank, pulling out the tape.

"I guess it's shot," I said, smiling. "Now you'll

have to play that other tape that you never play."

I was so happy that we'd finally get to listen to something else.

Hank tossed the broken 8-Track tape over his shoulder and it landed on the backseat. He then reached into his glove compartment and pulled out the new tape. I couldn't see the tape's title until he finished unwrapping the cellophane. To my horror, it was a brand new exact copy of Neil Young's *After the Gold Rush*.

"No way." I wailed, "It can't be."

"Yes," he smiled, "it can." He then pushed the new 8-Track into his stereo. The song "Tell Me Why" began to play.

When Hank dropped me off at my home, I found Carissa Johansson parked there in her white Volkswagen convertible. I had no idea what she was doing here. Hank went home to nurse his hangover as I walked over to Carissa's car. She was as stunning as ever.

"Hi," I said, standing on the curb by her car.

"Hi," she replied, "Could you get in so we can talk?"

"Sure," I said, as I got into the car. I noticed our nosy neighbor, Mrs. Castagnola, peering out from her window. "Would you mind just driving us somewhere, I have nosy neighbors."

"Okay," said Carissa. She started the car and drove east for a block and then turned right onto Pacific Avenue heading toward the ocean. "I had to see you, to apologize."

"It's alright," I said. "Your dad died, you were emotional, I understand."

"The things I said were not very nice."

"Did you really mean that about my stories?"

"No, I liked them a lot. You were writing about sports, but you were also dealing with history. The writing reminded me of my dad."

"I never got to thank him for being such a great teacher."

"I know. It's too bad."

"He taught me to appreciate history."

We continued south on Pacific Avenue, the wind causing her blonde hair to flow.

"I'm sorry about saying that your 'parts' don't work," she said. "I'm sure they probably work just fine."

"They probably do," I smiled.

Carissa parked her VW at the lookout spot where Pacific Avenue stops at the sea cliffs overlooking the ocean.

"What are you going to do about the prom?" I asked.

"I'm going to go with Tony. I'm sorry, but I think it's the right thing to do."

"I understand, you should be with your boyfriend."

She looked out at the ocean. "I like you, Niko, and I think we would have had a good time too."

"I think we would have."

She looked right at me with those beautiful blue eyes. "Maybe we can still have a dance, if that's okay."

"A dance would be great."

I didn't know what Carissa was thinking, but as I looked at her, I was thinking how lucky I was to get to know my first real crush. Even just having one dance with her at the prom would be memorable. Now, I just needed to find a date for the evening.

"I got my acceptance to Berkley," she said, with a smile. "I'm going to be a journalism major, and I hope to write for their school newspaper."

"They'll be lucky to have you," I said. "You're a good editor."

I knew that Carissa's life was just getting started, but she would do fine. She had so much going for her. But I didn't have any plans, or even know what I was going to do with my life. I had never really thought much about college, mainly because I figured that I'd be in Vietnam, but now there was no Vietnam.

"So," asked Carissa, "do you have any college plans?"

"Not really," I smiled, "I'll probably end up at a junior college for a while."

"That's okay, then you can transfer to a four year school. Just major in something that you enjoy."

"That's good advice."

Carissa dropped me off at the Twenty-Second Street Landing where Cousin Vlatko kept his boat. Before I'd gone to church that morning, my dad had told me that Vlatko wanted to see me. It was something about a trip that he was going on. I found Vlatko standing in the marina's parking lot, taking things out of the trunk of his Fiat 124 Spider. He couldn't help noticing Carissa as she dropped me off. As I walked over to him, I could tell that he liked what he saw in the white Volkswagen.

"Now that's mighty fine," said Vlatko, "mighty fine."

"She's a nice girl," I said.

"That's okay, Niko, nice girls are good. But bad girls are so much better."

He finished getting everything out of his trunk and onto the ground.

"Your father told me that you're selling your car." he said.

"I sold it, it's gone."

"Good. Then you can do me a favor."

"What's that?"

"You can take care of my car while I'm away."

"Really?" I asked, looking his car over.

"Yes, unfortunately they don't make a trailer that fits on the back of a sailboat."

"Where are you going?"

"Did Columbus know where he was going when he discovered America? No, the poor guy thought he was going to India. What did he know?"

"So, you have no idea where you're going?"

"I'm going where the winds will take me. Do you want to go?

"You know I can't. I have to finish school, it's my senior year."

"Ah, school," he said, "the place that teaches you things you'll never need to know, for a life you'll probably never get to have. But other than that, it's a swell place."

"You really want me to take care of your car?"

"Yes, here are the keys." He handed me the keys. "Oh, and there are some conditions."

"Conditions?"

"You must only drive it to school, to work, or to run errands for your parents. There will be no going to parties, and definitely no picking up girls."

"Are you serious?"

"Hell no. I want you to have fun. Put the top down, let the breeze blow through your hair, and seat beautiful women of every color, shape, and size next to you. If the car is in one piece when I return, that's good. If it's not, that's even better."

"Let me make a solemn pledge to you." I noticed that he had several books that he'd removed from his trunk. "What books do you have?"

Vlatko picked up one of the books. "This is Hayden's book, *Wanderer.*

"Hold it out flat," I instructed him.

He held out the book flat, as if it were a Bible. I placed my left hand on the book and I raised my right hand.

"I, Niko Petrovich, do solemnly swear that I will have fun in this car, and I will try to seduce women to the best of my abilities. So help me, Vlatko."

"A noble endeavor."

Vlatko then proceeded to tell me everything I needed to know about the car and its quirks."

"I think the name 'Fiat' stands for Fix-it-again-Tony," he said. "You'll need to find an honest mechanic."

"Do you have one?" I asked.

"Unfortunately, they're difficult to find, especially for Italian cars. Mechanics are all like Ali Baba and the Forty Thieves. But I have a fellow named Pasqual, who, what he lacks in honesty, makes up for with charm."

"Well, if that's the best that I can do."

Vlatko started to pick up his things from the ground.

"Here, give me a hand with this stuff."

I managed to grab the last of his things and I followed him along the wharf to his boat.

"Hayden's leaving today for Sausalito," said Vlatko, as he ambled down the dock carrying his belongings, "he's done with his movie promotions."

"Too bad he's not sailing with you," I said, following along carrying the rest of his things."

"Yes," said Vlatko, "It would have been like old times."

Sterling Hayden sat in the sun on the deck of Vlatko's boat. He had a portable typewriter set up and he was typing away. His hair was uncombed and his beard unkempt. He also had a large duffel bag packed and ready to go. Sitting there, Hayden reminded me of the character Captain Ahab from the novel, *Moby Dick*. I started the book once, but never finished it. Fortunately, I'd seen the movie.

"Hey kid," said Hayden, greeting me. "Good to see you."

"Hi Mr. Hayden," I said, climbing on board the Illyrian Queen.

"Sterling, please," he said, "not Mr. Hayden, okay?"

"Okay," I said, setting everything down on the boat's deck. "What are you writing?"

"I call it *Voyage*. It's a sailing yarn, takes place in the 1800s."

"I know you've done a lot of things in your life," I said. "How long have you been writing?"

"I wrote my first story when I was about your age, sent it off to the *Reader's Digest*. I received a wonderful rejection letter," he laughed. "That stopped me writing for a long while. But then I read, and read, and read everything I could find."

"And eventually you got back to it?"

"Yeah, I did. Next to the ocean and beautiful women, it's what I enjoy the most."

"With me," said Vlatko, "beautiful women stand alone as a strong number one."

"You crazy Slav," said Hayden. "I'm going to miss you."

"I'll be back," said Vlatko. "Maybe then I'll swing up to Sausalito and pay you a visit."

"I wish you would," said Hayden, "I'll have a bottle of Black Label just waiting."

I helped Vlatko carry his things down into the cabin. As he found places for everything, I again found Hayden's book *Wanderer*, which Vlatko had just set on a shelf. I cracked it open and glanced through it. I quickly found one quote that stood out for me.

"Voyaging belongs to seamen, and to wanderers of the world who cannot, or will not fit in."

I thought that sentence perfectly described Hayden and Vlatko. These were two men who were living life on their terms and no one else's.

Most people, I thought, lived pretty ordinary and dull lives. These two weren't interested in that kind of life.

As I put Hayden's book back on the shelf, Vlatko was just finishing putting his things away.

"How's your Adamic Report coming?" he asked, starting to head back up to the deck.

"Fine," I said, following him out of the cabin. "I have to finish it tonight, it's due tomorrow."

After we'd climbed out of the cabin, Vlatko and I grabbed a seat on the deck. Hayden had gone back to his writing and he was typing away.

"I found out that Adamic had killed himself," I said, "I hadn't known that until yesterday."

Hayden had stopped typing when he heard what I'd said.

"It made me really sad to know that his life had been ruined when he'd been accused of being a communist."

Vlatko and Hayden looked at each other. It was a look of recognition. Like I'd said just said something that I wasn't supposed to.

"Did I say something wrong?" I asked both of them.

"No kid," said Hayden, "It's just that it sort of happened to me too."

"Sterling," said Vlatko, "You don't need to go into all those things."

"It's okay," said Hayden, "the kid asked, I don't mind telling him. It's no secret."

Sterling Hayden turned from his typewriter to give me his full attention.

"During my time in Yugoslavia during the war, I came to admire Tito and the Partisans."

"We all did," said Vlatko.

"Yeah, anybody who witnessed how they fought the fascists couldn't help but admire them. But they were Communist, right? So you weren't supposed to admire Communists, but I did. Then after the war, in Hollywood, I was invited to some of their meetings, so I said; Why the hell not, and I became a Communist."

"So, you really were a Communist?" I asked.

"Yeah, for about ten minutes. Then I got tired of it, stopped going to their meetings, and moved on. They wanted a commitment, and I'd never been one to commit to anything. They said to be here for the next meeting on Tuesday. I said, hey, I might have a hot date that night; I might not be able to make it. They didn't like my answer, and I was done."

"So, that was it?" I asked.

"For me, but not for J. Edgar Hoover and the House Un-American Activities Committee. I had to sing."

"Sing?"

"I had to rat on everyone, name them as Communists, ruin their lives, their careers. It wasn't enough that I renounced my membership in the Communist party, I had to squeal about my friends' memberships."

"You told on your friends?"

Hayden had been looking right at me, but now he couldn't look me in the eye.

"It's the only thing in my life that I'm truly ashamed of."

For a moment no one said anything, then Hayden looked toward me again.

"You mentioned Adamic," he said. "I'd read a lot of his writing, it was damn fine, and I agreed with everything he said about Tito and the Partisans."

"But as far as I know, he never became a Communist."

"You didn't have to be, many a life was ruined anyway."

Vlatko looked my way and got my attention.

"Adamic found himself sailing head-on into a giant wave," he said, "and that wave came crushing down on him with all of its destructive power."

"I'd read about his suicide," said Hayden, "it was very sad."

For a moment, we didn't say anything, and then Hayden started to put his portable typewriter away in its case. He shut the lid and placed the typewriter beside his duffel bag. I wished Vlatko good luck on his journey and thanked him again for allowing me to watch over his Fiat Spider.

"Next time I see you," said Vlatko, "I want to hear that you're no longer a virgin, that's your mission."

"Ay ay, captain," I said, saluting. Vlatko

returned my salute.

Hayden grabbed his duffel bag and his typewriter, and then both of us stepped off of the boat. Just then, we noticed Vlatko's two college-aged girlfriends approaching the boat. These were the same two that I'd met earlier in the week. They each carried a duffel bag of their own.

"Ah, my crew," shouted Vlatko.

Sterling Hayden and I watched as the two pretty girls tossed their bags to Vlatko. As they boarded the boat, he gave each one a big hug and a kiss.

Hayden and I smiled at Vlatko's good fortune before we continued along the dock to the parking lot. We said our goodbyes, and then Hayden drove off in his Karmen Ghia. He was planning to stop in Santa Barbara for the night, before heading home the next morning. But his plans were open, and if he found a good place to write on his trip, he might just stay there for a while.

I put the top down on Vlatko's 124 Spider and then got in. The sun was starting to set, so I drove over to Point Fermin, and then along Paseo Del Mar toward Royal Palms. Near White Point, the sunset was on my left and it was spectacular, oranges and yellows. At Royal Palms, I angled right on Western Avenue toward home.

After dinner, I closed myself off in my bedroom, gathered my papers, surrounded myself with books, and then got to work finishing my report on Louis Adamic. It wasn't difficult to fin-

ish. With all of my research, finishing the report was actually pretty easy. I completed it around ten o'clock at night.

Easter Monday

It was a little odd to be back at San Pedro High School after a long Easter Vacation. For some reason, the first day back at school was always jarring. In spite of that, I actually got there early so that I could work in the photo lab. I needed to develop my rolls of film into negatives, so that later during photography class, I could make some prints. I started with the roll of Randy and his streaking prank, and then the rolls of Beacon Street. Neither of those sets of photos would have rivaled nude pictures of Nancy McClay, but I was okay with that.

At the beginning of English class, I turned in my Adamic Report to Mrs. Coleman. She looked surprised to see that I'd actually finished it. For the next hour, Mrs. Coleman

asked the class to write a journal entry about
their Easter Vacations. Some students had gone
off to Palm Springs, Catalina Island, or even Mexico. I had just stayed home, researched my report,
gone to work, went to a party, and sold my car. I
really didn't think I'd done anything that anyone
would really want to hear about. For that hour, I
just sat there frozen, unable to put down a single
word on the paper. While the others wrote about
their vacations, Mrs. Coleman read and graded
my report on Louis Adamic. She handed me back
the paper. It had an "A" at the top, but that was
crossed out and a "B" was drawn next to it. The
words "One week late!" were also written there.

"It's pretty good," she said. "Next time, turn it
in when it's due."

Later, when everyone read aloud about their
vacations, I had nothing to share.

During my photography class, I managed to
quickly make a proof sheet of Randy's streaking
photos. A couple of students saw the images, but
stayed quiet. Then I made a proof sheet of all my
Beacon Street pictures; there were a lot of good
ones. My photography teacher really liked what
he saw, and asked if he could make a few prints to
display. For myself, I picked the photo of the Bea-

con Light Mission to blowup into a large photo. After it had dried, I borrowed a pen and wrote something on the bottom of the picture.

At lunchtime, I met my friends over at the outdoor lunch area by the cafeteria. Randy, Dean, and Jake were there. Melissa was noticeably absent. Randy was a little down because of it. He perked up when I handed him the proof sheet of his streaking photos. Dean and Jake looked them over.

"It must have been cold that day," said Jake, smiling.

"Is that what Mrs. Coleman means by a dangling participle?" asked Dean.

"Man, those Catholic school girls went crazy," bragged Randy. "They loved a good Italian sausage."

Randy circled several of the photos on the proof sheet. "Those are the ones I want copies of."

"You've got it," I said.

After school, I made my way over to Miss Martin's class. She was still there, grading papers.

"Hello, Niko," she said.

"Hi Miss Martin."

"Did you turn in your Adamic report?"

"Of course," I said, "Mrs. Coleman gave me an 'A,' then made it a 'B' because it was a week late."

"That's okay, it was good enough to earn an 'A,' that's what counts."

I noticed that Miss Martin had put up a new poster by the artist Sister Corita Kent, whom Miss Martin had been a nun with. The poster read:

"Let it be your privilege to have no privilege." A quote from St. Francis of Assisi.

I pulled the large photo of the Beacon Light Mission from my three-ring binder. "This is for you," I said, handing it to her. At the bottom of it I had written:

"To the world's best nun,
Thanks for the hug. I'm sorry I smelled so bad.
Your friend,
Gerald"

Miss Martin held the picture with one hand and placed her other hand on her chest. She closed her eyes, as if to hold back tears, and then finally spoke.

"Thank you, Niko. It's amazing that you tracked down Gerald after all these years."

"I'm very resourceful."

Miss Martin turned to the bulletin board

behind her and pinned the photograph beside a photo she had of Sister Corita Kent. In the photo, Sister Corita is in her nun's habit, standing there behind a red Harley Davidson motorcycle.

Epilogue

That day, J.P. Watterson's demolition company began the process of tearing down the Beacon Street area. The old, it seemed, needed to make way for the new. With the pictures I had taken, I managed to preserve a photographic history of a place that had lived for over a century, but would now be completely gone in just a few days. I couldn't watch the destruction, and avoided the area until it was finished.

I attended two funerals that spring, one for my former teacher, Mr. Johansson, and one for my old friend, Chad. The services were both up at Green Hills Memorial Park, where most of the citizens of the town eventually make their way. Both funerals were sad, but since he was so young, Chad's funeral seemed much more tragic. There was a lot of talk in town of finding a location to build a new drag strip, so that kids could race more safely. Finally, a new spot was approved on Terminal Island, not too far from where East San Pedro had once stood, before its Japanese-American citizens had been placed in relocation camps. Lion's Drag Strip had been built many years earlier for the same reason, but everyone had somehow forgotten that. Like my father always said, "Those who don't learn the lessons of history are forced to repeat them."

Before graduation, I signed up for classes over at Los Angeles Harbor College. Since I had no idea what to major in, I picked classes in journalism, theater, and education, hoping that one of those classes would lead me to something. I took Carissa's advice, and picked classes that thought I might enjoy.

I figured that I would ask Chad's girlfriend, Cheryl Patterson, to go with me to the senior prom. She had lost Chad, but she knew everyone in the graduating class, and I thought she should be there. I was so happy that she agreed to go with me, and she ended up having a good time.

The prom was originally going to be held at the *Queen Mary* in Long Beach. But because of some scheduling issues, the location was changed to the Disneyland Hotel. I was a little disappointed that the prom wasn't going to be at the *Queen Mary*, since the ship had been my transportation to America. Although I was only two when I made that trip, and obviously didn't remember any of it, it still would have felt like a homecoming of sorts, like I'd somehow come full-circle.

But I wasn't really disappointed because Carissa and I had that dance; it was a slow dance to a song by Rod Stewart. She was so lovely, and she even put her head on my shoulder. It was all that I imagined it would be.

ABOUT THE AUTHOR

Peter Adum studied theater at The University of Southern California. After graduation, Peter worked on the staff at the Mark Taper Forum in Los Angeles. During this time, he wrote screenplays and plays. At the Taper, he adapted John Fante's novel, *Dreams From Bunker Hill,* for their literary cabaret. Eventually, he and John's widow, Joyce Fante, collaborated on the play, *The Boys in the Backroom*, about the group of writers who once gathered at the Stanley Rose Bookshop in Hollywood during the 1930s. He also adapted John Fante's novel, *Ask the Dust,* into a screenplay. For the past twenty-four years, Peter has been a teacher living in the Seattle area with his wife, Elizabeth, and their overly demanding cat, Ellie.

ACKNOWLEDGMENTS

I'd like to thank my friend and colleague, Shelley Keller, for proofreading a very rough draft (twice) and helping me make it look somewhat professional. And also, I'd like to thank my friend, Tim Hannon, who after reading it, told me that it was at least as good as *Bill and Ted's Excellent Adventure*. Finally, my sincerest appreciation to John Budz and Vee Sawyer at Ward Street Press, for their expertise, advice, and creative energy. Without their help, the book would not have turned out looking this good.

COLOPHON

A typeface can recall an era in memory. For that task Clarendon was chosen as the face of *A New Day Yesterday*. Originally created in London in 1845, this wide slab-serif font was designed by Robert Besley and engraved by Benjamin Fox. Though always popular with designers, in the late 1960s and 1970s Clarendon was ubiquitous: on posters, logos, movie title sequences, magazine spreads, headlines, and book text. A new digital version was created in 2007 by Ray Larabie, the Super Clarendon family. It is this face with the distinctive Clarendon round ends (called ball terminals) on the lower case a, c, f, g, r & y, that help to anchor this story in 1973.

Made in the USA
San Bernardino, CA
21 November 2018